Niki Valentine is an award-winning writer who, under a pseudonym, has been published internationally to huge acclaim. When she isn't working on her next psychological horror novel, Niki teaches Creative and Professional Writing at Nottingham University.

Also by Niki Valentine

The Haunted

POSSESSED
NIKI VALENTINE

sphere

SPHERE

First published in Great Britain in 2012 by Sphere

A CIP catalogue record for this book
is available from the British Library.

ISBN 978-0-7515-4538-8

Typeset in Caslon by M Rules
Printed and bound in Great Britain by
Clays Ltd, St Ives plc

Papers used by Sphere are from well-managed forests
and other responsible sources.

MIX
Paper from
responsible sources
FSC® C104740

Sphere
An imprint of
Little, Brown Book Group
100 Victoria Embankment
London EC4Y 0DY

An Hachette UK Company
www.hachette.co.uk

www.littlebrown.co.uk

For Chad, my lovely husband.

Acknowledgements

Special thanks to Luigi Bonomi, Cath Burke, Thalia Proctor and all at Little, Brown. Also to Chad, Mum, Dad, Deborah, Paul, Adam, Danielle and Natalie, as well as all my family for encouragement and amazing support, as always. And to my writer friends, especially Richard Pilgrim and Maria Allen. Finally, a big thank you to my students at Nottingham University, who inspire me and keep me grounded.

One

Emma was sitting on her bed. She had been there for an hour, since her mother left. She was paralysed. She knew that she should leave her room and try to meet some of the other students, start her new life, but she couldn't make herself move. She kept staring across the landscaped gardens of the university and towards the building where she would be spending most of her time. *The Conservatoire.* Its name whispered through her head but the building stared back at her with the blank eyes of its windows and the black maw of its doors, and she felt like it might swallow her up, completely consume her, if she wasn't careful.

The first time Emma had come here, for her interview, she had imagined the place as a jolly castle and university a bit like boarding school, except with bank accounts and much more freedom. Coming from a state school in Manchester, Emma's idea of boarding school was a romantic one, story-book stuff about midnight feasts and hockey matches. Now she was here, she knew better. She felt the reality of being away from home, completely alone. She had never realised before how safe it had been, wrapped up in her family.

Now, as she looked at the Conservatoire, she couldn't imagine how she had ever thought it friendly. It loomed on the top of a hillock, quite a distance from the halls of residence. The sky was dark with clouds, casting shadows over the building. It was more like a stately home than a castle, in fact, with two north towers and large picture windows. Above the main hall there was a silver-green dome, a smaller version of the one that loomed above St Paul's Cathedral. An exact replica, she'd been told at interview. There was a staircase up to the main doorway. The stone was grey and aged and the whole effect was like the gothic churches she'd loved in Paris when she'd gone with her mum, a treat for doing so well in her A levels. That holiday seemed an age away now, as did school and her family life. Emma felt like she'd walked through a portal and into another world. In the books she'd read that started that way, there was evil in that other world. *The Subtle Knife*, the wicked queen with her Turkish delight; these things lurked in her imagination. But she didn't believe in nonsense like that and had never bought these stories, preferring adult fiction instead. She wasn't going to let them scare her now.

She thought about getting her clock out and checking the time, but she still couldn't budge. She knew she needed to break the paralysis but she didn't know how. Then there was a knock at the door. And it was as if it broke a spell, because Emma found she could move. She got up.

Emma opened the door, and a girl stared in. She was tall and slim, with hair that was almost jet black and eyes that were powerfully blue. So blue they seemed to glow with ultraviolet. A sense of unease settled over her. Why was she letting herself get spooked? It wasn't even her style.

'Hello,' said the girl, holding out a hand. She had a cut-glass accent, the kind of voice Emma associated with villains in James Bond movies.

Emma looked at the hand for a moment as if she

didn't know what it was there for. Pulling herself together, she shook it, and smiled. 'Hello,' she said. 'I'm Emma Russell.'

'Yes.' The girl's eyes were sparkling. They looked mischievous, and Emma could imagine messing around in class with this girl, playing knock-a-door-run on the street like she used to with her cousin. 'I know who you are. I saw you play in Birmingham.'

'Oh.' Emma was still unused to this reaction. 'What's your name?' she asked. She felt suddenly very young asking this question, like a kid in primary school.

'Can I come in?' The girl didn't wait for an answer, but flew past, rushing into the room and sitting on the bed. 'Oh,' she said, turning with a broad grin. Her face seemed to glow. 'You haven't unpacked yet.'

'No.' Emma laughed. She found this girl's company infectious and wanted to confess everything, getting the sense that she'd understand. 'I've been sitting feeling sorry for myself and staring across at the Conservatoire building.'

The girl smiled at her. 'I had to get away.' She leaned back on the bed and looked up at the ceiling, her eyes following the cornice work and the stains. 'My sister was driving me crazy.'

'I know what you mean. It was the same at home. It's just me and my mum, see, and she can be a bit over the top. Overprotective. You know?' Emma heard her own voice, the harsh nasal tones of the north, echoing around the room. For the first time in her life she heard how she must sound to other people and she didn't like it.

The girl on the bed looked confused, as if Emma had missed her point altogether. Then there was a sound at the door. Emma turned. She hadn't realised she'd left it open. For a moment, she thought she was seeing things. There was another girl in the doorway, the absolute image of the one on the bed. Emma looked from one to the other. Her head went dizzy trying to take them both in.

'I was looking for you, Sophie,' the girl at the door said.

'I've been meeting Emma. You know, the prodigy. We saw her play in Birmingham.'

Emma winced at the word 'prodigy'. She had always hated it. She found that people her age used it against her more often than as a compliment.

'Yes, I remember,' said the girl at the door. Her voice was flat and unenthusiastic. Emma got the distinct impression she was stuck in the middle of a row between the twins, something unpleasant.

'This is my sister Matilde,' Sophie told her, gesturing towards the door. She was hugging her legs and looked at home sitting on the bed, as if she owned the place. Emma would never have dared behave like that in someone else's room. She wished she could be more like this strange, confident creature.

'Come in,' Emma told Matilde. She wasn't sure she actually wanted company, not even these two bright, beautiful girls. Perhaps especially not girls like these. She felt out of her depth. But Matilde smiled then and there was a real warmth in the smile. She walked over to the bed and sat near her sister but on the edge of the bed. Emma looked at her and she smiled again, and Emma realised she was looking for some reassurance that sitting on the bed was all right.

It was odd. Emma had read about twins and seen documentaries, knew all about how they were supposed to have divergent character traits despite the identical DNA, but it was still strange to see this, right in front of her. Whilst the appearance of the twins was dazzlingly similar, she immediately sensed the difference in their personalities. It was as marked as the difference in the way they sat on her bed. Whilst, judging by their accents, the twins' background was about as different from hers as it was possible to be, she sensed that Matilde was somehow like her. If it hadn't been for Sophie, they would probably both still be sitting on their own beds, staring out over campus. Emma caught Matilde's eyes again and the two girls shared a smile of recognition.

'I'm bored,' Sophie said, stretching across the bed like a cat. 'Let's go out. For dinner or something.'

'I need to be careful with my grant,' Emma said, straight away. She was so programmed to think this way that it came out before she could stop it, before she could think about how that might sound to girls like these.

'Grant?' Sophie said, at once. She made the word sound ridiculous. 'I thought that was something people got in the eighties.' She let out a shot of laughter, and Emma flinched, knowing what was coming next. 'Ah, you got a scholarship, though, of course you did, being such a vicious talent. I forgot about that!' She sounded very pleased with herself for working it out.

'We can pay,' Matilde said, quietly, seriously. She was chewing on a nail, quite intent at biting something off it. She frowned and pulled away her hand. 'In fact, I insist.'

'I'm not sure,' Emma said. She wanted desperately to go out with these girls and get to know them, but she was scared, and proud. She felt a kind of dizzy feeling just sitting with them, something she imagined was a little like falling in love. She felt danger.

'Don't be silly,' Sophie said. 'Of course we'll pay.' She stood up, and Matilde too, then Emma found that she was reaching for her bag. They both followed Sophie through the door and Emma locked it.

She turned towards the twins, two strangers now, in a strange hallway at a university in a city she knew nothing about. She was terrified, but she also felt she would follow Matilde anywhere. And she looked at Sophie, and knew that she was a girl who was used to getting her own way.

The girls had taken a taxi into the city centre which the twins had paid for. Sophie told the driver where to go with more confidence than Emma could ever imagine having about such things. Her instruction was very specific, a bistro on Henrietta Avenue, and Emma realised they knew the city already.

The bistro was the kind of place Emma had passed by in the posher parts of Manchester and Salford and had always wanted to go in, but they'd never been able to afford eating out. Only on holiday. It had those French doors all the way across its front that opened on to the pavement. There were no tables outside, but sitting near the window felt almost the same. The twins sailed in, clearly used to the luxury, but Emma hesitated at the door. Even though she wasn't paying, she felt scared. She felt like going inside would change the world somehow, her world. It felt like a test.

Sophie didn't even notice, rushing in and looking for a table, but Matilde turned. Emma knew it was Matilde because she was wearing the red top, but she thought she might have worked it out anyway, just by the fact that she was waiting for her. She came back and reached out a hand. 'Come on,' she said. 'Papa knows the owner. It's really good.'

This was enough to get Emma through the door. Sophie had picked a table and they all sat down. Emma looked around. The restaurant had high ceilings and there were even chandeliers. She stared up and they sparkled at her. She couldn't believe there were chandeliers. It was like something out of a Jane Austen novel. She turned to the other two girls to find they were both staring at her. She felt self-conscious then, like the subject of a study or an animal in the zoo. She realised that she was as exotic a creature to the twins as each of them was to her.

'You know the city well,' she said, to break the silence.

Sophie smiled. 'Our parents live nearby, in the countryside.' Emma noticed another tone to her accent then, something she hadn't heard before. A slight European twang.

'Are you from France?' she said. The question came like a breath out and she regretted it immediately. Sophie had just told her they were from around here.

'Our parents are. I mean, we were born there, but we've lived here for as long as I can remember.' It was Matilde speaking, and her soft voice felt like a rescue.

Sophie looked rather annoyed, as if she thought Matilde had spoken out of turn. As soon as Emma saw it, the expression disappeared, and she wondered if she'd imagined it after all. She realised she hadn't looked at the menu yet, and tore her eyes away from the twins to do that. She had missed a meal, sitting on the bed in a daze earlier, and felt hollow inside she was so hungry. She couldn't believe how stalled she had been. It seemed ridiculous now, in a plush seat in this posh bistro, with these beautiful, polished young women. She looked up at them and smiled. They had helped her remember what an opportunity she had. She remembered what her mum had said to her about wanting to go to university but her parents not supporting her and she was thankful again.

The menu was confusing and Emma didn't understand half of the descriptions. She had no idea what carpaccio was and she could translate *chèvre chaud* but couldn't imagine it really meant hot goat. She was too embarrassed to ask, so she played it safe with a bowl of pasta. Sophie fussed over the wine list for a while and eventually settled on a 'passable' Bordeaux, after tutting and complaining about the years they had listed of almost everything else. Emma knocked the candle over and, flustered, grabbed for it, just in time to stop the tablecloth lighting up. She spilled hot wax on her hands, though, which was painful, but she tried not to show that it hurt. She was certain that if she was herself around Sophie, even for a moment, she would end up regretting it. She couldn't imagine Sophie having anything but contempt for this unsophisticated creature brought up on council estates by just her mum.

'Who will your piano tutor be, Emma?' It was Matilde who spoke. Even her voice was less harsh than Sophie's somehow, lilting and kind.

'Professor Wood,' Emma said.

Matilde seemed to wince at the name and Sophie became all distracted, signalling to the waitress and asking about the whereabouts of the wine she'd ordered only minutes before. Then something changed and she looked straight at Emma. 'He's a friend of Papa's,' she said, pronouncing Papa the old-fashioned way with the stress on the second syllable. 'We've known him for years.'

'And you don't like him?' Emma heard her own voice, sounding panicked. She had warmed to Wood at her interview and he was one of the reasons she'd chosen this university. He had seemed honest, and fatherly.

Sophie made a strange sound, a strangled laugh that sounded bitter. 'I wouldn't exactly say that.'

'You can be such a bitch sometimes, Soph,' Matilde said, frowning.

Emma flushed a little and the atmosphere frosted

over. She was confused. She got the distinct impression that Sophie was implying some romantic connection. She couldn't mean that, surely? Wood was so much older than Matilde, and he didn't seem the type.

'Tell us about how you taught yourself to play,' Matilde said. 'I love stories like that.'

Emma smiled awkwardly. She could tell by the tone of her voice that Matilde wasn't making fun or laying a trap. 'It was such a long time ago that I barely remember it. I just got a book from the library.'

'Such a talent,' Sophie said. It wasn't as clear from Sophie's voice if her intentions were honourable.

'What's Wood like then?' Emma's turn to change the subject.

'He's the best,' Matilde said. 'By far the best piano tutor you could have,' she added quickly. Her cheeks had turned pink.

The waitress returned then with the Bordeaux. She looked flustered as she showed the label to Sophie, who nodded her assent and told the girl to pour it. Emma swilled hers around in the glass, the way she'd seen people do on the television. She took a sip. It tasted bitter and made her throat close up. Perhaps wine was an acquired taste.

'Probably it needs to breathe,' Sophie said.

Emma had no idea what that meant but she guessed it was something to do with mixing with the air. She placed her glass on the table carefully and looked at the twins, searching for signs to tell them apart. Now she looked, they were not so much identical as mirror images of each other. Mirror twins. She had read about that before. It was a subtle difference, though, as their faces were so symmetrical. The pair of them looked happy and perfect, but she imagined they must be hiding some dark secret.

Then she smiled at herself. How ridiculous. She had read too many Daphne Du Maurier novels. Real life wasn't like that at all.

Two

Emma woke with a dry mouth and throbbing head. She ran her tongue over her teeth and found them sticky. She couldn't remember if she had brushed them before bed. She had definitely forgotten to take out her contact lenses, which lent a milky aspect as she blinked her eyes. She had been out with the twins, again, the previous evening. It was becoming a habit.

The last few hours of their night out were hazy at best. She remembered being in a taxi and feeling sick. She hadn't thrown up; at least, she didn't think she had. She sat up on her bed and her head swam. She thought she might vomit and took deep breaths. After a few moments, the nausea abated. She looked at her clock radio. Its display showed a random time, flashing so that she knew it hadn't been set yet. She remembered struggling with it just before she went to sleep, trying to focus on the LCD digits and failing, then giving up and falling into bed, gritting her teeth against the way the room was spinning. Emma's watch was on the dressing table and she reached for it. It was five to six. She had woken early, despite the late night, and would have to face her first day of lectures with a hangover and wearing glasses. She sighed and rubbed her temples.

Dragging herself up, Emma leaned for support on her bed. The room was tiny and it was only a few steps to the shower. This was one of the things that had stalled her when she'd first arrived. She really couldn't imagine spending a year living here. When she'd got the application pack for the room in halls, it had sounded lovely. Single room with en suite and a study area. The description failed to mention that you had to sit on the bed to use the desk, or that the en suite was basically a cupboard with a toilet and shower in it. She went inside the tiny space but didn't close the door. It was too claustrophobic, shutting herself in like that. She pulled the shower curtain around her and turned on the water. It flowed over her head and against her skin, the heat making her feel a little better.

Dried and dressed, her teeth brushed now and her contact lenses out, Emma examined her face in the mirror. Her skin felt dry and looked sallow. Her glasses were an emergency pair and didn't really suit her. She considered for a moment putting the lenses back in but she knew her eyes were too sore. Where had all this chaos come from? It wasn't her usual style at all. The twins had brought this into her life, with their expensive tastes and credit cards and all the champagne. She could live with that. There were worse things than champagne and chaos in Freshers' Week. And the twins were worth it. Especially Matilde.

It wasn't as if Emma didn't like Sophie; she had hardly ever liked anyone more. It was just that, with Matilde, it was different. The quieter twin hung back more often to walk side by side with Emma. She was always the first to reach and point to the right fork or knife, or explain something else Emma didn't understand. What she had with Sophie felt like friendship already, but with Matilde it felt deeper. As if it was Emma who was the other twin, not Sophie. Emma wondered what Sophie would think of her if she knew that she thought this sometimes.

The lecture theatre was half full when Emma arrived. She probed the room for the twins, and spotted them sitting with a boy she hadn't met before. At least, if she had met him, she had forgotten him, which was certainly possible with the levels of alcohol she'd consumed in the previous week. It was normal, though, to drink like this in the induction and Freshers' weeks. Everyone had been doing it. Emma told herself she could calm down later, when her lectures started.

Which was today. Hugging her notebook to her chest, she made her way over to her friends. She stood at the end of the aisle and wondered how to get their attention. She lifted her hand in a wave, but neither of the girls saw her. She stood and watched them. They didn't notice her looking. Both girls were talking animatedly to the boy. Emma noticed he was good-looking, blond and blue-eyed, with the appearance of privilege about him, something she was beginning to recognise when she saw it. She also saw right away that he was enchanted by the twins. No. She looked again. It was Matilde he liked. Sophie was gesticulating and throwing herself into whatever she was saying. Emma knew the other twin from the way she held back, and because she was the left-hand-side reflection. The boy's eyes were fixed on Matilde. Then Matilde looked up and noticed Emma, and she seemed to light up.

'Excuse me,' Emma said to the girl on the end of the row, who tutted as she got up and moved her bags. Emma was irritated but then her attention was drawn to Sophie, the way she seemed to be fixing Matilde with a puzzled look. Then the look melted and both of the twins beamed at her. Sophie was in the seat nearest, and she stood up and kissed Emma, one cheek and then the other, all impeccable manners and polish.

'This is Henry,' Matilde said.

Henry looked up and smiled at Emma. He seemed a little shy. 'Hi,' he said. He looked like he didn't quite know what to do with his hands. Emma felt a shiver down her spine as she sat down beside him. But he was Matilde's already, she was sure of it, and Emma wasn't about to make a fool of herself.

'Henry's staying on your corridor,' Sophie told her. 'He's just a few doors down from you. Isn't it funny we never met until this morning?'

'Yes,' Emma said. 'Funny.' She felt like an echo or a shadow. She often felt this way around the twins.

The soprano voice rose up into the very top of the recital hall, and Emma was so struck by its beauty that she stopped playing. It was Matilde, singing *Ave Maria*, the Schubert version. It was only a rehearsal but the young woman's voice was so beautiful that several people who weren't involved had been drawn inside the hall.

Matilde stopped singing. She flushed bright red and turned away from all the people watching. She caught Emma's eyes across the room and they shared a smile. Emma was enjoying feeling close to Matilde. They were spending lots of time together thanks to the rehearsals. Sophie was not in the choir and when Emma asked her why she had scoffed and said these things were for kids. Emma was still getting used to how different the twins were. It was such a contradiction when they looked so much the same.

'From the top.' It was Joanna, the third-year student who was organising this performance. She looked a little frustrated with how Matilde's voice had stopped everyone dead, but Emma thought she should be glad that Matilde was singing for them. Emma could have listened to her all day.

Joanna counted them in and Emma began to play. She half watched the notes and half Matilde. Her friend was dressed casually, in jeans and T-shirt, but she looked more beautiful for it. When it was her cue to come in, Emma felt like the whole room held its breath. Matilde opened up and the music came from within her. The *Ave Maria* floated around the room like a spirit. Emma could imagine being haunted by a voice like hers.

After working with Matilde in the rehearsal, Emma felt inspired to play her own pieces. With all the socialising, she'd neglected her practice recently. It made her feel as though she'd missed something vital, eating, drinking, breathing even.

Sitting in front of the piano, she found she was drawing a blank. She pressed down chords, then discordant groups of keys. She found the latter more convincing. Something about Henry's presence in the lecture earlier had bothered her. She wasn't sure why. She let her eyes go in and out of focus and pounded the keyboard. It was very satisfying, even more so for how bad it sounded. She felt like she was smashing glass, destroying something beautiful.

Something tickled her face like a whisper. 'Hello.' The voice was in her ear.

Emma turned, sharp. She felt like all her breath was being sucked out of her. She found herself face to face with one of the twins, their noses almost touching. She stared, trying to work out if it was Sophie or Matilde. It was so much harder to tell when there was just one of them. Then she realised that, whoever it was, she'd been in the room for a while. She had heard the rubbish Emma had been playing. So much for the prodigy. Emma felt the heat glow from her cheeks.

'That was interesting music.' The voice was hard in tone. Not that friendly. Matilde would never have spoken to her like that and so Emma knew it was Sophie.

'Just getting the stresses out,' she told her. She had to look away from Sophie's intense glare and stared down at the keyboard.

'So I see.' That same voice, not easy to interpret but definitely not kind.

Emma didn't say anything. She didn't dare. She was terrified of making an even bigger fool of herself. She closed the piano case and turned away. 'Modern jazz, eh?' she said, trying to crack a joke, but her voice sounded weak and strained and it didn't come off.

Sophie didn't even appear to register the attempt at humour. Emma felt as if her neck would be burned open by the other girl's gaze, although she was facing the other way and couldn't even see if Sophie was looking at her. She felt breath against her neck again, hot like pepper. The heat made her shiver.

'You should know,' Sophie hissed. 'Nothing comes between my sister and me.' There was no ambiguity now in her voice. It was menacing. 'Nothing,' she said again, like a full stop.

Emma wanted to turn and face Sophie, she wanted to challenge her, but she couldn't move. She realised she hardly knew this girl at all. She wasn't trying to come between the twins, though. They were her friends.

'I saw you, the other day, when you went off together. You thought I was asleep but I wasn't.'

The sound of the door swinging shut punched the air. Emma breathed easily again. Sophie was gone.

Emma thought about what she'd said. She'd had no idea that this had been brewing. She was usually good at reading people, and the idea that she'd missed this chilled her slightly. It would be unpleasant if Sophie was going to get jealous and oversensitive. Emma had to admit that she would like to see Matilde on her own more. But she really liked both of the twins. She didn't want to stop spending time with either of them.

One word came to her then, something she was sure was about to cause a whole load of trouble. *Henry*. Sophie wasn't going to like Henry at all, at least not when she discovered he preferred Matilde.

Later, after Matilde and Sophie had swept her away to a wine bar in town, Emma couldn't see a trace of the earlier malice in Sophie. She began to wonder if she'd imagined the whole encounter. They stood by a tall table, chatting and drinking champagne. The novelty of champagne had worn off and Emma wasn't even sure she liked it. It tasted sour and the bubbles burst harshly over her tongue.

Sophie was her animated self, holding court about one of the professors. The woman she was talking about was the beloved Professor Margie. Professor Margie was Emma's supervisor and unusual among their lecturers because the students called her by her first name.

People studying in other schools at the university laughed at the rather formal, archaic way the music students stuck to surnames but it was just the way it was at the Conservatoire. 'No one could really be *that* nice,' she'd begun. Now she was spinning a story around Margie, turning her into a witch who ate children, playing up to the shrieks of laughter she was getting from the girls around her. Emma's cheeks were sore from laughing and her tummy muscles tight. She took some deep breaths to calm herself.

After a moment, Sophie's monologue didn't seem funny at all. Despite her jokey manner, there was something poisonous there. Emma felt some distance, like she was watching from above. She wondered if the earlier incident was affecting her still. Matilde seemed to notice her disquiet and nudged close. 'You okay?' she said. Emma noticed Sophie shoot them both a look. She nodded but then she rushed off to the toilets.

Staring at her own reflection, Emma splashed water on her face. She was a little drunk. Coming into view in the mirror was another girl from their year, Hannah, as she walked through the door. Her reflection smiled at Emma.

'Hi,' she said.

Emma turned to look at her. She knew her from the choir, but they had never spoken before. She tried to smile back. 'Hey,' she said. Hannah disappeared into one of the cubicles. Emma tried to move out of the bathroom but she was feeling something akin to the panic she'd felt that first night at the university. If she didn't have the twins, she might as well be right back there again.

The toilet flushed and Hannah came over to the basin beside her, washing her hands and smiling into the mirror again. She flicked at her hair. She had some of that same, upper-class confidence Emma admired in the twins. She didn't glow the same way they did but still, Emma recognised it.

Hannah examined her lipstick and eyeliner but didn't put on any more make-up. Then she turned to Emma. 'So, you knew the twins before you came here?' she said.

Emma looked up from the sink, surprised. 'No,' she said. 'Just since the first day here.'

Hannah looked surprised. 'That's odd,' she said.

'What do you mean?'

Hannah paused, looking at her like she was deciding whether to reveal a secret or not. She took a breath, and Emma thought she wasn't going to come out with whatever it was. 'I went to school with them, that's all,' Hannah said. 'They don't usually let people in like this.'

Emma stared at her, trying to take this in.

Hannah shook her head. 'It's like you're one of them,' she said. The way she used these words struck Emma. She made it sound ridiculous. She pushed her hair back one more time and then smiled at herself in the mirror. 'The prodigy, people call you, did you know that?'

'I've heard it before,' Emma said, with a shrug.

'They don't mean it nicely.'

Hannah was still smiling and Emma couldn't help feeling that shiny hair and good teeth hid a lot of things. She never would have guessed someone so clean and healthy-looking could be so bitchy. Except, she had experienced it before.

'Jealousy is a terrible thing,' she told Hannah. The comment was barbed and hit its target.

The smile had been knocked off Hannah's face. 'Nobody would have anything to do with you if it weren't for the twins,' she said. Her voice was flat and unpleasant.

Emma didn't respond to this final dig, but turned away and staggered back to the bar. She must have been drinking too fast for her body to register, because the alcohol hit her in waves now. She looked at the group of students from afar, wondering if Hannah was right, suspecting her comment probably had at least some truth in it. She wasn't sure if it was the effect of the drink or something deeper, but Sophie and Matilde seemed to stand out a mile. They were taller than the others and, of course, very beautiful, with such flawless skin and those ultraviolet eyes. Sophie was still playing entertainer and almost all eyes were on her. *Almost all.* What Sophie couldn't see, hadn't seen yet, was that Matilde was slightly off from the group and with her, there was Henry. They had eyes only for each other.

Emma saw Henry's hand as it reached for Matilde's. She saw him lean in. Matilde did not move away. She saw the moment when their lips touched.

The kiss did not last long. As soon as their lips came together, Sophie jerked and then was still. She stopped talking and turned, staring at Henry and Matilde, neither of whom noticed. Emma held her breath as she saw both of the twins and Henry, between them. She saw Sophie's smile drop and her eyes narrow. She saw the break between the twins and she felt it too, the crack like lightning. She could smell it as if it had charred a trail in the air.

Three

Everyone met in Sophie's room for drinks before the Choral performance. Emma sat nursing the glass of whiskey that she'd been given. This was the only drink that the twins actually kept in their room and they served it straight in highball glasses. Emma thought it was a bit of an affectation.

Matilde had gone quiet; Emma was concerned about her friend, anxious that she wouldn't enjoy the limelight. Henry seemed to be worried too and kept asking her if she was okay, and if there was anything he could do. She was working through her drink a little easier than Emma but it was only Sophie who was downing them with any regularity. She didn't seem too drunk, but perhaps she was drinking them so fast that half hadn't taken effect yet.

The four of them walked down to the recital room together. Sophie kissed her sister and friend goodbye. Henry waved awkwardly at Emma, then turned to Matilde. They shared a tender kiss. Then Matilde and Emma walked into the backstage area. Emma was glad to find herself alone with Matilde; she relished their time together without the others. But there was something about leaving Henry with Sophie that made her feel a little sick inside. Maybe it was nerves about the performance.

From the changing rooms backstage, Emma could hear the strings tuning. The way they scratched and slid the notes set her nerves on edge. She was gritting her teeth and tried to relax as she undressed. She heard the orchestra start up outside, and soon after, the choir began. She unzipped her garment bag and took out her dress. It was lovely, dark blue and silky, long and straight. It was the same dress she'd had for her first big concert when she was fourteen and, these days, every time she went to put it on she breathed in, worried that it wouldn't fit this time. She wondered how long it would be before people at the Conservatoire noticed that she wore the same dress every time.

Matilde smiled at Emma. 'I'll zip you up if you'll do me,' she said.

Emma slipped into her dress and let the skirts fall down around her ankles. She was relieved as Matilde pulled on her zip and it closed easily. The contact made Emma shiver.

Matilde unzipped her own dress cover and the fabric flooded out. It was stunning; a deep, dark red studded with sequins. Matilde climbed into her dress. Emma zipped her up and Matilde checked her reflection. She fluffed up her hair and picked excess mascara from her lashes. Then Emma stood back and looked at her friend.

'You look amazing,' she told her.

Matilde beamed; she looked transformed and ready for the occasion. She turned to Emma and kissed her on the cheek. 'Break a leg, Ems,' she said.

Emma nodded. 'And you.' Although she hated that expression; she was always worried it might actually happen.

Standing in the wings, Emma checked her music, obsessively touching the edges of the pages. The choir were coming to the end of their last piece of music. The strings faded out to their final note.

Matilde strode on to the stage, beaming. The sequins on her dress were like stars under the stage lights. She was stunning and for a moment Emma forgot what she was there for. Then she remembered where she was and rushed over to the piano. She placed the manuscript sheets on the music stand and sat down. Taking a deep breath, she began to play.

Matilde's voice soared above the audience, who stared up at this heavenly creature. Listening to her sing, Emma had to concentrate hard to remember to play. She understood why people spoke of angels and sopranos in the same breath. Schubert's arrangement of the prayer was beautiful in itself but Emma had never heard it sung this way.

'Do you think they'll stay together and get married?' Sophie was lying on her stomach on Emma's bed, kicking her legs as she hunted through her CD collection. 'Don't you have anything that's not classical?' Both questions were asked in the same tone, as if they were equally important to her, although Emma knew her well enough now to know better.

'No and no, I don't think so.'

Sophie turned and stared right at Emma; her expression was tense. She looked like she was trying to work out which answer was which. Then she broke into a smile and all the lines of tension faded as if they'd never been there.

Emma never quite trusted what appeared on the surface with Sophie. She had never felt able to, not since that morning in the practice room when she'd acted so strangely. She liked Sophie, though, very much; she was charismatic and wild. The twins were her best friends. It was just that she couldn't get used to being on a stable footing with both of them. She kept looking for cracks, with Sophie particularly. But it seemed that whatever fissures had been there, Matilde's evident case of first love with Henry had healed them right over.

'They won't get married,' Emma said. She watched Sophie going through her CDs and felt a knot in her stomach. She'd spent her life collecting that music; it was more than her music collection, something vital, and she didn't like to see Sophie's fingers digging through and the faces she pulled. She had a lot of it on her computer too, but that wasn't the point. She liked the physicality of the CDs, their covers and the notes inside; she chose them carefully.

Sophie being in her room at all made her nervous. She couldn't imagine what her cheap keepsakes looked like to her sophisticated friend. Sophie was a girl who could choose wine and who knew about designer dresses. Emma's belongings each had a story, a reason for being there, like the piece of Berlin Wall her mum had picked up with her very own hands when she'd been in Germany to see it torn down. Emma knew that Sophie's dismissal of these things would hurt, that it would cheapen them somehow and spoil them for ever.

Sophie rolled over on to her back. Emma watched her stare at the ceiling and wished, not for the first time, that she could be so comfortable in her own skin. To be comfortable in her own room would be a start. She was sure that anyone observing the two of them would assume that it was Sophie's room and Emma was the visitor. 'I hope to God they don't get married,' Sophie said. 'That would be tiresome. I don't mind Henry, not really, but he's just a little bit dull.'

Emma shrugged. She didn't really know Henry but he seemed good company. He made her laugh, sometimes. She wouldn't call him dull, except, she supposed, compared to the twins. 'Yes,' she said. 'He is a bit boring.'

Sophie's face glowed then, enjoying the affirmation. 'Let's go and find them,' she said. 'If we can just get them out and away from their rooms, get him drunk, maybe he wouldn't be so dreadfully dull. And Matilde might be more entertaining again too.'

Emma felt more knotting in her stomach at this idea. She didn't think Sophie's motives were about being entertained at all, or getting to know her sister's boyfriend. 'Okay,' she said. From inside her head, her voice sounded like a squeak. Sophie bounced up from the bed, though, all enthusiasm and with a glow of a smile for her. A reward, like scraps on the floor, Emma thought, and she didn't like the way she warmed inside at the sight of it.

Standing outside Matilde's door, Emma's stomach tied itself tighter. She watched Sophie knocking. 'Maybe we shouldn't ...' She heard her own voice trail off.

'Don't be silly,' Sophie said. 'She's my sister.' Like she felt that excused anything she did.

A sleepy-looking Matilde appeared at the door. Her hair was mussed and untidy and her face slightly red, like she'd been kissed too many times. 'Hey,' she said. She looked drunk but Emma was almost sure it was the effects of love rather than alcohol.

Without waiting to be asked, Sophie bounded in. Emma stood outside, looking past Matilde into the room. Her friend opened the door wider like an invitation, and so, hesitantly, she walked in. Henry was sitting on the bed wearing shorts and a T-shirt. He looked slightly embarrassed to be intruded on. Sophie either didn't notice or was ignoring this as she plonked herself on the bed right next to him. She smiled at him in that full, attentive way she had of looking at you like you were the only person in the room. Matilde sat back down on the bed too. Emma settled herself on the armchair nearby.

The quieter twin smiled at Emma, not looking like someone upset at the invasion, but Emma felt guilty. 'Did you hear?' Matilde said. 'I have a masterclass. Dominique Bouton.'

'That's fantastic.' Emma tried to sound enthusiastic, but the idea of a masterclass terrified her. She couldn't imagine playing in front of everyone just to get picked apart afterwards. She would have to go through this, she knew, but like dying, she chose not to think about it until she had to. 'Bouton is the best.'

'Yes, he's amazing. Although I must admit, I'm dreading it,' Matilde told her.

'And he's fucking gorgeous,' Sophie said. She didn't look at the other two girls when she said this, though. Only Henry. Emma didn't feel it was beyond the realms of possibility that Sophie would just lean in and kiss him.

A breath later and Emma had a sudden realisation about the situation. She saw the way Sophie looked at Henry and how Matilde was sitting apart from the other two. She felt like the wind had been knocked out of her. Of course Sophie didn't like Matilde being close to Henry and wanted to get in the way; that Emma had never doubted. It was just that she hadn't realised before the way Sophie would stop them. Now it was totally obvious what her strategy would be.

Emma could hardly believe she hadn't seen it before.

That night, Emma struggled to sleep. What she'd noticed about Sophie's behaviour around Henry was preying on her mind. That and the way that Matilde had backed off. It was as if the quieter twin knew her place and would accede to her sister's claim on anything she wanted. Emma sat up in bed after a while, and then got up.

She had suffered from insomnia before, in the lead-up to her exams, and half of what kept her awake was worrying that the problem had come back. There was no reason it should, though. Her life was pretty much perfect, with the twins in tow and her piano going well. She knew that there wasn't a girl in the entire department who wouldn't swap places with her right then, whatever Hannah Meredith had said. She got dressed and had a drink of cold water from the tap. Then she pulled on her coat and left the room.

Outside, the air was sharp. Emma could see her own breath as she walked across the landscaped gardens. She thought about going to practise, but she wasn't in the right mood for it. Instead, she took the path around the Conservatoire and headed towards the lake. Mist was hanging over the water and did nothing to improve her mood. She picked up a stone and tried to skim it over the water. She never had been very good at that kind of thing. She gave up and threw the stones, overarm, harder and harder. She enjoyed the sound they made as they split the lake's surface and the circles that grew from the places where they'd sunk.

It was then that she heard voices, the sound of a boy and girl, both laughing. She wasn't the only person awake, then. She turned and saw them heading her way. As they came closer, she saw it was Henry and Matilde. They looked wrapped up in each other, the way they always did. She realised then that the answer she'd given Sophie about them was a lie. Emma did think they would stay together and get married. She couldn't imagine any other outcome.

Emma smiled and waved at her friends as they hurried over.

'What are you doing up?' Henry asked her. 'Dirty stop-out,' he added, and then he turned and kissed Matilde.

Emma shrugged. 'I couldn't sleep,' she said.

'We didn't want to sleep.' Pleasure carried on Matilde's voice as she explained. 'It felt like a waste. We've been exploring campus all night. It's amazing what's here. Have you been down to the maze?'

'No,' Emma said. Her unease was growing so strong that she felt sick.

'Oh you should, darling,' Matilde continued. 'It's such fun.'

Emma tried to smile at Matilde, who grinned and

winked at her. It was then that Emma realised what was unsettling her. She wasn't at all sure, now she thought about it, that it was Matilde she was talking to.

'You know, we could go for a dip, in the lake,' the twin said, her eyes flashing at Henry.

'We don't have swimming costumes,' he said.

'I know.' The words felt like they'd been shot from a gun.

Emma looked from Henry to the twin and back again. She saw the possessive hand on Henry's back, the tilt of the girl's neck. Now she was almost sure it was Sophie standing in front of her. She wondered if Henry knew.

'Come on, darling,' the girl said, touching Henry's hand. 'Let's go over to the school of nursing and see if we can find any of those strange creatures in their natural habitat.' She flashed a smile at Emma. Henry shyly smiled too, and then the two of them were off.

Emma watched them walk away. What could she do about it? She needed to find out for sure. It was only fair to Matilde. She deserved to know what Henry and Sophie were doing to her and Emma was sure her friend would thank her, even if it meant being woken up in the middle of the night. She turned heel and headed back to their halls of residence. She walked fast, energised by her mission. She needed to get back before the other two did.

Making her way up the stairs towards Matilde's room, Emma's heart was beating fast. What would she say if she found her friend there? She didn't think she had the words or the courage for it. Something made her carry on, though. An inbuilt sense of right and wrong. A moral compass, like her English teacher talked about when they studied *To Kill a Mockingbird*.

Finally Emma found herself outside Matilde's room. She thought she could sense her friend on the other side of the door but couldn't be sure. She hesitated before knocking. If the door was answered, she knew it had to be Matilde. Sophie's room was at the other end of the corridor. She took a deep breath and knocked.

At first there was no movement from inside and Emma experienced momentary relief. It didn't last long. There was the sound of scraping, of someone getting out of bed and gathering themselves together. Then the door opened. All at once her friend was standing in front of her, her eyes gummy with sleep, their colour muted in the dark hallway.

'I'm so sorry to wake you,' Emma said.

Matilde's eyes widened. 'Is everything okay, Ems?'

'Not really, no,' Emma told her. She felt her neck tense up and her mouth tighten, and thought she might cry if she wasn't careful. 'Tilly, I just saw Sophie, with Henry, out by the lake.'

Matilde's face crumpled but she didn't look surprised. As if it was bad news she'd been waiting for, like when a relative has been ill for a long time. 'You'd better come in,' she said, matter of fact. She walked over to her bed like she was sleepwalking. Emma half hoped she was. Maybe she could pretend, tomorrow, that this had been Matilde's bad dream and not real at all. That it hadn't happened. Maybe Emma didn't have to be the one to break her best friend's heart.

Four

Moonlight glistened on the surface of the water and every ripple seemed to have significance as Emma sat and stared from the concrete of the bank. She'd woken up early and hadn't been able to get back to sleep. Being here, awake, while all around her on campus everyone slept was the weirdest thing. It felt like being the only person in the world. In these lonely moments she could imagine those science-fiction scenarios where a gas cloud or virus or some other catastrophe had killed everyone else and she was left completely alone. She hugged her legs and shivered.

There was a sound in the distance, a screech.

Something animal. In a horror movie it would be a portent, a sign that she shouldn't go down to the cellar or a foreshadowing of someone watching her from the trees to the left, ready to pounce and do unspeakable things. But horror movies were just fiction. For some reason, Emma always felt safe here, at the university. Perhaps it was naïve but she didn't feel that danger could find her here. It was as if the place was cut off from the real world. A shadow of it, a play space where, if you died, you got another life, like in a computer game. That could have been the lack of sleep, though, the way it made everything feel not quite real, leaving you with an edge you carried into the day and that coloured everything.

She tried to remember how good life had felt before what happened between Sophie and Henry smashed her world apart. It was like she had dreamed it all. Stress had woken her in the middle of the night recently, more than once. She'd sat bolt upright in bed with an intake of air like she had forgotten to breathe, sheer panic filling her up as if she had been dying. She knew, really, that she was never dying. These were night terrors, panic attacks, whatever you wanted to call them. It didn't help to know the name. She'd found her only release recently in playing more again. The practice rooms were open all hours, so she could have gone there but she hadn't. It never felt right being there alone. The high ceilings, the echo of the hallways, the history she felt there: these things were too much; overwhelming. The electric piano that she'd brought from home never gave the same satisfaction either and so, she'd come here. The scene of the crime.

She thought about the twins. Sophie, who now had a boyfriend, and Matilde, who did not. They hadn't rowed about it. Matilde had simply stepped aside. Emma supposed it had to be that way but it had still been strange to watch. She worried that there would be consequences to come.

A dizzy edge reminded Emma how much she'd had to drink the previous evening. She was bored of all the drinking. It had been a rush, out with the twins in the best places in town and getting champagne and dinners bought for her, but she was beginning to feel trapped by their lifestyle. She didn't want to drink and celebrate all the time. She didn't want to take advantage of the twins' generosity, no matter how freely given, but she couldn't afford to pay her own way.

Emma wanted to curl up in a ball by the lake and stay there, rather than face up to the world or the course and the other students. She didn't have a choice, though, not really, because Matilde had her masterclass with Bouton that morning and Emma had to be there. There was a sinking in her stomach as she thought about it. The visitors varied remarkably in their sensitivity to the students' discomfort. If you were lucky, there'd be moments of slight embarrassment. The visitors with the bigger egos, although funnily enough often the less successful careers, these musicians could crush a young student. You had to take it well, though. It was part of the act they all put on. *That was amazing I learned so much oh my God amazing,* the cry of the masterclass participant at the end in one breath out. They couldn't all be so happy at having their faults and bad habits pointed out to the world. At least, Emma hoped not. She didn't need to find yet another way they were different to her, better, more poised, and so much happier with themselves. She refused to believe it.

The recital hall was buzzing ahead of the masterclass. All the university's flautists and many invited from other local institutions were sitting in pairs and threes on the seats that floated from the stage up to the back of the room. As Emma walked in, she felt the room vibrate with their talking, with their excitement about the class. Bouton was a member of the National Philharmonic and a heart-throb among the girls on the course. Emma had tried to explain to Maggie, a good mate from home, how excited everyone was about his visit, but her friend, who was training to be a nursery nurse, didn't get it. She had never heard of him. Outside of the musical circles Emma found herself in, no one would have recognised his name. For some reason, this was the kind of thing that made her feel further away from home than ever. She should be at college or in a job in Manchester with her mates, getting excited about going off to see Take That at the MEN Arena. She felt as if she'd slipped from one existence to another, through a magic door or a wardrobe or some other enchanted portal.

She scanned the hall for any sign of the twins. She saw Sophie sitting about halfway up; the perfect part of the room to stay inconspicuous. She was a little surprised as, often, Sophie would choose to sit right at the front, and Emma would find herself well out of her comfort zone just to stay near her. As she walked up the steps in the middle of the hall, Sophie noticed her coming, smiling and moving over to make room. Emma shuffled up along the row, taking out a notebook to write down useful points from the class. She glanced at her friend, and just for a moment, wasn't sure it was Sophie. Something about her demeanour, the way she touched her nose. She stared at her and then Matilde came in, with music and her flute, some water, which she arranged in appropriate places at the front of the room. Emma looked from one to the other but they were too far apart for the reflection to become palpable.

The room began to hush, excitement rising. A few stragglers rushed in, grabbing seats where they could. Matilde was sitting waiting, looking uncomfortable under the scrutiny and chewing on a hangnail. Now Emma was certain she was looking at the shyer twin; this habit was something that Sophie told her sister off about all the time. She turned to look at Sophie, catch her eye, but her friend was staring right at the stage, immersed before they'd even started. She looked like she was willing her sister to do well. They both knew how this went, the heat of expectation, of the crowd looking down at you as you were picked apart. Somehow, the fact that it was someone young and attractive like Bouton who would scream and shout and criticise her playing made it worse, not better.

Dominique Bouton walked onto the stage and sat down, looking benevolently into the crowd. One of their lecturers, Professor David Davis, introduced the professional flautist, citing details about his career and achievements that fluttered over Emma. The room was deathly quiet as Dominique stood up to begin the lesson. He turned towards Matilde. She was looking at the floor. He stared at her, waiting for her to get up and join him at the music stands, in front of the mics that had been set up to capture everything they said and did. But Matilde just sat there. The silence in the room seemed to rise and take them over. It felt like people had stopped breathing. This went on for way longer than was comfortable. Then Bouton cleared his throat and raised his eyebrows pointedly at Matilde. Finally, she looked up at him. She stood up and walked forward as the room collectively breathed out. *It's going to be all right,* Emma thought. But she felt like she was persuading herself.

Matilde had been rehearsing Vivaldi's *La Notte* for as long as Emma could remember, so she wasn't surprised at all when this was the piece they started with. Her friend had become obsessed with this particular concerto. Emma knew that Matilde had several issues with the piece and wished she hadn't chosen it. She knew that for a masterclass there was no point choosing music you could already play, although many of the student musicians did or, at least, pieces they believed they played well. *La Notte* meant 'The Night', and Emma couldn't shake the feeling that the dark of the night was coming for them, Matilde's choice of music an omen that it would all go wrong.

Bouton asked Matilde to play the first movement and let her go right through once without stopping for commentary. Then he made marks on her copy of the piece, cutting it into manageable chunks to be examined more closely. Emma noticed Matilde's fingers were shaking. One of the problems with playing in public was that nerves were impossible to hide. They showed themselves all over the instrument and in the notes that came out. Playing was such a physical thing to do that once the shakes took you, it was impossible to get it right. You needed steady breathing and steady hands. You needed to keep your nerve. The buzz that was running through Matilde was probably imperceptible to most of the crowd, but to Emma, and Sophie beside her, it was the obvious start of something. Sophie had gone tense all over. Emma grabbed for her hand and her friend welcomed her contact, her support.

The nerves inside Sophie must have been building too because soon she was squeezing Emma's hand just a little too hard.

Emma watched Matilde, expecting the shakes to get worse but they didn't seem to. A phrase she was playing over and over just wouldn't go right, though. Bouton should have moved on. He should have seen that she was struggling and realised that perfection was neither attainable nor possible. But either he didn't see or he didn't care. As he made her repeat and repeat the phrase, her face went redder and her mouth began to curl up. Emotion twisted her lips and the sound the flute made became less pure. The tension in the room grew as it became clear just how uncomfortable Matilde was feeling. Bouton wouldn't stop, though. He turned to the audience and Matilde narrowed her eyes, trying to do what he wanted even though Emma could tell she was getting angry with him.

Making her play the phrase yet again, Bouton let out a loud tut as she finished and rolled his eyes in frustration. Matilde turned then, and stood very still, staring straight at him. She didn't look scared any more, but furious. Emma supposed there was often little to tell between these two strong emotions. Matilde stood there for what seemed like an age, and then finally she moved, throwing down her flute and storming towards the stage door. Bouton watched after her, his mouth hanging open. There was a collective gasp that filled the hall. Students had looked nervous, or angry, or even argued in masterclasses before but not one had walked out. As for throwing her flute; that was sacrilege. Even Emma was shocked. And she was worried too. She didn't know if Matilde could live this down; even in all the years she had left here, she might remain in people's minds as the girl who stormed out of the masterclass and couldn't hack it. Fear stuck in Emma's throat as she thought about this.

Sophie had let go of Emma's hand. She was staring at the stage, where Matilde had been just a moment before, as if she couldn't believe she was no longer standing there. Bouton had turned towards the crowd with a wry smile, and he made some joke but it flew past Emma and she didn't laugh.

'Bitch,' Sophie said.

Emma stared at her friend. She couldn't believe that this was her reaction to what had happened. 'That's a bit harsh,' she said.

Sophie's face hardened. Emma had never seen her look so disgusted. 'You don't understand,' she said. She let out a big sigh, then got up, walking from the room.

Emma watched her go. She felt like she had to concentrate just to breathe. She had never seen a cross word between the twins, or either of them look any more than slightly annoyed with one another, not even over what had happened with Henry. Sophie had said, that very first night, that her sister was driving her insane, but Emma had never seen any evidence of this before. It was confusing.

As she listened to her friend's heels click against the floor, Emma wondered if she knew the twins at all. The girl walking towards the door of the recital hall looked like a stranger.

Five

After the class, Emma had gone to the practice rooms to lose herself for a while in some of the pieces she'd been working on. She needed to wash the masterclass off herself with music she loved. When she played and it was going well, it made the world and all its problems dissolve away. She took out the books and manuscripts she'd been keeping in her case and the new things she'd picked up from her tutor the previous week. There was a special piece in there. It was just a sonata but it was a Rachmaninoff. She had never learned any Rachmaninoff before, not even for her diploma. She had asked Professor Wood if she should fill this gap.

He'd shrugged. 'One piece of music is as good as another.' But he had pulled the Rach from his shelf and suggested she go copy it. She placed it now on the music stand and examined it, hearing it in her head. She closed her eyes and imagined playing it.

Then Emma changed her mind and put the piece away. She would tackle it but not yet. She was feeling emotional about what had happened in the masterclass and didn't want to invest that kind of anxiety in such a beautiful piece of music. She would wait for the Rach until she felt more stable, more like herself. Emma pulled out a book of music she'd bought from a shop in town, popular songs, and flicked through. She fancied learning something new, but something light that might raise her mood. There was a good Coldplay track. She folded the book back on its spine so it would stay open on the music stand. She began to play. It was easy enough that she could practically sight-read it, and after three times through she was more or less fluent.

After that, Emma went back to some of the technical pieces she'd been learning in her piano lessons with Wood. He was a hard taskmaster, but she felt lucky to have him as a teacher. He'd been a concert pianist back when he was younger but had to give it up when he developed RSI. His experience was invaluable, though, and it was as if every lesson she had was a masterclass, except without the audience. She practised a Bach sonata he'd given her, then an accompaniment part in an orchestral arrangement by a modern composer. She found these orchestral pieces hard. When she didn't carry the main melody it was difficult to make sense of her role, especially with some of the more avant-garde pieces. She had to imagine the solo flute or violin, or whatever the instrument was, floating above what she was playing.

Finally, Emma closed the case of the piano and took a big breath out. She knew she needed to stop hiding and find the twins. They had been there for her when she had needed it, when she had been missing home so badly she hadn't even been able to move. Now it was her turn. She turned off the 'busy' light and left the practice room, closing the door carefully behind her. She realised she was creeping around, trying to make as little noise as possible, and wondered why. It was with a bit of a jolt that she realised she felt guilty. She should have been there for Matilde right away.

Emma rushed away from the practice rooms and through the quiet corridors of the Conservatoire. The place was deserted now. She had been playing for much longer than she'd intended. She often found this when practising, that time ran away from her and it would be dark outside before she knew it, or she would feel so hungry that it felt like her stomach was eating at her from the inside. She left the building and walked across campus. It was only a five-minute walk from the Conservatoire building to her halls of residence but it was like she was walking on the spot; she couldn't get from one place to the other nearly as quickly as she wanted to. She rushed through the door, almost smashing into Henry, who was walking the other way. He frowned at her.

'Have you seen the twins?' she asked him, breathless.

He shrugged. 'No,' he said. 'They rushed off together and no one's answering either of their doors or phones.'

Emma nodded at him and then walked on, wondering if the twins might be ignoring him. They would answer the door to her, she was sure. Both girls had rooms on the top floor of the halls, above Emma's but on the opposite side, with a lake view. She rushed up the stairs, taking them two at a time, but had to stop at the top to catch her breath. She knocked on Matilde's door, once, then louder, but there was no answer. She walked along the hallway to Sophie's room and bashed on the door there like she was trying to raise the dead. Still no response. She pulled her mobile from her pocket and tried to ring both of her friends. Their phones rang and rang but were not picked up. She pressed her ear to each door in turn but there was no sign of life, nothing. It felt like the girls had vanished completely.

With a heavy heart, Emma walked down the stairs to her own room. She unlocked her door and walked in, collapsing on to her bed. She wanted to be with the twins more than anything right then, even more than she wanted to be a pianist. As she sat back, she noticed an envelope near the door. She walked over and picked it up. It was an expensive notecard, quality stationery, and she recognised it immediately from a set she'd seen on Matilde's desk. She opened it up.

We're going away, just for a few days, to regroup. I think Tilly needs a break, poor love. We'll be back soon, sweetness, so don't fret. Love Sophie X

Emma was touched that they'd written a note for her. It was like something out of another century, when they could have texted or sent an email. She liked the way they were archaic like this sometimes, traditional. It fitted them. She wanted to rip the card up, though, as if by doing that she could erase the mistake she had made. The twins were gone, and now she couldn't be there for Matilde. She'd missed that chance. Hiding away in the practice room had been a selfish decision and she could never take it back. The mistake tied a knot in her chest that she couldn't undo.

The twins stayed away, two days, then three days with no sign, then almost a week, and Emma felt so alone. She found it hard to be at the Conservatoire without them. There were other people on the course who she could have met for drinks or dinner, people she was out with all the time when the twins were around, but she didn't want to. The memory of what Hannah Meredith had said, in the bar in town, put her off but nothing appealed to her without her best friends anyway. She didn't even try to have a social life without them but instead threw herself into practice. There were auditions coming up for a piano recital and she was determined it would be her who was chosen. She needed it to be. She needed to prove to herself that she was worthy of being here; that it had been the right decision to come.

Emma spent all hours in the practice room,

hunched over the tricky Rachmaninoff sonata Wood had given her. A girl from a year above walked in on her at some point and breathed out an 'oh pul-lease'. Emma wondered then if she'd chosen the right piece. Had she gone for show-offy and would the other students see her choice and think she lacked class? She remembered her piano teacher in Manchester, his voice firm on the subject. 'You are good enough for music school,' he'd told her over and over again. 'Christ, you taught yourself to Grade 4.' Then he'd given her advice that she tried her best to follow: 'Don't let them intimidate you, because you deserve to be there and if in doubt, choose anything by Rachmaninoff for auditions.' She could, at least, follow the second part of his orders and so she would, no matter how disparaging other students might be about those choices. It was not their opinions that counted, in the end, and they were all so competitive. Their reactions to whatever she was rehearsing could not be trusted.

When the twins had been gone for nearly a week, Emma had a bad dream about them. She woke early morning full of fear but at first the details were hazy. The sense of unease stayed with her and strong, clear images from the dream came back to her. She had been fighting with one of the twins. She couldn't tell which but she could still see her face, twisted with rage and looming above her. Then there had been a struggle to breathe underwater and so much blood, and screaming. There had been pools of blood but pink and frothy on top, as if it was bubble bath. She could almost smell the iron of it. She tried to shake the unease off as she showered. She headed down to the practice room again, hoping to take her mind off the dream.

Emma sat at the piano, banging away on the keys. She hammered the Rachmaninoff from the instrument and demanded it join her in the room and shake off the sense of unreality she felt. It didn't help. She played until she had blisters but still the dream stalked her thoughts. She continued playing until she felt raw with frustration, and then she pounded a random selection of keys several times, as hard as she could. She turned, and almost jumped to her feet when she saw Sophie standing right behind her. Straight away she remembered the last time she'd appeared in the rehearsal room like this. Her stealth was almost supernatural.

'They're not the real final chords,' Emma said, without a hint of humour.

Sophie smiled, but there was something off about the smile, something not real. Her eyes looked red and puffy; she had been crying not long before, Emma thought. 'You were really banging that one out,' she said.

Emma closed the lid of the piano and stared at her friend. She realised she'd had no doubt that this was Sophie, not from the instant she saw her. She normally had more trouble than this with the twins when she saw one of them alone. She breathed out her name. 'Sophie.' The word hung in the air.

'I don't know how to tell you,' Sophie said. The curl of her lips looked involuntary, and reminded Emma of something she couldn't quite place, except that it made that knot come back again, the one right in her chest that restricted her breathing. She could smell the blood from her dream.

Staring at Sophie, Emma tried to keep breathing. She knew, though, that Matilde wasn't coming back. She just knew.

'She killed herself.' Sophie's voice wasn't more than a whisper but it echoed around the soundproofed room.

Emma's head felt hollow as she stared at her friend. Seeing the truth in Sophie's eyes, the facts hit her so hard in the stomach she felt physical pain. That was when she remembered, realised, where she'd seen the weird smile that had played on Sophie's lips. It had been her uncle, when he came to tell her mother that Emma's grandad had died. It was the involuntary grin of the bearer of the worst kind of message, news so bad it played with your synapses and the physical signs got confused.

She threw herself forward, bent double and hitting the piano's case. She breathed deeply and told herself she would not be sick. Her reaction played surreal and ghostly in the small practice room and she could hear girls crying but it all felt far, far away.

Six

The next thing Emma knew, she was coming to on the floor of Professor Margie's office, arranged on her side in the recovery position. Her vision was cloudy and her head swam. She pushed herself up to sitting and nausea hit her in waves.

'Are you okay?' Margie asked her. She was leaning over, full of concern.

'I think so,' Emma said. She turned to see Sophie sitting on the chair behind her. Her friend and the professor got out of their seats to help her stand up. Then they sat her down in one of the comfy chairs in the corner of Margie's room. The students had their jokes about the staff of the Conservatoire, but one of the mainstays was about Margie and her chairs. You knew she thought there was a problem if she took you to the comfy end of the room.

'Do you remember anything?' Margie asked her.

Emma shook her head. 'The last thing I remember is Sophie coming into the room. Telling me about Matilde.' She paused. 'That did happen, right?'

The professor and Sophie exchanged a meaningful glance that Emma couldn't help but notice. Margie cleared her throat. 'Yes,' she said. 'But let's focus on getting you properly conscious before we talk more about that.'

'I feel fine,' Emma said, trying to stand up. Dizziness made her grab for the chair and Margie came over and made her sit again, pressing a firm hand on her shoulder as if to keep her down.

'I need to be sure you're okay before I let you leave,' the professor told her.

'You kind of lost it in the practice room. I had to come and get the professor to calm you down. I thought you were going to hurt yourself. Then you passed out.' Sophie didn't make eye contact as she spoke, as if she was embarrassed. 'Don't you remember any of it?'

'No!' Emma was horrified. What had she done?

'Don't worry,' Margie said. 'It's fine. It was a moment of extreme stress hearing about your friend.'

There was a silence then in the room and it felt very awkward. Emma stared at Sophie and then at the professor. Her eyes rested on her friend. 'How can you be so calm about this?' she said.

Sophie shrugged. 'I already freaked out when we found her. I've run out of energy for crying.'

'People grieve in different ways,' Margie added. 'There's no point judging.'

Emma took in what she was saying. She was grieving. Her friend had died. She played these phrases in her head but they did not ring true. Silence was hanging over the room again and Emma realised the question she was supposed to ask, the one that the others were waiting for. 'How did she do it?' she said.

Sophie cleared her throat. 'She slit her wrists in the bath. Mama found her and I came when I heard the screaming.'

Emma had to stop herself from heaving. Everything Sophie was describing brought to mind the dream she'd had the night before, the screaming, the blood and water, the foam fluffy and pink, at odds with the pools of blood that coloured it. She didn't believe in premonitions but it was uncanny.

'Margie, you know what would be good for me would be just to get on with things,' Sophie said. 'I'll never get over this, so, you know. I want to try to get back to normal.'

Margie looked at Sophie and Emma watched her appraise the situation. She gathered from the professor's studied gaze that she was as confused by Sophie's reaction as Emma was, even if she was choosing not to judge it. 'I'm not sure that either of you should be here right now. You'd be better off with your families.'

Sophie shrugged. 'I'm as well off with Emma. Only Emma really understands.'

Emma turned sharply at this. It seemed strange coming from Sophie. It was how she felt too but she'd had no idea it was mutual.

'We can look after each other,' Sophie said.

The professor hesitated, looking at Sophie as if trying to weigh it up. 'Okay,' she said at last, nodding. 'Yes, that's a good idea.'

The two girls left the room and headed back towards their halls of residence. Emma didn't feel herself at all. She was still dizzy. It felt like she'd had too much to drink. Sophie kept turning towards her, asking if she was all right. Emma answered her at first, but after a while she just nodded each time. It was all out of balance, though. Sophie had lost a sister. It should have been Emma who was looking after her. She needed to be stronger and to be there for Sophie. They'd only known each other a few months, but they'd have to be there for each other. Emma had no strength, though, and for the moment she focused on putting one foot ahead of the other.

Emma and Sophie stayed together that night, lying in Emma's bed facing each other. They talked about Matilde until the early hours, things they had done together and all the ways they would miss her. Sophie told Emma that she had often shared a bed like this with her sister and Emma felt very privileged to be taking Matilde's place that way.

When she woke up in the morning, though, Emma had a few moments when she forgot what had happened. Then she noticed that Sophie was no longer with her in the bed. She sat up and looked around the room; Sophie had gone. Emma felt cold and alone, more so than she ever had in her life, even more than in her first few hours at university. They said it was better to have loved and lost but Emma wasn't sure at all. Why did you have to lose people at all? The leaden sensation that came to her every time she remembered she would never see Matilde again was achingly familiar; she had felt this way when her grandad died years before. The horrible finality was almost too much to bear. She'd spent her entire life worrying about her mum dying. She'd never thought it would be a best friend she'd lose first.

After a shower and a few minutes spent splashing water on her face, Emma emerged from the room for her morning lecture. She wasn't keen on learning or worried about falling behind. In fact she didn't have any particular feelings about her course right now. All she knew was that it would be better to be in the lecture theatre than not. In the lecture, she could switch off and listen to the words. Maybe not in order, trying to make any sense of them, but one at a time. Nonsense to fill her head with. It was all preferable to thinking about what had happened to Matilde.

It was usually busy in the cold, draughty hallways by this time of the morning, as student musicians rushed between practice rooms and lecture theatres, checking schedules for auditions, masterclasses and instrument lessons or practice. This morning was different. People were quietly going about their business and no one was really chatting. There was a strange buzz, despite the calm. It filled the air like a plague of insects and made Emma feel sick again. She walked like some kind of zombie through the other students. She heard someone calling her name and turned to see Sarah, another one of the first-year pianists. She stopped and tried to smile. Sarah came over and grabbed her hand. Emma wanted to pull away at first and couldn't work out what was going on. Then she saw the look on her face, full of sympathy and concern, and she realised that Sarah had heard. Another couple of the girls from her year and one of the boys were by their side soon too. Emma stood there weakly as they gabbled on about what a shock it was. All she could think was how news travelled fast.

The group surrounded her and shepherded her into the lecture theatre. As they walked in, Emma spotted Henry sitting about halfway down the hall, completely alone. He turned and looked at her. His face was imploring, she felt, asking for her forgiveness. She had never considered before the idea that it might be his fault, but it struck her now. Henry's lips curled as he tried a smile and she could tell he was hoping she'd return it, give him a sign that she didn't blame him. She couldn't do that, though, and turned away.

The lecture theatre was about half full. Students looked up as they saw Emma walking down the aisle. Many turned to whisper to friends sitting nearby and Emma tried to ignore them, slipping into a row near the back of the room. Sophie arrived soon after, and it was as if a ghost had walked in. Emma had never considered this before; how one twin would always remind you of the other, how when a twin died they remained absent and present at the same time. Sophie would see her lost sister every time she looked into a mirror. Emma wasn't sure she could have stood it. Unlike Emma, Sophie didn't look as if she'd not slept. Her hair was straightened and shiny and her make-up perfect, as usual, and her ultra-blue eyes flashed a challenge as she walked to the front of the room. The place went very quiet. Emma shuffled from her seat and past the others to where Sophie was sitting, slipping into the front row beside her. Sophie turned towards her and smiled, grabbing her hand.

Then it was like the whole place breathed out, a

few subdued mutters building into the usual pre-lecture chatter. Sophie put a hand to her forehead and looked down at the slab of desk that ran across in front of them. 'How embarrassing,' she said, as if the lecture theatre's hushed reaction was the worst part of all.

They sat through the lecture, Sophie sighing a lot and chewing hard on a pencil. Emma suggested they go back to her room afterwards and skip the rest of the day. She wanted to be away from the scrutiny and she wanted to talk to Sophie. She was worried about her friend. She knew that Professor Margie was right about people dealing with grief in their own way but Emma was worried Sophie might be in denial. Sophie was resistant at first; she said she didn't want to miss lectures and practice time at this stage of the term, with auditions coming up. Emma put her hand on her friend's shoulder, but Sophie batted it away. Emma felt stung but decided to rise above it.

'Your sister died,' she said. She heard her own voice telling Sophie something she knew already and cringed, but she didn't know what else to say.

Sophie looked back at Emma blankly, a look that said it all. But then she nodded. 'Okay. Just today, though. After that, I'm back to business. I don't have time to waste.'

Emma's room was small but it was now her favourite place on campus. She had made it her own with posters of art, Monet mostly, and her keepsakes from home. There was that piece of the Berlin Wall and an old snow globe of New York City. The snow globe still had the Twin Towers in the skyline, trapped in time as if by amber and shooting above the other buildings in a massive 11. Her mother had been given the snow globe by Emma's father; he had brought it with him from home, which was America. It was all Emma had of her father and sometimes, late at night, especially when she couldn't sleep, she would stare into the globe and imagine she could see him there, walking the streets.

As they walked in, though, Emma was embarrassed by these keepsakes. She placed an opened book on top of the snow globe and put on some music. Vivaldi. It was bright and comforting but at odds with the mood. Sophie sat on the bed and bit her nails. Emma noticed this and thought it odd after all the times she'd seen her scold Matilde for her nail-biting. She didn't say anything, though. It seemed petty to notice.

'This must be so hard for you,' Emma said, gnawing at her lip and wishing she had better words. She filled the kettle with water from the sink and took milk from the mini-fridge her mother had given her as a going-away present. *Students always steal milk*, she'd said. Emma didn't know how she'd known this but she'd been right. It had been the best present she could have got her.

'I can be honest with you, right?' Sophie said.

Emma looked up from what she was doing, surprised. 'Of course.'

'Well then, if I'm being honest, it's a relief.'

Emma put down the cups and had to steady herself against the desk. She turned and stared at her friend.

'Oh don't look so shocked. You said I could be honest, so I thought you could handle the truth.' Sophie's face had hardened and Emma had a moment's panic, hardly recognising her. 'You didn't know the half of it,' Sophie said. 'Matilde suffered for a long time and she made the rest of us suffer too. There's nothing more selfish than someone who's depressed, did you know that? All she could talk about was herself, and doom and gloom. It was getting impossible to live with.'

Emma went back to making the tea, hoping to distract herself from what Sophie had said and the cold tone of her voice. Her hands shook. She tried to make her moves strong and confident but her fingers vibrated against the spoon. It reminded her of so many music exams and auditions she'd sat over the years. In those, she found the way out was to lose herself in the music. There was no music in this situation, though, only the Vivaldi playing behind them, sounding uptight and fake. Emma remembered that Vivaldi had been what Matilde had chosen for the masterclass, and wished she'd picked a different CD.

'I'm not glad she's gone or anything, that wasn't what I was saying. I miss her.' Sophie's voice was quiet. 'I'm just glad she's not suffering any more.'

Emma abandoned the tea, walking over to Sophie and sitting beside her. She put a hand on her friend's shoulder but it felt all wrong, out of place and useless. Sophie turned and looked at her, then stared at her hand as if she was thinking the same thing. Her eyes narrowed and she pushed Emma away.

'Oh you think you get it but you just don't,' Sophie said. 'She wasn't your sister. You'd only known her a few months.'

Emma felt as if she'd been slapped. Her eyes stung with tears but she forced herself not to cry. She pressed her lips hard together and tried to calm her beating heart. She didn't deserve this from Sophie, but that wasn't the point. She guessed it was some divine right of the newly bereaved to be rude if they wanted to. She stood up and went back to making the tea.

Turning with the two cups in her hands, Emma saw that Sophie was getting up. She didn't say a word, but picked up her bag and left the room. The door swung fast shut; not quite a slam, but near enough. Emma stood looking at its white surface, holding the two hot cups. She wanted to drop them and fall to the floor. She had lost one of the sisters. She couldn't bear to lose the one she had left.

Seven

The night before Matilde's funeral, Emma hadn't been able to find Sophie or get her on the phone. She was worried that her friend might have gone home without her, a day earlier than originally planned, and she couldn't stop thinking about this. She stared out of the window into the black of the night. It was consuming; no moonlight or stars to break it up but like a black curtain across the window. Just for a moment, she felt like she'd died and not realised. It was like time had stopped, as if this moment had been for ever. She imagined all the memories in her head planted there to make her believe there was this thing called life but that it was a lie.

Being Jewish, Matilde's parents had wanted to bury their daughter right away, but had been made to wait because of the autopsy, leaving everyone in limbo. Life couldn't go on until death had been dealt with. She could only imagine how hard that was for the family. The black of the window seemed to grow as she thought about the practicalities. Matilde's body, cold and blue in a casket somewhere. Beginning to smell and rot. She couldn't picture it. It was like it was happening to someone else; someone she didn't know. A doll rather than the girl she had been friends with. When she thought of Matilde, she thought of her friend's laugh, her smile, the way she took so much delight from small things, like a vase of flowers in her room. Emma hadn't really thought too hard before about life after death because she hadn't thought hard about death at all. Now she was forced to stare straight on and she had to believe there was something left of the person she had known. The alternative was too much to accept, no matter how much more logical it appeared.

The blackness outside was getting to Emma. She didn't want to face the dark any longer or think about Matilde. She knew if she fell asleep the pain would go away for a while but she knew also that she'd wake and it would hit her all over again. She rinsed a cup and clicked on the kettle to boil it, waiting just long enough before pouring the water over a herbal tea bag. She held the mug like it was a comforter as she walked back to her bed. She felt wide awake.

She placed her tea on the desk and looked at the electric piano. It was never as satisfying, playing the fake piano. The plastic click made by the keys sounded more real than the sound that came out of the speakers or, more usually, her headphones. It had been all she'd had at one point, though. Her mum had not been able to afford a real piano. In fact, before the electric piano she'd had a Casio keyboard, not even full-sized keys or touch-sensitive and only four octaves. She'd taught herself to play on that, though, and she remembered it with affection. She'd spent more and more time on the tiny keyboard, and had asked for lessons at school. They'd said she needed a real piano to practise on, so she'd lied and said she had one. Once she was whizzing through her grades, her mum saved up and bought her this one, second hand. It had been such a luxury at the time. Now she had played on the pianos here, as well as on the grand in the recital room, she had been spoiled.

Emma needed to lose herself now, and she had always done that through playing. She turned on the piano and plugged in her headphones. She shot through some scales, just to warm up her fingers, then played some of the jazz she'd learned years ago but rarely played now. Then a more classical piece; something she'd written herself. She'd not got around to transcribing it and she hadn't even shared it with anyone else. She was too worried it wasn't original but something she'd picked up subliminally at some point. She would explore this more when she did composition, which didn't start until the second year.

It was hours later when Emma came out of her trance. She had played through the night and dawn was breaking. She was glad to see the blue of the morning cracking open the night sky. She didn't know where she went when she was playing, but it was almost as refreshing as sleep. She couldn't even remember the pieces she'd gone through now she came back into the room. She had been completely taken away.

One of the lecturers in their theory classes had talked about music being a way to forget you were going to die and that being the reason people loved it so much. Emma wasn't sure about this. For her, music was more than that. It was a way to forget she existed at all. To lose herself completely.

Later that day, Emma examined the schedule for rehearsal time on the grand in the recital room, where the concert and the audition would take place. She needed the feel of the piece on that specific piano. It turned out the entire cohort felt the same and there were very few spaces left. For some reason she turned, sensing a presence behind her. Even so, it made her jump to see Sophie so close by, her face just inches away.

'Hello,' Sophie said. 'Sorry about last night.'

Emma shrugged. 'Don't be silly. I understand.' She wanted to reach a hand out to her friend but wasn't sure if that was what Sophie wanted. She held back. 'I would've hidden away somewhere if I'd been you. I'm sure everyone understands that you want to be by yourself.'

Sophie pulled a strange face. 'I haven't been hiding,' she said. She looked a little annoyed at the idea she might hide from anything.

Emma didn't understand. She stared at her friend trying to work out where she might have been. For some reason she didn't want to know. Something had turned in Sophie since the night she'd stormed out of Emma's room. She was worried that Sophie was still avoiding facing the truth that her sister was gone for ever. Emma was spending a lot of time facing that herself and couldn't believe someone so close to Matilde could be anything but crushed by it.

'Don't you remember?' Sophie said. Her head was held to the side and there was something odd about the smile that played on her face.

Emma stood and stared, wondering what she had forgotten this time. 'You said you were sorry about last night.'

Sophie looked like she was trying to work something out. Then she smiled. 'Henry took me out,' she said. 'I know you want me stay in and grieve more, but this is my way of getting over it.' She paused, then said 'sorry' again.

A voice calling Emma's name carried across the hallway, making them both turn towards it. Professor Margie had tipped open her door. 'Emma, can we have a chat?' she said. Emma turned to look at Sophie, who was studying the schedules on the wall as if she too needed to practise on the grand, then nodded and made her way towards the door. The professor was heading for the comfy chairs at the far end of her room. Emma followed her, dreading what would come next. She liked Margie but she didn't want to talk to her about this terrible situation. She didn't want to talk to anyone except Sophie. No one else understood.

'Please take a seat, Emma,' the professor said, indicating towards the chairs. 'Tell me, how are you coping?'

Clearing her throat, Emma tried to speak. 'Well . . .' She felt tears coming and she didn't want to cry here. She took a deep breath.

'We had a staff meeting about this situation yesterday and I should tell you, we're all very concerned. You've been seen around the building late at night. I understand you might feel that throwing yourself into work is the right thing—'

'No, it's not that.' Emma heard her own voice, weak and squeaky, but she didn't cry.

The professor leaned across from her chair and put a hand on Emma's shoulder. 'Are you sure it wouldn't be better for you to go home for a while? We can arrange a leave of absence very easily.'

'No.' The answer shot out, fast, without Emma having to think. 'I don't want to go home.'

Margie looked like she was thinking deeply about the situation, about Emma and her state of mind. Emma wondered if she suspected her a second suicide risk, which she wasn't. Far from it; she was too scared of dying to do anything like that. And yet she knew, without asking, that the professor hadn't had this worry about Sophie. Whether her friend had been hauled in for a talk she couldn't be sure, but she was certain that Margie wouldn't think Sophie was likely to hurt herself. That was perhaps what was so odd about Sophie's reaction. She wasn't crushed, she didn't seem depressed at all.

'Why isn't Sophie sadder?' Emma's voice cracked as she spoke and she let out a little sob, despite her best efforts.

Margie shook her head and leaned forward again. She placed an arm on Emma's shoulder and sighed. 'Grief is a journey we have to take by ourselves. Everyone responds in a different way.'

Emma refused to let go and actively cry but tears were leaking out. She tried to wipe at her face subtly but knew she was fooling no one. Margie was gently rubbing her shoulder but now Emma had had enough and wanted to be out of there. The professor stood up and walked over to her bookshelves. She pulled something down and handed it to Emma. It was a leaflet about grief and bereavement.

'Can I go now?' Emma asked, looking up through her tears.

Professor Margie half smiled and nodded her head. 'You know where I am,' she said. It was the kind of nothing sentence that teachers and professors used all the time. Of course Emma knew where she was. That didn't mean she'd come looking for her if she had any choice in the matter.

Back in her room, Emma read the leaflet. She felt bad about what she'd thought about Sophie's reaction. Margie was right; who was she to say how you had to behave when your twin sister died? Sophie had said she could never understand, and that had hurt at the time, but it was true. The leaflet didn't really explain Sophie's reaction, though. It said that grief was a process and that there were stages. But this was the problem; Emma wasn't sure that Sophie was going through any of the stages she was reading about, except perhaps denial. She'd been angry too, that day she'd stormed off, but not since. You couldn't exactly call that one incident a 'stage'. She threw the leaflet across the room and watched it slip under the desk.

Emma had fallen asleep and was shocked to be woken by a knock on her bedroom door. She sat up and called that she was coming, checking her face in the mirror. She saw that there were marks from the pillow but there wasn't much to be done about it. Her mouth was dry and she took a big swig of water and swilled it round before swallowing. She looked at the clock. It was eight p.m. and they'd be leaving pretty soon. Sophie's father was coming to get them at nine thirty.

In case it was someone she didn't want to speak to, Emma opened the door just a crack. She saw it was Sophie and opened the door wider. Her friend walked in and sat on the bed. 'I came to check you were packing,' Sophie said. 'Well, that you were packed. You know.'

Emma indicated the suitcase beside her bed; she'd packed days before. How could Sophie think she wouldn't be ready? 'Of course. Did you think I wasn't coming or something?'

Sophie was looking at the floor and then Emma felt bad, because she looked like she might cry. 'I don't know,' she said. 'I know I've been weird recently. Since ... you know.' She looked back up and into Emma's eyes and hers glowed with moisture. 'It's just my way of coping.'

Emma wanted to get up and grab her friend but she didn't dare. Instead, she nodded and looked away. For some reason her eyes found the suitcase again. 'Of course I'm coming.' She got up and put on some music, to drown out all the feelings in the room. It had been unfair of her to judge her friend the way she had. How could someone cope with losing a twin, being torn from the person you'd spent your entire life with, from the moment you were conceived? It was even more than that in a way, because the girls had started their lives as one person. Worse still was the way Matilde had died; it was like she'd chosen to leave Sophie. Emma shivered, wondering where that thought had come from. Maybe the only way to deal with this was to pretend it didn't matter, hadn't happened, and to distract yourself as much as you could. It was understandable.

'Dad'll be here soon,' Sophie said. Her voice was flat.

'Yes,' Emma said, thinking how useless words were. She decided to take action instead, and picked up her bag from the side of the bed. 'Let's go to the refectory and get a coffee, wait for him there.'

'Okay. I'll text him,' Sophie said.

The refectory was deserted when they arrived. Emma was used to seeing the practice rooms and hallways this way, but the café was normally a busy place and it seemed eerie without the usual crowds. They waited by the counter for a while, convinced it should be open. A sceptical-looking assistant appeared eventually, avoiding making eye contact while she tidied and fussed under the counter. Finally she peered up. Emma thought she was about to tell them she'd finished for the night, but instead she looked expectantly in their direction. They ordered two lattes and carried them to a table, where they had to take down their own chairs before sitting.

The drinks were very hot. Emma sipped hers but Sophie stirred in two sugars then didn't touch her drink. She sat playing with her iPhone instead and they didn't talk. Emma felt so tired she was frayed at the edges. She realised she didn't remember falling asleep. She was sure she had been awake and playing the electric piano and then, next thing she knew, Sophie was banging at the door and waking her up. It was frightening, the sense of losing time, losing control and not remembering. She didn't like it one bit.

Sophie's father came in. He walked through the door and strode over to them. He was tall and appeared confident and capable, just as he had when Emma had met him before, when he'd come to collect both of his daughters one weekend that seemed a lifetime ago. Emma wasn't sure if it was what she knew that made her notice but she thought she saw a stoop to him now, an edge of disappointment. She was sure she could see the mark of what had happened, there in his gait. Sophie pushed her drink away. There was a thick skin over the top where she hadn't broken its surface.

'Time to go, girls. Let's get this over with,' he said.

These were good words. They summed it up.

Eight

Emma stood nervously behind the funeral party at the graveyard gates. The service hadn't started yet, but the hearse sat in front of them, a reminder of why they were here, and of the body, hidden away behind wood. Emma had only been to three funerals her whole life but she already knew they were terrible things. Part of that was the inherent sadness of the occasion but it wasn't just that. Everything about funerals was dire and dreary: the dirge of the organ music, the dull, dark colours everyone wore.

Emma had learned in sixth form that funerals in some cultures were different, like in India they wore white, and she figured that must change the nature of the event. Or maybe it just changed the nature of the colour, so that you saw white and felt sad. Matilde's family were Jewish and Sophie had told her that this changed everything, even though they weren't especially strict or religious. Emma looked around for the differences. The clothes people were wearing were generally dark but not necessarily black. There were no flowers. It seemed inexplicably sad to have a funeral without flowers. Emma was sure that Matilde would have liked some lilies or roses.

There was something foul about the reality of disposal, when you thought it through. The body that was once a person you knew and loved was reduced to something that needed getting rid of. Emma knew you couldn't change it; you could hardly leave people to rot where they fell, but it was still hard to take. Especially when it was your friend, your young friend who'd been so full of life and now she was gone and you'd never see her again. The final nail in the coffin, they said, and as she stared at the wooden box that held Matilde, Emma felt that she understood that saying in a new way.

As she was thinking about this, the coffin was lifted from the car. The men who carried the casket all wore kippah, the small caps that covered the back of their heads, a reminder to Emma that they came from a different culture. They made their way along the graveyard path. Close family followed. Emma saw Sophie, wearing a dark blue dress and matching hat, looking mature and sensible but stunning as ever. She wished she could be closer to Sophie and Matilde but she stayed back a respectful distance. She followed what other people did, hoping that would be right. Everyone was chanting but Emma had no idea what the words meant. It sounded very musical and she was disappointed not to be able to join in. It was unusual for her to be excluded from the music.

She lost sight of Sophie and stopped walking to look for her. Her guard was down and she didn't care any more what the other mourners thought. Sophie turned and caught her eyes, smiled. It was a small movement of her lips but one that Emma couldn't miss. She looked away and to the edge of the mourners and then she saw Matilde. It couldn't have been Sophie again because there was no blue hat; her hair was loose and she was wearing a flowing white dress that blew in the wind. Emma clutched her chest and took a breath in at the sight of her dead friend and staggered as she walked. A lady nearby reached over for her. 'Are you all right, dear?' she said. Emma was blinking. She could still see Matilde but that was impossible, wasn't it? She closed her eyes tight.

When Emma opened her eyes again, there was no sign of the second twin. Just Sophie walking ahead with her parents. Emma felt all the air leaving her. She thought she might faint and swayed to the side of the path, sitting down on the grass. The concerned lady followed her over. 'Put your head down, between your legs,' she said, and Emma did as she was told. Her skin felt cold as ice, wrapping around her. Slowly the dizziness abated. Emma pulled her coat around herself tightly but she still felt freezing. She knew she must have imagined it but she felt like she'd seen a ghost. She didn't believe in that kind of thing but it was how it felt.

The funeral party had stopped again and Emma guessed that this was part of the Jewish ritual. She searched the crowd ahead of her for her friend. Sophie was facing away from her now, no longer offering a smile. She looked small, and paler than she normally was. She looked as if she'd cried all night. Emma wondered how she had seen both twins. Matilde, standing on the edge of the crowd, staring at the coffin in front of them, and in it at the same time. She saw the twins' mother reach a hand towards her husband. Emma was taking big deep breaths and the concerned lady knelt in front of her, a hand on her arm. She saw the rabbi then. He was ripping at the clothes of the family at the head of the mourners, tearing at them as if he was deeply distressed himself. It was more physical than the Christian burials Emma had witnessed and the force of emotion behind it was terrifying.

'Were you a friend of Tilly's?' The voice cut through the air. It was the woman who had broken away from the other mourners to look after Emma.

Emma nodded, slowly.

The woman's face twisted with sympathy. She patted Emma's arm. The cold, clammy touch of her hand filled Emma with nausea. She hoped she would wake up soon from this nightmare and find that no one had killed herself, no one had died.

The wake was a very different affair from the couple of funeral parties Emma had attended for family members. Those had been in small, poky rooms, different places but had the same dark, cheap feel about them.

Both times there had been a buffet with sandwiches that were curling at the edges, cake, sausage rolls, that kind of thing. The spread at Matilde's final party was something else altogether.

The get-together was held in the twins' family home. It was the first time Emma had visited, which she thought was a shame, as she would now forever associate the place with this sad event. Not that you would have guessed someone had died. The gathering was a sophisticated affair, with cocktails and canapés. It was more like an engagement or anniversary party. People clumped in small groups and discussed the weather, the holidays they were planning. There was a photograph of Matilde on a table by the piano and a candle burned beside it. Emma couldn't help thinking that apart from this small touch, Matilde wasn't there at all. Her death, the burial they'd just come from, all of that was being ignored, pushed aside. As much as it was hard to face, she was disturbed by the way everyone was so steadfastly avoiding it.

Emma sat in a corner of the room, looking at a plate of food and nursing a drink. She watched people circulate, holding glasses high, air-kissing. She had never felt so far out of her depth in all her life. Not even in the grand old concert hall at the Conservatoire. There was the music there, though. It was always possible to lose herself when she had music. She saw the grand piano, with the picture of Matilde. The keys winked at her. But she knew it would be bad form to go and play it. Her hands itched for the feel of ivory, but she ignored the feeling and sat with her drink. She had made a fool of herself once already. Noticing the mirrors covered, she had said something to Sophie. She had assumed it was because of the surviving twin's reflection and how that might be too much for her family and had made the mistake of saying as much. Sophie had been aghast. She had told Emma about shiva, a Jewish mourning period during which they covered their mirrors. Emma had felt such an idiot.

In the far corner of the room, Sophie came just into sight. If her sister was dead then she looked the opposite of that, bursting with life, so full of it that Emma could imagine she had sucked the life out of Matilde. Emma had seen documentaries on the TV about twins, and how one could dominate the other to the point of destruction. The images from that documentary had stayed with her and come back to mind when she'd got to know the twins. Sophie was pouring a drink, holding the bottle high and letting the liquid arc into her glass. She looked relaxed and happy.

The way Sophie was standing as she poured, how content she seemed, it was out of sync. Everything about the party was. Emma had a sudden feeling that she was getting everything wrong, that reality had fallen in on itself and she was imagining things that weren't true. Matilde wasn't dead at all. This was a birthday party for the twins, and they were happy, pouring drinks for each other in the corner of the room, smiling and talking about how old they were getting, even though they knew they weren't. All of a sudden, she felt it so strongly that it was as if it had to be true. She was certain that Matilde was there, just out of view, that all she had to do was get up and find her.

She stood, sharply, making herself dizzy.

Emma rushed across the room as fast as she could, heading towards Sophie. She pushed past a couple of girls. One of them spilled her wine and called after her, but Emma was only just aware of this; it all played out on the periphery. Then she was beside Sophie and caught a glance of Matilde, just like she was expecting. She pushed Sophie to the side. She needed to see Matilde; she knew her friend was there somewhere, behind the curtain. She pulled the black drape open but saw just the silvered view of herself. Her eyes looked red and manic. Around her there were audible gasps at the way she had broken everyone's mourning.

Emma touched the mirror's cold surface, letting out a small sound. She had seen a glimpse of Matilde but it had just been Sophie, reflected in the sliver of mirror that had peeked from behind the drape.

Matilde's face appeared again, coming slowly into view behind hers. 'Are you okay?'

Emma turned, dropping the cover, and saw Sophie standing behind her. 'I think so,' she said. Her hand was still on the mirror, but she let it drop.

Sophie's hand went to Emma's, covering it and squeezing. 'I know,' she said. 'It keeps happening to me too.' She smiled and brought her mouth right up to Emma's ear. 'Thank fuck for shiva,' she whispered.

The whisper made Emma shudder; she turned and caught Sophie's smile. She couldn't bear it any more, and rushed out into the garden. She needed fresh air more desperately than she could say. She stood outside, bent over with her hands on her knees as if she'd been running. She thought she might vomit. She took big deep breaths and stared into the sky.

Sophie came flying out after her. 'Are you all right?'

It was one of the stupid questions people asked at times like this, and there was no good answer. Emma was too busy taking deep breaths to talk anyway. Sophie put an arm around her and looked down at her full of concern. Emma felt like a fake. She should have been the one taking care of her friend, the girl who had lost her twin. And yet it was Emma who was lost and Sophie was coping. She was dealing with her sister's death far better than a twin should cope with losing the other half of herself.

Later, Emma lay awake in the guest room. The house was cold and dark. She wanted to get up and walk around, fetch some water or a drink of something stronger; maybe that would settle her down. Something about the house oppressed her. It was odd because the rooms were airy and spacious, with high ceilings and picture rails, but Emma felt everything closing in on her. She closed her eyes and the room spun a little. She'd had a few glasses of wine at the wake, but she didn't feel so drunk that this should be happening.

She would have liked to have been able to play piano right now, lose herself in the notes. But there was no electric piano here, or practice room, and she would wake up the house if she went downstairs to play her Rachmaninoff in the middle of the night. She was itching for it, though. The piece she was practising for the audition was one of the most challenging she'd ever tried. It had been coming together and she was worried that the days off would set her back.

Professor Margie couldn't have been more wrong about what she needed right now. Going home was the last thing she should do. She would have been suffocated in the semi in Manchester. What she needed now was music, to carry on, push forward, prove to herself that the Conservatoire was where she belonged, the way her tutors had told her. She needed to feel it for herself. She needed not just to claim her place there but to show she was even better than that; that she was the best. Silence the jealous whispers once and for all.

Matilde came to mind again. Emma thought about the masterclass that had pushed her over the edge. She had known that Matilde was shy and found being exposed that way hard, but she'd had no idea how bad things were for her. She wished she'd realised. She would have talked to her, done anything. Sophie had known, so why hadn't she said anything? Why hadn't she done more? Emma tried to stop these thoughts racing around her head. She tried to stop all the thoughts, all the white noise. She closed her eyes. She slowed her breathing.

Her eyes snapped open. She had a sudden sensation that she wasn't alone. There was a noise like wind in the room, then a sound like distant crying. That was when she saw Matilde. Her friend shot through the air from above and straight at her. It felt like being thumped in the face. The last thing she saw was Matilde's eyes, the ridiculous blue of them that glowed of ultraviolet. It was as if they had been burnt into her retinas.

She sat straight up in bed with a sharp intake of breath. Then her breathing came in sharp and rapid. She could feel her heart thumping in her chest. She tried to calm down. What had just happened? She had been dreaming but it had seemed so real. She had been asleep. It took a few minutes before her breathing went back to normal. The room felt cold and very empty. She was terrified that she wasn't awake, even now.

Emma got out of bed. Her fear of the room she was sleeping in outweighed how she felt about the rest of the house now and she put on her dressing gown. She had a thought that this might have been Matilde's room when she was alive. She dismissed this idea; she couldn't believe they would have put anyone in Matilde's room so soon. They were her family and wouldn't have done that.

The house was completely silent as she closed the bedroom door carefully. She walked towards the stairs and then slowly down them. Despite the care she was taking, the second stair creaked. She carried on, almost on tiptoes. The dream had put her in a strange, freaked-out place and she imagined a hand reaching out, touching her shoulder in the dark. She imagined a door opening abruptly and someone rushing out, not necessarily a living occupant of the house. But that was stupid. Emma did not believe in ghosts.

In the kitchen, she turned on a light. The fluorescent strip flickered several times before it came on properly. There was a sound from the garden; an animal calling into the night. Emma searched for a glass, opening doors as quietly as she could. She found the right cupboard and located a tumbler. She filled it, then placed it on the draining board and splashed more cold water on her face. It was the second time recently that she'd woken and couldn't remember falling asleep. It felt like chunks of time had escaped her and she'd been cheated out of her own sleep. It felt out of control.

She took big sips of the water. The creak of that second top stair made her start. Who was coming down? She scared herself with thoughts of ghosts again. The door squeaked as it opened and a figure appeared. She looked pale under the fluorescent strip. Ghostly. Her dark hair cascaded down her back and her eyes shone out like they didn't need illumination.

'Emma?' the twin said from the door, as if there could be any mistaking her friend who stood there.

'Sophie?'

Emma walked towards her friend and put her arms around her. She was solid and warm and real and the opposite of a ghost. The two girls hugged like this for several moments, then pulled away. Emma was relieved. And yet she couldn't shake the feeling that they had both been expecting someone else.

Nine

The alarm cut through the air like an assault. Emma sat bolt upright in bed. She had overslept. She rubbed sleep from her eyes, then sat up, feeling for fingers and toes and checking she was alive, and not dreaming.

She had been dreaming, she remembered as she reached full consciousness. Details came back. There had been a house, rooms with high ceilings. There had been something she didn't want to drink. A cold feeling spread on her skin and down her throat. Something had been wrong in her dream. She remembered then what had been different. In her dream Matilde had still been around. She had been there with Emma and Sophie, sitting beside them. But it had been like Matilde couldn't see them both there. She had sat and stared like she was catatonic. She had not spoken and when Emma asked why, a voice had come from somewhere telling her it was because Matilde was dead. That was what had woken her.

Emma pulled the quilt around herself as tight as it would go. She shivered. Then a thought came to her, something far scarier than the dream. She had her audition this morning. She had overslept and needed to be there in twenty minutes. For the first time in days, the time she got up was important and she had slept in. She tore herself from bed.

The music she needed was sitting on the electric piano, where she'd left it the previous evening. She couldn't believe that she hadn't been more organised and got all the things she needed ready before she went to bed. It felt like someone had come in the night and stolen her time from her. She rushed around the room, grabbing clothes that looked clean and shoving her music into a portfolio case, putting this by the door to make sure she didn't forget it on her way out. She had a moment's doubt about the piece she'd chosen. She remembered the girl who had walked into the practice room when she'd been playing it, the contempt in her voice. She examined her hair in the mirror. It needed a wash really, but it would have to do.

There wouldn't be time for breakfast either, Emma realised. Her stomach growled and she hoped it would stay quiet while she played. She could have done with the energy from some food to throw into her piece. There were a couple of bananas on her desk so she grabbed one and peeled it. She tried to eat and put on clothes at the same time. She found she was doing neither, so she ate the banana as quickly as she could and threw the skin across the room, towards the bin. It landed on the floor but she left it where it fell. She pulled on tights and a skirt, a black T-shirt and cardigan. Straight away she was too hot, so she took off the cardigan and tied it around her waist. She walked over to the sink and cupped water in her hands, sucking it up for a drink. It said clearly on the sink that it wasn't drinking water but she didn't care. She needed to rehydrate and she hadn't time for other options.

Staring at the mirror, she pulled her hair around in the vain hope that she could hide the fact it wasn't clean. As a last resort, she scraped it back and held it in place with a hair band. She didn't think it would be fooling anyone but she examined the image in the mirror and thought she looked passable. She had a sudden sense of someone standing behind her. She even thought she saw a person there, in the mirror, at her shoulder. She turned, but there was nothing there. Her breath came in fast.

She needed to leave, right there and then, or she would be late. She held out a hand in front of her. She was surprised to see that she wasn't shaking. She remembered auditions before where the stress had vibrated right through her so strongly that anyone could see it. It was one of the hardest things about doing something so physical. Almost any other subject at university would be easier, in a way, because cerebral things were. You could learn them. With music, there was no replacing natural talent and pure graft. There were no short cuts and no guarantees. She could really have used a coffee but there was no way she'd have time, not even to grab one to go from the café.

Checking one final time that she had everything, Emma closed her door and locked it behind her. She turned and leaned back against it, taking a big deep breath. What was the worst that could happen? Well, it already had. There was this saying her mum used to have about how no one would die, which had never really put her mind at rest but now someone had and it didn't work any more. Sometimes, people did die. They died and there was nothing you could do about it. It was one of the most frightening things about life and she had only just found it out.

On her way down to the recital hall, Emma bumped into Sophie, who was going in the opposite direction. She watched as her friend tried to rush by with a little wave.

'Where are you going?' Emma called after her.

Sophie stopped in her tracks and then turned. She looked at the floor, blushing slightly, caught out. 'I can't do it,' she said. 'I can't come and listen to you play that piece. It was one of her favourites.'

Emma's breathing became faster. She didn't need to ask whose.

'Look, she used to play that piece, years ago. Hearing it will bring it all back to me and I just can't do it.' With that, Sophie was off, dashing down the hallway to escape saying anything more.

Watching her friend rush away from her, Emma was confused. The Rachmaninoff she'd chosen was a very challenging piece. It wasn't the kind of thing you learned unless you were a pianist. She couldn't imagine trying to play something so technically difficult on the flute, her second instrument. Why would Matilde have played it? That made no sense.

The hall was busy when she arrived. It wasn't as packed as it had been at Matilde's masterclass but there was still a quiet buzz about the place. Auditions always made the students excitable. The nerves and adrenalin and late nights practising followed by early-morning coffee meant a lot of people were wired, and they fed off each other. Emma walked into the hall and saw people turn to look at her. A couple of tall girls from her year, people she didn't know so well, whispered to each other, both staring as she passed them. She brushed herself down and put down her bag, taking the music out of the portfolio case. She breathed in and out, deep, the way her piano teacher had told her would take away the nerves. She tried to rid her head of thoughts about Matilde and Sophie and all those recent events.

The audition was open, which meant that students could sit and watch as if part of an audience. Their tutors said that this was a better way to do things; it gave them a sense of who could play in front of others.

There was the odd person on the course who, despite being talented enough to get in, just couldn't take it and lost it all in front of an audience. For the public recitals, that would be a real problem. It had never happened to Emma and she hoped it never would but a little flutter grew in her stomach as she thought about it. It might be that she had a limit. She might not be able to perform in front of a big public audience without crumbling. She realised then that she had a real chance of getting this. She was a contender.

The auditions were about to start and the tutors took their seats. The way it worked was that all the participants had to come for the beginning of the session, and would be called for in an order which was never published in advance. A handout was coming around now with the audition slots. Emma hoped hers would be in the first few. She knew she'd get more nervous as she watched others play and waited for her turn. She was passed a sheet by the girl in front and grabbed it, staring for her name. At first she couldn't see it and she had a panic that she wasn't supposed to be here after all; she'd come to someone else's audition. Then she found herself, about halfway down. Not too bad. She could hear whispers all around her and felt paranoid that people were talking about her and her dishevelled appearance. She wanted to start playing because then she could forget it all; forget everything she'd ever known and just be one with the instrument. She knew the piece so well by now that the idea of playing it was like an anticipated trip to see an old friend.

The first student sat down to play. Alex, she thought his name was, from the year above. She didn't know the students in the other years so well, not even the pianists. He placed his music confidently on the stand and began. He had chosen a prelude by Bach. It wasn't nearly as difficult a piece as the one Emma had picked but he played it well. With aplomb, her piano teacher would have said. He made flourishes of important chords and didn't put a finger wrong. The excellent performance set Emma's teeth on edge. He folded up his music in his own time and walked away from the piano looking pleased with himself.

Emma phased out. She didn't want to appreciate how strong the competition was for this recital. She had so set her heart on it. It was something to do with what had happened to Matilde. That had made her throw herself into the piece even more strongly and led to a sense that she was doing this for her dead friend. And now, it turned out, it was one of Matilde's favoured pieces. It was such a strange coincidence. Emma took herself away, to a deep place in her mind, and though she heard the odd note and saw people moving around her, she wasn't taking it in. Then she heard her name being called from somewhere far away. This dragged her back into the room.

'Well?' It was Professor Dyer. 'Do you want to play the piece you've prepared?'

Professor Wood was smiling in her direction. He raised his eyebrows in encouragement. Emma stood up and made her way to the piano. She looked down at her feet as she went, not making eye contact with any of the lecturers or the students littering the seats that sloped up and away from the stage. The grand piano loomed in front of her and she felt sick. If she got this recital, then she would have proved herself. If she didn't, she doubted she'd have the confidence to pick herself up and try again. She remembered the things Mr Nicholls, her old piano teacher, had told her so many times. *Take your time. Take your seat. Take a really deep breath and then start playing. Let the music take over.* He'd repeated this to her like a mantra and it had helped her so many times. It had got her this far.

The room was very quiet as everyone waited for Emma to start. She didn't look up. She didn't need to see their faces to know that there were quite a few people in the room who would love to see her fail. The working-class girl from Manchester who had taught herself to play; the *prodigy*. Emma unfolded her music and placed it on the stand. She remembered the girl in the practice room, the reaction to the piece that Emma knew now was too obviously technical, show-off stuff. Why had she chosen a piece like this? It wasn't her usual style. She couldn't change her mind now and so she placed her hands on the cold white keys and tried to centre herself. She would do what Mr Nicholls had told her and give herself to the music.

When Emma finished playing she looked up at the audience in the half-empty recital room. There were lots of faces staring back at her but no one was talking now. She had silenced them. She didn't know if that was good or bad. She was half expecting the silence to fold up into applause, but this wasn't a performance, it was an audition, and it was bad form to clap or cheer for one candidate when they finished playing, she knew that. When the previous students had done, though, the general bubble of chat had continued in the room, she was sure it had. The crowd watching were either impressed or mortified but she had no idea which. She could feel her face turning red, heating up with her growing discomfort.

Gathering the pages of her music, Emma stood up as fast as she could, making the piano's case close with a bang and causing a couple of the professors to look at her sharply. She had to be out of there. She had to be away from this room, these people. She clumsily pulled her belongings together and rushed towards the door. She saw Professor Wood out of the corner of her eye, getting up and heading in her direction, but she dodged him, running up the other aisle of the hall and as fast as she could out of the door. Her heart was racing and she felt short of breath.

Outside, it was raining, just a light drizzle. The water felt cool on her face and she walked in the rain, over grass, no idea where she wanted to go except away, away from what just happened. What was she thinking, that she could fit in here? It was never going to happen. She was not of the set, the class, and she did not belong.

What had happened back there? She wished she knew if she had played well or badly. She stomped through the rain until the Conservatoire looked small, in the distance. Only when it looked like she could pick it up in her hand would she really feel safe from its draughty halls and towers. She found a tree and sat down, hugging her knees and trying to get her breath back.

She had no idea how the audition had gone; she didn't even know if she'd played the piece at all. That was the thing; she couldn't remember any of it. She remembered getting her music out and setting it down, she remembered sitting on the stool and putting her hands on the keyboard ready to start. She could recall thinking she was ready and looking at the music on its stand in front of her. But of the Rach she could remember not a single note. Not one chord or moment or any of the difficult transitions she'd struggled so hard to learn.

She was used to getting lost in the music, but this was different. This time she had been lost somewhere else entirely and she didn't remember a single thing about where she had gone.

Ten

Emma woke to the surreal feeling of coming back from the dead. Her eyes were sticky and she sat up sharply in bed, breathing hard to pull in a rush of air. She switched on her bedside lamp. It took a while to fade up and then it glowed ominously. Hers was a small room and the bed was close to the window. Emma pulled the curtain open. The sun flooded in like a slap and threw her from her sleepy mood. It was later than she'd thought. The curtain was made of a heavy material that kept out the light, and this could be deceptive.

It was today that the audition results would be posted. Emma remembered this with a sense of dread and then some excitement. She was still unable to remember a single thing about her audition. Of all the things she could have blanked from her memory, an audition seemed too petty to bother with, irrelevant. She'd had so many over the years that they were simply part of her life. How badly could it have gone for her to have erased its existence completely? She didn't want to think about it. She needed this recital. She needed it to begin to heal the badness of the last few months. There was no meaning to Matilde's death, to the sad fact that her friend had killed herself, but at least being here could make sense. It had to make sense.

Emma pulled herself from bed and got dressed, checking the time. It was half eight. She had a piano lesson at eleven but the audition results would be out at nine, first thing. She sat on the bed with her head in her hands. She wanted to rush to the noticeboard and wait for one of the professors to come out and post the notice. She knew that wouldn't be a cool thing to do and, anyway, the waiting would kill her. She had to find things to do in the half-hour between now and then. She could shower, dress, eat something. She doubted she'd be able to stomach much in the way of food. For now, it was all she could do to sit on the bed with her head in her hands.

Finally, Emma pulled herself to standing. She felt light-headed and steadied herself on the dressing table. She caught her reflection in the mirror. Just for a moment she didn't recognise herself. She stared; it looked like a stranger, there in the mirror. Then it was her reflection again, just as it should be. She bent forward and lowered her head to the same level as the dressing table. Blood rushed to her head and she began to feel better. She looked in the mirror and there she was: Emma Jane Russell. She wondered why she'd felt so disconnected from herself the moment before. It was crazy, but she guessed she was entitled to feel a little crazy, everything considered.

Nausea settled over her but she forced herself to move and grabbed a towel. This was nothing that a good cool shower wouldn't cure. She peeled off her pyjamas; they felt stuck to her with the cold sweat. She walked the few feet to her shower room in the small student digs. One of the many strange things about living here was these confined spaces. How was anyone supposed to live like this? There was a kitchen and the common room, of course, but these places were shared and she never quite felt comfortable there. She spent her time between her room and the rehearsal rooms and out with the twins. Well, with Sophie, now.

It had blown her away, at first, all the parties and recitals and the beautiful people. She had felt a part of it, like she belonged. Looking back, she couldn't believe how naïve she had been. She wondered just how much the other students made fun of her behind her back, and if the twins had ever joined in. There were so many things she didn't know. Simple things the others had been brought up with, like which fork you needed for which course of the meal. Emma hadn't cared that she hadn't known these things until she'd come here.

The shower was cool on Emma's red-hot skin and made her feel better. She scrubbed at her hair. She wondered how much scrubbing it would take; when would she feel clean again? She put on more shampoo and lathered it up. Her eyes felt dry and sore, even though she'd slept. She tried not to rub them as she showered. She stepped out of the tiny cubicle and dried herself down. The towel smelled damp. She leaned out from the en suite and threw it into the plastic box that she used as a washing basket.

As she brushed her hair, she caught the reflection of her clock in the mirror. There were a few minutes still before the notice would go up. She thought about breakfast, even a cup of tea, but a sick feeling settled over her and she knew she wouldn't have been able to swallow a thing without it coming straight back up. She sat on her bed and hugged her knees. There was a loud knock at the door, startling her out of her reverie. She didn't get up to answer it because she didn't want to see anyone. Then a voice came quietly through the flimsy wood. 'It's me.' Sophie. Hearing her voice softened Emma and she went over to let her in.

As usual, Sophie was full of that energy and confidence Emma had always loved about her. Except that in Matilde's absence it seemed so strange; inappropriate. Emma couldn't get used to the fact life had to go on. Sophie bounced on to the bed and looked up at her. 'Well?' she said. 'Are you excited?' The slight European twang to her accent reminded Emma that Matilde and Sophie's family were international types who'd lived all over the world and owned 'property'. It was too far outside of Emma's experience and upbringing for her to really understand it.

Emma shrugged. 'I'm not sure.'

Sophie grinned at her. 'You're not sure? But you aced it. You must know that. You knocked the Rach right out of the park, Em.'

Emma was stalled; completely floored. 'You were there?'

Sophie screwed up her nose and it looked like she was trying to work something out. 'You didn't see me?'

'No.' Emma tried to find the words to explain it. 'I kind of lost it. Lost myself, you know how it is when you're playing?'

Sophie looked right at her. She had an expression on her face like she was thinking deeply, trying to make it all add up. 'But . . .' She didn't finish whatever it was she'd been about to say and straightened. Her mood changed like she was a doll that had just been wound up. 'You aced it. You remember that?'

'Actually, Soph, I really don't remember at all. I know this must sound weird to you, and I'm sure I'm coming across as a right nutter, but it was like I blacked out, then woke up when I'd finished playing, on literally the final chord.' She ran fingers through her hair. 'I think I'm losing the plot.'

The expression stayed firm on Sophie's face for a moment, then she looked as if she'd worked something

out and smiled. If it was meant to be a reassuring gesture, then it missed its mark. 'You've been working
hard,' she said. 'And things are bound to be strange for a
while because of Tilly.' She paused and laughed to herself. 'That's what everyone keeps telling me, anyway,
and we were all three so close I guess the same applies.
I'm sick of hearing about how I'm grieving, though.'

Emma nodded. She understood; it was like the way
people kept asking her, too, if she was all right, stopping her in the hallway to tell her she looked pale. As if
they thought that was helpful.

'We should go and find out if they picked you.'
Sophie motioned at the clock's reflection in the mirror.

Emma turned to look and then flinched a little. It
was a shock, seeing Sophie and her reflection. She wondered if she'd ever get used to seeing her dead friend
conjured up by a simple mirror. She had to look away.
'Come on,' she said, picking up her bag and portfolio
case. 'I want to practise anyway.'

Sophie tutted. 'A thing like this and you're just
going to practise like it was a normal day.' She was
shaking her head. 'You're more of a musician than I'll
ever be.'

Emma looked at her friend to see if there were any

traces of sarcasm there. She couldn't tell. If Sophie felt that Emma belonged here, then that was reassuring. She could begin to believe it herself. She hoisted her bag on to her shoulder and headed towards the door. Sophie followed. As Emma locked the door behind them, Sophie reached across, her hand on Emma's arm. Emma looked at the hand as if she'd never seen anything like it. 'You're going to get it, you know, hon.'

Emma studied her friend's face, the certainty in her eyes. She felt the flutter of a new fear building in her gut. What if she did get it? What then? Could she really do this? She wasn't ready for a recital, to play a Rachmaninoff sonata in front of hundreds of people. Her breathing was getting faster. She pulled in a big deep breath and tried to smile, but it felt very fake.

There was a crowd around the noticeboard when the girls arrived. Emma felt like she was shaking but, when she looked at her hands, she couldn't see them move. She hoped it wasn't obvious how nervous she felt, how much it meant to her. They all cared, her fellow students, and everyone knew that underneath but the trick was not to let it show. It was a little bit of magic that Emma wasn't sure she'd ever pull off.

As she came towards the noticeboard, people turned and the crowd parted for her. She knew then that she'd got it. She could sense what people were feeling as she walked by; that heady mix of admiration and resentment. It was strange, to feel this so strongly as she walked. Her feet moved, light as air. She felt like she was floating. And then she was there; she was in front of the announcement and the letters were blurred by the water in her eyes. She would not cry. She had to concentrate to find her focus. She read it once, then again. It wouldn't sink in. She turned and saw that all eyes were on her.

Pulling her music portfolio in towards her chest, Emma walked out through the crowd. She was holding it together; her eyes were wet but she hadn't let herself dissolve into the tears she felt rising. She would have liked to rush away, get back to her room so she could be alone, but she didn't have the strength. It was only then that she noticed Sophie, still at her side. Emma sat down without speaking and Sophie sat beside her, her hand on Emma's shoulder. 'Are you okay?'

Emma nodded. 'I think so.'

'I can't believe that you weren't expecting it. You're the best pianist here by a mile.'

Emma smiled at her friend. Her throat felt dry and scratched. A guy from the year above waved as he passed by; the sort of bloke who wouldn't usually take much notice of her. 'Well done,' he said. 'Well deserved.' The girl who'd tutted and huffed about the piece when she'd been rehearsing walked past but she didn't stop to congratulate her, looking pointedly away. Emma had no idea what the girl held against her.

After a while, the hallway calmed down and emptied out. A few stragglers stood talking. The drone of their gossip did not make any sense to Emma. She saw that Sophie had brought her water. She picked up the cup and took a big sip. The chill slipped down through her chest and into her gut and made her feel better. 'I don't know what's wrong with me,' she told Sophie. She had no idea how long they'd been sitting there. It could have been minutes or hours. 'I've been waking up and not remembering going to bed. Like I'm losing time. And feeling sick and weepy.'

Sophie took one of Emma's hands in hers. 'Maybe you need some help. You're not coping.'

Emma let out a sharp sound. 'You're coping.' She looked up at her friend. 'You're doing better than me.'

There was a silence.

'Matilde was a pianist, really,' Sophie said then. Her voice sounded far away and wistful.

Emma looked up sharply, and saw that her friend was staring into middle distance. It was the first time for ages she'd seen Sophie's grief, even though she knew it must be there, somewhere under the veneer. Her eyes were glowing with water.

'Tilly was a pianist, first. But she changed to flute so we could be together the whole time. It wasn't the right decision. She was better at the piano.'

'I never knew that.' Emma's voice carried her emotions, the utter surprise she felt. How could the twins have kept this from her for so long? It was almost as shocking as the loss of her friend. Like she hadn't known Matilde at all, or she'd never existed. Emma took another big sip of the cool water. She was feeling a bit better now. 'I need to practise,' she said. It was an excuse to get away, although it was also true. She had no idea how she was going to pull this off. She had wanted the concert so badly but now she was terrified about playing such a difficult piece in front of so many people. What on earth had she been thinking to put herself forward for this?

*

The Rachmaninoff sonata vibrated around the practice room as Emma played. It seemed to bounce off the walls and make fun of her for even trying. She kept stumbling on the same phrase, over and over. This kind of thing could drive you insane. She'd had her moments with certain pieces through the years, times when she wanted to bash and thump the keyboard with frustration.

Emma stopped for a moment and drank some water. She ran her fingers through her hair. She was ready to give up. She would have to meet with Professor Wood and beg him to let her choose a different piece. She didn't rate her chances. He was one of the hardest, most difficult of the tutors there, famed for his stubbornness. She certainly wouldn't have dreamt of calling him by his first name, not like she did with Prof Margie, not even behind his back. She'd put herself forward and she'd done it with the Rach, and Wood would insist she lived up to what she'd promised. She sighed and turned the music back to the first page. It was the first movement she had perfected for the audition and so she knew it from the inside out. She would play it again and that might make her feel better.

The piano keys were cold under her hands as she

paused before starting. Then she gritted her teeth and threw herself into playing. She let her head float off into the music. It was a good place to be. Before she knew it, she had achieved that trance state again and was away. The music drifted around her. She was still there, in the room, unlike when she'd played the piece in the audition, but at the same time she was miles away. Her fingers made the notes without her having to think about it, exactly as if she was walking, or running, or dancing wildly in her bedroom when no one was looking.

The door flew open and Emma stopped playing, turning around to see who was bursting in. She had definitely put the busy light on so that no one would interrupt her. It had not bothered Sophie. She stood in the doorway, looking dazed at the room around her, as if surprised to find herself there. She walked towards Emma with wild eyes. Something about the intensity of her stare, the madness in her expression, made Emma start back on the piano stool like she'd been slapped.

'This was her piece,' Sophie said. Her eyes were red, as if she'd been crying.

'Whose piece?' Emma asked. She stared at her friend and then she knew she was talking about

Matilde. 'This piece? The Rach?' She remembered Sophie had talked before the audition about her sister playing the Rach. She needed Wood to let her change it. He would think she was trying to cop out but it just wasn't like that. Not at all.

The door was swinging in the breeze from where Sophie had rushed in without knocking. Emma closed the piano's lid and turned towards her friend. Sophie reached for her face, touched her cheek and held her hand there. It was a tender, gentle gesture and yet it sent shivers right through Emma.

'She played this. Auditions, recitals. She always played that piece. It was hers, and now it's yours.'

Emma examined her friend's face; her eyes were darting around and she looked manic. 'It's not mine,' she told Sophie. 'It's just a sonata.'

'Don't be silly, darling, it's yours. It's ours. It's our piece.' Sophie's eyes were wet with happiness but it looked all wrong.

Then, all at once, Sophie calmed right down. She looked like she'd just woken up and found herself in the practice room. She looked like herself again. 'I don't know what I was thinking,' she said, 'barging in here like this. So rude of us.' She gathered her things, which she'd abandoned near the door on her way in, then waved and walked away as if her behaviour had been normal.

Emma sat staring at the upright piano. She would have liked to take an axe to it. She needed to practise but she couldn't do this piece any more. It was Matilde's. A couple of phrases echoed in her head. *It's our piece. So rude of us.* Sophie had been talking in plurals. She hadn't even done that when Matilde was alive.

It struck Emma that it might be an act: Matilde being a pianist, the Rach being her audition piece, all of it. Sophie was viciously competitive and it was possible she'd go this far to throw Emma off course. But they were best friends, so surely not? In a way, Emma wished she could pass this off as some kind of game. It was preferable to the idea that her friend was losing her mind.

Sophie was gone but Emma didn't feel alone. She couldn't shake the feeling that Matilde had been here, watching as she played. It was just a sense she had but she felt like Sophie had pulled something of her sister kicking and screaming into the rehearsal room behind her.

Eleven

As she waited outside Professor Wood's office, Emma chewed at her nails. She tried to stop herself but the moment she let her focus go, she was biting them again. She hadn't been a nail-biter when she was younger; she couldn't remember exactly when that had changed, except that now it felt like something she'd done for ever. It wasn't great for a pianist. You needed your nails short but your hands were on show and could be filmed up close; they needed to look good. In a way, it was your hands that were your instrument as much as the piano. That was the way Emma saw it, anyway, and so she wanted to stop the nail-biting but for some reason she couldn't.

Professor Wood opened his door. 'Come on in, Emma,' he said, smiling. As he stood there, he looked affable and eccentric; every bit the university professor. Except that Emma knew better. She'd heard the stories of his shouting fits and temper at the student musicians, even if she'd never felt the brunt of them herself. He was well known for his refusal to compromise with them about the smallest thing and his insistence that the students under his supervision practised until they could no longer move their fingers. The students respected him; it was well known he got the best out of people. That didn't make the prospect of working with him on the Rach any less terrifying, though, and Emma found she was shaking as she walked into his office.

The professor was sitting at his desk and Emma saw there was a chair facing him, so she sat down too. She had a moment's doubt as to whether she was allowed to sit down, and was about to get straight back up again until she realised how silly that would look and stopped herself. Anyway, he surely couldn't expect her to stand to attention as they spoke. Anything was possible, though, if rumours were to be believed. She had rehearsed so many times in her head the words she would use to explain she no longer wanted to play the

Rachmaninoff. It was show-offy and clichéd. She could do something subtler; better. But now, as the words ran through her head, she could hear them the way the professor would. It sounded like a cop-out.

'So,' he said. 'You're excited about the recital?'

Emma hesitated, just a moment, long enough to show her true feelings. All she felt was fear. She considered telling Wood the whole story. He would think her stupid, she was sure. He would laugh at her assertion that it was her dead friend's piece of music. Matilde, the suicidal flautist, what a story. 'Yes, I'm excited,' she said. 'And a little bit scared.'

'That's as it should be,' Wood told her. 'You should feel scared.'

That didn't help Emma's mood. She looked down at the floor and a hand went automatically to her mouth. She chewed on a nail.

'But not too scared,' he said, considering her.

Emma looked at the professor and decided she had only truth on her side. She would tell him. And then she found she was talking, words flowing from her mouth like she was vomiting. The things she was saying choked her, just like too much sick, and she could feel the squeeze of her face as she cried.

'Matilde ... the masterclass ... and flute wasn't even her first instrument and I don't know if I can perform. I can't do this piece. It was Matilde's piece, her audition, she was a pianist first—'

'Let me stop you there.' Wood had his hand held out towards her and Emma found his gesture stopped her dead. She couldn't even remember exactly what she'd said; she had lost control. 'What happened to your friend is a terrible thing. Terrible. But this recital is what you need right now.' He shuffled papers on his desk. 'I've seen it before, believe me. In my years here I've seen just about everything.'

'But I can't play the Rach,' Emma told him. Her voice was clear and firm now; poised. She had regained herself.

Wood leaned over his desk and gave her an intense stare. 'I know you want this,' he said. As he spoke, Emma remembered she did. She wanted it more than anything. The man was having a hypnotic effect on her; bringing her back from whatever space she'd gone to since her friend had died. 'I'll tell you something for nothing: Matilde didn't kill herself because of a bad masterclass, or because of being a frustrated pianist, and it had nothing to do with that sonata you played when you auditioned. Tilly had a lot more fucking problems than that.'

Wood's use of Matilde's pet name jolted Emma like an electric shock. She remembered the conversation she'd had with the twins that very first night, and the implications in what Sophie had said.

'You're going to play the Rach and that's that.' His voice carried the air of finality of someone who was sure of his authority. There were a hundred 'buts' running round Emma's head and she wanted to throw them at him, and yet she knew it was no use. He had made up his mind. It was her own fault. She had learnt the piece and played it at audition, and now she was committed. She wished Sophie had said something about the sonata earlier. She'd known that Emma was practising it.

Professor Wood moved from his desk and was digging through his shelves. He removed several practice books. 'This étude will help,' he said, pulling a book open at a page and marking the top corner. 'And this. Copy them both and put the book in my pigeonhole.' He did the same in a second then a third book and handed them across to Emma. 'We'll meet again in a few days and I'll hear you play these. But I don't want you to touch the sonata. What you played ... ' He paused. 'Well, it wasn't right, although it had the potential to be so much more than right. I want you to forget it for a while. You mustn't play it again until I tell you different. Okay?'

Emma nodded. That bit, at least, suited her just fine. She didn't want to play the sonata again ever. No matter how she thought about it, she couldn't dismiss the idea that the Rach belonged to her dead friend. The last time she'd played it, it had made her disappear so completely that she still couldn't remember a single note. That scared her more than anything else.

Back in her room, Emma considered packing and going home. She hadn't felt this low since the day she arrived. She respected Professor Wood because he'd never pretended it would be easy for her here. At her interview he'd been clear from the outset that it would be a hard three years; *more like a prison sentence than a holiday*, had been what he'd said.

'It's not like other degrees,' he'd said. 'You can't slack off and not turn up and spend your whole time out drinking with your mates.'

Emma had been shocked at the idea that students

would waste their opportunity like that. She smiled at that memory now, at how ridiculously naïve she'd been. Many of the students she knew learned more in the SU bar than they did in their lectures or, at the very least, they spent more time in the bar. There was practice and lessons that made this harder for the musicians but even then, there were students who did the bare minimum.

There was no way she could quit, Emma knew that. There were so many people out there who would have killed for the opportunity she had. Sophie would have cut off another flautist's hands to get a recital spot. Emma told herself she was being silly about the Rach, about it being Matilde's piece. It wasn't. Matilde had majored in the flute, and whatever her reasons, that was what she had decided. Wood was right: Emma would do the recital and she would play the sonata. She had no idea how she'd pull it off but she was determined.

There was a rap on the door; the sharp taps she'd grown so used to. The twins knocked in exactly the same way and it was a moment before Emma remembered that it couldn't be Matilde. As she realised this, she knew she'd been hoping it was. The quieter twin had had none of the edge that Sophie had. She wasn't competitive or arrogant or manipulative. She was just poor sweet-natured Matilde.

'Come in,' Emma said, but the door was opening already.

Sophie flew into the room like a rush of wind and landed on Emma's bed, bouncing her up and down with the force of it. 'How was your meeting? Did you tell Wood you wouldn't do it?'

Emma's breath caught. She hadn't told Sophie that she was hoping to wriggle out of playing the sonata.

'What?' Sophie sounded indignant; she must have read Emma's look. 'You told me last night.'

Another blank. Sophie looked convinced and sincere. Emma wondered if she was going mad or had a brain tumour or something. She couldn't remember the most important audition she'd done all year and now a conversation had gone missing too.

Sophie looked at her friend, concern brimming in her eyes. 'I've been all over the place too,' she told her. 'The grief counsellor, well, she says it's all part of the "process".' She made speech marks with her hand at that last word.

'That must be it,' Emma said. Her eyes had watered up, something that happened to her easily these days. This was to be expected too; as Sophie said, it would be the grief. Sophie reached for her, placing a hand on hers.

As their hands touched, a feeling rushed through Emma, something like an electric shock. She had a picture then, a flash of a childhood scene. It was a garden in France somewhere, Paris maybe, although Emma had no idea why she thought it was France. She was in the garden, picking daisies, and so was Sophie, skipping through tall grass. She gasped and pulled her hand away.

'What's wrong?' Sophie said, reaching for her again. She looked confused and fascinated as Emma arched away from her. Of course, being Sophie, she wasn't taking no for an answer. She grabbed her friend by the arm and stared into her eyes. 'What just happened?' she said.

Whatever had passed between them was gone now. Even though Sophie held Emma's arm firmly, there were no more gardens or parks or long lost summers. Just the stillness of the room. Emma realised how quiet it was.

'Nothing,' she told Sophie.

But Sophie looked at her with an expression that said it all. Emma knew right away that her friend didn't believe a word. Whatever it was she'd seen when Sophie had touched her hand, Sophie had felt something too. But that didn't make sense. She was going insane. Sophie let her go and they both sat together on the bed as if nothing had happened.

'I'm playing the Rach,' she told Sophie. 'Wood was pretty clear that he wanted me to and anyway, it's what I decided.' This was almost the truth; it would do.

'Oh well, darling, you should do what Wood tells you.' Sophie didn't sound convinced.

Emma remembered the first time she'd spoken to the twins about her piano teacher, and the strange vibes she'd got from them about him. She shook her portfolio case at Sophie. 'He's given me loads of shitty preludes and études to learn. Says I should leave the piece alone for a bit.'

Sophie nodded, as if this wasn't news at all. 'He did that before. I remember.' As she said this, her eyes narrowed and she studied Emma's face, as if she was looking for something there, something she apparently didn't find. She laughed; just a small sound without too much joy to it. 'Silly me, I'm thinking of something else.'

'I should practise,' Emma told her.

Sophie nodded and got up from the bed. 'I'll leave you to it.'

As she turned, Emma caught a glimpse of her friend in the mirror. It was an awkward angle, from the end of the bed, and for a moment Emma could see both twins. But it was odd because just for an instant, there was a doubt. Was it Sophie or Matilde in the mirror? Was it Sophie or Matilde in the room? She knew they'd had fun swapping round when they were younger and even fooled their parents, because the girls had told her the stories. A sudden, terrible thought flashed through Emma's head about a much bigger deception.

'Sophie?' she said. She was half expecting the girl in the mirror to turn towards her but it was the other twin who did. Things were back to normal now, everything in its right place, and she felt silly and twisted for thinking it could be any other way.

The living mirror twin was staring at her expectantly, waiting to find out what she wanted.

'I just wanted to say that I'll do this for Matilde. I'll make us all proud and remember her.' Emma wasn't sure where these words had come from, or if the sentiment would come across as twee and forced. She lacked sophistication; she knew that.

'Oh, I know you will.' Sophie was smiling as if she knew a secret.

Scratching at the door woke Emma in the middle of the night. It sounded like an animal, a cat or a rabbit or some other creature with claws and gnawing teeth. She lay in bed listening for a while, hoping the noise would go away. It only got more urgent. Fear built inside her stomach. There was something unnatural about the sound, something that set her teeth on edge.

Emma pulled the quilt closer. She didn't want to get up and go to the door, but it was impossible to lie there and ignore the sounds. She wasn't going to get back to sleep with the scraping going on and on like this. Worst case, it could be some wild animal that had got in, a fox or a squirrel, and she might have to chase the thing off. These animals were becoming less scared around people, she knew that, and that it wouldn't necessarily run for the door at the sight of her. Then she had another thought: it could be a rat. That would be worse. She could picture it now, a rat scratching at the door. She shivered.

A voice floated into the room, nothing like a rat. It was a woman's voice; singing Schubert's *Ave Maria* and singing it beautifully. Matilde's song. Tremors passed over Emma and her skin went cold. What kind of person would come to her door singing this particular song with all the resonance they must know it would have for her? She couldn't imagine anyone being so cruel. She forced herself from her bed and grabbed her dressing gown, pulling it on in a rage and heading to the door.

The scratching stopped as she threw the door wide open. The source of the noise nearly stopped her breathing. Looking up at her from the threshold to the room was her friend, singing like the performance of her life but on all fours. It had to be Sophie, but she was singing Schubert's *Ave Maria*. She looked like Matilde and she was singing that hymn just as well as her sister had and it was hard to believe that it wasn't Matilde. Emma watched her friend crawling across the floor and into her room. Sophie looked up at her blindly. She reached for her legs, snatching at her dressing gown but without much purpose.

'Sophie?' Emma called to her, reaching down, placing a hand gently on her shoulder. She needed to feel the solid, warm heat of her, be sure it was the living twin and not some apparition. She was as real and alive as Emma was. Emma waved a hand across her face. She didn't flinch or move and Emma realised she was asleep. She had never seen a sleepwalker before. She didn't know if people singing in their sleep was a common phenomenon. She remembered hearing that you weren't supposed to wake someone in this state but Sophie's blind eyes and the singing were both making the skin crawl on her scalp.

Worried about Sophie hurting herself, Emma guided her over to the bed and sat her down there. Sophie carried on singing, staring blindly out in front of her. Then she stopped abruptly, like someone had switched off a CD player at the wall. Emma guessed she should have known that both twins sang. Matilde and Sophie were made of the same genes, and would have the same skills and talents if developed in the right ways. It was just that Sophie had no involvement in the choral works, not even the choir. Now she was muttering, words coming out of her so fast that Emma couldn't follow what she was saying at all. She heard her own name, and Bouton's, then Sophie's too, but mostly the words blurred into a undecipherable mess.

There was something other-worldly about Sophie in this state. Her blue eyes wide open but unseeing, her voice slurred with sleep. Emma was fearful as she watched her friend sitting there, gabbling. She couldn't understand a word Sophie was saying and the way she was rocking backwards and forwards, spewing out the words, it was disturbing. *Speaking in tongues* was the phrase that came to mind, an idea from the Bible she'd learned about at school. Someone being totally taken over by the spirit and talking God's own language. Emma wasn't religious but that was what this looked like. The *Ave Maria* fitted with that too, except that there didn't seem to be anything holy about Sophie right then. Nothing holy at all.

Finally, Sophie stopped speaking, lying back on the bed and falling into a deeper sleep, a stillness. Emma sat on the chair near her desk and stared at her friend. Her heart was pumping fast. She didn't care that Sophie had the bed; she wouldn't have slept anyway after all that drama. She was fine with Sophie sleeping there, even with her shoes up on the covers. All she cared about was that she stayed there, still and quiet. Whatever it was that had come over her, she didn't want to see it again.

Twelve

Emma was sick of the sight of the inside of a practice room. If someone had told her she'd feel that way a year back, even a few months ago, she would have laughed. She'd been looking forward to university so much and to her whole life revolving around music, around playing her beloved piano; she hadn't been able to think of anything better. No other A levels to worry about, no facts to learn or books to read that weren't about music. With the piano, it had never been like learning. Well, she supposed it had, but it had been more like learning to walk or talk, a skill you assimilated without thinking too hard. Coming to the

Conservatoire had been her dream but it was fast turning into a nightmare.

One of the many études Wood had picked out for her was sitting on the music stand. She couldn't play it. Well, that wasn't entirely true. There were phrases that she could sight-read. But there were others that she'd practised and practised but still didn't sound right. The piece was very technically challenging but it had no soul. She found that, no matter how she tried, she couldn't get taken by it. So then it was just the technique, a matter of one finger in front of another, and she could hardly bear continuing. She'd swapped and changed the studies several times and they were all similar; every single one of them took the joy out of playing. She wanted to thump the keys until she broke strings inside the instrument and cut her fingers. She wanted to rip up all of the music. But, most of all, above all of these feelings, she wanted to play the Rach. She ached for it.

Wood had made her promise that she wouldn't, though, and she trusted him. If he'd said she wasn't to play it, then he had done that for a reason. She'd had enough of playing the soulless pieces he'd given her, though. Emma switched off the practice room's 'busy' light and closed the door behind her. Turning, she almost banged heads with Sophie, who was standing right in front of her.

'I woke up in your room,' Sophie said. 'What happened? I don't remember anything.'

Emma looked at her. Had she been waiting outside all this time? 'You were sleepwalking last night.' Emma wondered if she should tell her what she had been singing, how she'd been scratching at the door like an animal. 'Let's get a coffee,' she said.

Sophie nodded, and they walked away together.

The two girls sat opposite each other in the refectory. As she sat facing the twin, Emma felt she could have been the girl from the other side of the mirror. She felt like she had known Sophie all her life and for a moment her memory of Matilde was hazy, as if she'd never been real. It was very unsettling.

Emma had just a black coffee. She was hungry, but felt self-conscious about getting food; there was something about eating that wasn't especially cool. She wasn't even sure that Sophie did eat. It wasn't something she did publicly, that was for sure. Of course, she must eat or she'd die, she wasn't a vampire, although the image would have suited her. Emma thought about the way Sophie had acted the previous evening. It was the strangest thing and she didn't know what to explain to her friend and how to do it.

'You were definitely sleepwalking,' Emma said.

Sophie let out a small laugh. 'I've never done that before. Did I say anything weird?'

Emma relaxed a little. She didn't need to tell the whole story. It was a one-off; Sophie wasn't a sleepwalker and it wouldn't happen again. She smiled at her friend. 'Nothing I could decipher,' she said. 'Just a load of mangled words.'

Sophie looked relieved and Emma wondered what she had to be worried about. Everyone kept secrets, she supposed, but something nagged inside her that there was more to it. There was the radical way Sophie's expression had changed, the relief as the frown dropped was so palpable she could feel it hanging there in the air. She wanted to tell her then, that she had been singing Schubert's *Ave Maria*. She knew it would hurt her friend but she felt spite towards Sophie and it shocked her. She bit her tongue and then she felt ashamed about what she'd been thinking. She looked down at the table between them, unable to meet Sophie's gaze.

When Emma looked up again, Sophie's eyes were flitting around the room. She was chewing her nails, properly, like someone who made a profession of it. Like her sister used to. In fact, for a moment, Emma was so certain that it was Matilde sitting in front of her she almost called out her name. Then, just as quickly, Sophie was back, staring Emma down with that challenge in her gaze. 'What?' she said.

Emma shook her head. She certainly wasn't about to tell her friend what had gone through her head. It was a ridiculous idea really, because it wasn't Matilde's style. Sophie she could have believed it of, but not the sweeter, quieter twin. Matilde didn't have it in her to be so mean. Emma was certain that the twin who had survived was Sophie but there was something odd happening too. She didn't know how to explain it, but it didn't feel like Matilde had gone, not completely. When one twin died but not the other, it must always feel like that; the dead person's exact likeness haunting the world with your memories of them. But it was more than that.

Possession. The word hissed inside her head like water from a broken tap. She didn't believe in that kind of thing. She didn't believe in ghosts and vampires; that was all silly childhood nonsense. And yet she often didn't feel alone as she walked around the Conservatoire, especially at night. In her room, or by the lake, she would sometimes feel a presence that brushed against her neck or whispered in her ear, *there are more things in heaven and earth*. She knew that people took comfort from life after death but Emma wasn't sure. She preferred absolutes; to know where she stood.

Matilde was dead and there was nothing to be done about that, and so she should stay that way. Emma was sad to lose her but the feeling that she was still around was altogether more unnerving. She looked at Sophie. She was chattering away now about her own practise, things she was planning for the rest of the year. She wasn't waiting for answers from Emma and didn't seem particularly bothered whether she was listening or not. She was just getting it all out, and that was typically Sophie. But why had she sung *Ave Maria* the night before, scratching at the door? Why had she been chewing at her nails just moments before?

It was ridiculous to think that Matilde was here, possessing her sister. Emma refused to have anything to do with that idea. No; it was completely impossible. She studied her friend as she talked at her, or into the air. Was she capable of some kind of outrageous game just to spook Emma out? *Yes*, Emma thought, *she probably is*. In fact, it would be just her style. She frowned and looked away. She realised that she didn't trust Sophie one bit.

It had been a relief to leave Sophie and go off for her lesson with Professor Wood. It wasn't that Emma was looking forward to the lesson. Far from it; she was dreading it and knew that he'd be putting her through her paces on pieces that she didn't know yet.

She opened the practice room door and found Wood already there, waiting for her. He was staring at the piano keyboard and turned round to look at her in a weird, studied way. Emma checked her watch as discreetly as she could; she wasn't late. She felt like she was wilting under his gaze. She shuffled over to the stool and sat down, digging into her bag for the music. She felt Wood's eyes boring into her as she searched for the sheets. She finally located them and pulled them out, creasing the paper in her effort to get it on to the piano stand.

'Calm down,' he said, as if it was that easy.

Emma let her shoulders drop back and tried to do

as she'd been told. It was hard. She didn't know the pieces and although she'd only had twenty-four hours to learn them, she saw this as a failure. She turned and looked up at Wood. He was moving a chair to the side of the room. 'What do you want me to start with?' she said.

Wood sat down. 'The Bach prelude,' he told her. 'Are you fluent?'

Emma shook her head. 'Not with any of the pieces, not yet. I haven't practised them enough.'

Wood smiled. 'No problem. As I said, we'll start with the Bach.'

Obediently, she shuffled the paper to get the piece to the front. This was the easiest, which made her wonder if Wood was nicer than he liked his students to believe. She could sight-read many sections of this piece so that she could play it in faltering, jerky chunks, certainly not what she'd call fluent because she had to keep stopping. She glanced again at the professor, who had closed his eyes and was sitting ready to listen. This was his famous technique; he always listened without looking to begin with, to judge what his pianist was doing from the sound alone. Emma began to play the prelude. She stumbled at first, making lots of mistakes, but then she got into her stride in a couple of places and it wasn't an altogether bad job, not for sight-reading on a technical piece. She turned to look at Wood.

The professor opened his eyes. 'What are you looking at me for?' he said.

Emma tried to think of the right answer. She looked at the piano as if she might find it there.

'You're looking for my approval, maybe? I think you do that. I think you do that far too much.'

Emma could feel herself blushing. She didn't know if he was right or not but that he would think that made her die inside. 'I'm just trying to play it right,' she said.

Wood didn't reply to this but stood up, and began pacing around the room. Emma didn't think she would be able to play with him pacing like that but she saw him signalling with a spin of his hand that she should play it again. She turned back to look at the music. She placed her hands carefully on the keys and started once more. She'd played just half a phrase when he pulled her up.

'Stop,' he said, holding up a hand. 'Stop, stop, stop!' The way he was speaking made it sound like an emergency. Emma pulled herself up sharply.

Wood came over and leaned against the piano case.

His head was tilted as he spoke and he was looking at some random point in space. 'You need to get this exactly right, that's the point.' His voice had gone all sing-song. 'You can do the passion. I've seen that. That's the trick to pull off because we have far too many technical pianists here and we don't have enough who can do what you do.' He looked as though he was searching for the words. 'It's as if the music comes from a spiritual place and not your brain. When you're playing sometimes, it's like you remove yourself from the situation and give us just the music. That's a real talent.'

Emma smiled at the compliment. She couldn't help thinking he'd be shocked at how truly she'd removed herself when she'd played at the audition, though.

'We need to work on accuracy now. You can't do a piece like that sonata and not play it exactly right. That's why the specific studies I've given you, and why you're not allowed near the piece for a while.' He was nodding as he said this, as if he was agreeing with himself. 'Play it again,' he said.

Emma did as she was told. She was already bored of this prelude; it was far too easy for her. Maybe that was the point. She thought about each piece she'd tried.

She could see where Wood was going; each held a secret, an aspect of the Rachmaninoff sonata that she had struggled with when practising before. She wondered how many mistakes she'd made at the audition. She tried to put that to the back of her mind and play. She didn't feel like she was getting a note wrong now. Wood was there again, though, his hand in the air in that authoritative way he had about him. Emma had no doubt that he wanted her to stop.

'This isn't working.' He was pacing again. 'The rhythm's not right.' His voice was raised and stressed.

Emma wanted to snap back that she was trying really hard but the words didn't come. Her throat felt dry and rough. She bit her lip and started playing again.

Wood made her play it again. And again. He made her focus on each particular phrase. He even shoved on the metronome as if he thought she was a beginner.

Finally he waved his hand in the air. 'You have that one,' he said. 'More or less. But you still need to work on the rhythm.' He leaned over so that he was breathing in her ear when he spoke again. 'Practise just this one until we meet tomorrow. Use the metronome until the beat is really happening for you.'

Emma felt pure frustration. She was trying so hard.

She didn't need to practise this piece any more; she had it down. She definitely didn't need a metronome to count time for her; that stuff came from within her and she had never used one. What was he trying to do to her?

'Will you do as I've asked?'

Emma didn't answer. She wasn't sure she would.

'Do you trust me?' he said, then.

Emma remembered that she did. She was exhausted and wanted to stop. She didn't want to see this prelude ever again. But she trusted Wood. He would get the Rach out of her, she knew he would.

'Yes,' she said. 'I trust you and I'll do what you ask.'

Professor Wood nodded, as if he'd known the answer the entire time.

Thirteen

Emma sat on her bed and thought about Matilde. It wasn't getting any easier to accept that she would never see her friend again. She thought she might have been feeling a little better by now; she hadn't really known Matilde that long. She'd been a minor player in the dead twin's life and it felt sad to admit this. She tried to fill herself with the platitudes other people had repeated to her since Matilde had died: how her friend would always be there in her heart, how her memory kept her alive. She felt terribly sad about Tilly's death, and yet it was surreal sometimes because it didn't feel like she'd gone. There was no dark space where she should have been.

A shiver went through her; a breeze from the window she thought, but she checked and it was closed. She leaned over and pressed the play button on her stereo so that it would start the CD over again, then she pulled her quilt tightly around her. Emma's laptop flashed from the bedside table, where it was plugged in and charging. She reached for it; you didn't ever have to feel alone when you had the internet. She powered up her laptop and put in her password. It came to life and she opened a browser window.

That was when she had the idea: she would listen to the sonata. Wood had said she couldn't play it and she would obey him, but he hadn't said she couldn't listen to the piece of music. YouTube was such a gift for a young musician. You could always find a video of someone playing a piece well and learn from them, like you had twenty-four-hour masterclasses at your disposal. She turned off her CD player and searched for some Rachmaninoff. The first few links were of the man himself, playing his own concertos. She selected one of these and set it going. There was no video, unfortunately, just a still photo and the music, but it felt eerie to hear the sound of Rachmaninoff himself, the ghost of him playing. She thought then that she would

164

like to be a composer and put her mark on the world, leave bits of herself behind. It was the first time that idea had come to her. She had always wanted to be a concert pianist before.

Emma stopped the video clip. The room was cold. She thought about getting up to put on the heater but that meant getting colder first, so she wrapped herself tighter in the quilt. She focused again, searching for the particular sonata she was going to play. She found an appropriate link: *Masterclass, in Birmingham*. She opened up the video and listened to the familiar opening bars. As soon as she heard it, she longed to play it, to get lost in that piece. She hated Wood for stopping her; a feeling that came to her strong and then stuck in her throat. That moment passed and there was just the music. She closed her eyes and listened.

When Emma opened her eyes again, she almost dropped the laptop. She stared at the screen. The young girl playing the piece looked like Matilde. It surely couldn't be her dead friend? She pulled the laptop closer so she could make sure. Then, all at once, it wasn't Matilde at all. A girl who looked similar but not Matilde. Emma slammed the laptop shut. It was then she heard the sounds coming from the hallway outside, the unmistakable female vocal lead. *Ave Maria*. Sophie was sleepwalking in the corridor again. Emma leapt up from her bed and pulled on a dressing gown, flying out through her door and into the darkness of the corridor.

This time, she wasn't the only person who had noticed Sophie's presence in the hallway. Henry was out of his room a few doors down and staring at his girl-friend. He was walking over to Sophie and he looked furious.

'Why's she doing this?' he said. He looked as if he'd like to take her by the shoulders and shake her.

'I don't know. She did the same thing last night. She's sleepwalking.'

Henry snorted. 'I bet she bloody isn't.' He turned towards Sophie and stared right at her sightless eyes. 'Stop fucking around,' he said. But Sophie continued singing and didn't appear to have heard a thing.

'I'll sort her out,' Emma said, and she took hold of Sophie's hand, guiding her into her room. Henry walked away but he was muttering. Emma wondered what had passed between them that he could believe Sophie was faking. She wished Sophie would stop singing the aria. Her beautiful voice was penetrating and the way it shaped her face brought to mind Matilde far too readily. Emma felt haunted. She thought about all the glimpses she'd had, all the times she'd caught sight of her dead friend and been mistaken, like a few moments ago on her computer. It was just her grief playing out, but she couldn't help feeling spooked by it.

Sophie had stopped singing, which was a blessed relief. Emma was expecting her to mumble herself to sleep now, the way she had done the night before. But she just sat on the bed, staring into space. And then it was like she had shaken herself from a trance and was fully awake.

'I had a strange dream,' she said. 'I dreamed I'd died.' She was completely lucid but Emma wondered if she was awake yet, because she didn't appear to be at all surprised to find herself in Emma's room instead of her own. 'Oh, Ems, it was dreadful.'

A chill shook its way through Emma's body and made her jaw clench. Only one person in the world called her Ems, and it wasn't Sophie. What was happening? She told herself that Sophie was asleep and dreaming still, imagining herself as her sister. It was hardly a leap of faith.

The twin on the bed stared at her and she didn't

seem to be asleep. 'It feels like weeks since I've seen you,' she said, standing up and touching things on the shelves, Emma's little keepsakes. 'I love this snow-storm,' she said. 'We went to New York for Christmas once. Sophie was a pain, though. She so hates the cold.'

Emma wanted to wake her now, shake her until her bones rattled and she would stop talking like this. She didn't want to travel this path. She thought about what Henry had said and considered the idea that Sophie was playing a game with her. She didn't believe he knew her friend as well as she did, though. Sophie was a nightmare but she'd been through a lot. Who wouldn't go a little crazy?

'Please stop,' she said, and she wasn't sure if she was appealing to Sophie's better side or to the girl her friend thought she was in her dream.

Sophie snapped round to face her. 'Stop what? Touching your belongings?' She looked hurt. It was a look Emma recognised but once again it made her think of the other twin. She stared at Sophie. She didn't look asleep at all. There was no more sense of blind-ness about her eyes and her speech was completely normal. A thought came into her head, the idea of two twins in one body. Was that possible? She didn't believe in things like that. When you died, you were gone, and that was that.

'You're being hurtful,' Sophie said. 'I wasn't doing you any harm.'

Taking her friend's hand, Emma guided her back to the bed. She let herself be led and this settled Emma's mind a little; she must be dreaming. 'Sophie, Matilde's dead,' she said. 'She killed herself. I know you're asleep but you must remember.'

The other girl looked up at her, her face twisted with fear. 'Why are you saying that? Why are you talking to me like I'm Sophie?' She looked genuinely terrified by the idea and squeezed Emma's hand, harder and harder.

'You're hurting me,' Emma said. She let out a screech as her friend's hand tightened and tightened and then pulled her own hand away, shaking it to get rid of the pain.

Then the girl on the bed was talking, fast. 'Don't trust Sophie,' she said. She mumbled for a bit and Emma was glad to hear this; a sign that she was asleep after all. Her eyes rolled back in her head. Then she was talking again, faster still. 'Don't trust her. The masterclass.' It was like she was struggling to get the words out. *Struggling to come through* was the phrase that came into Emma's head. But that was ridiculous. As if she believed her friend was possessed by her sister, in a supernatural way. Then Sophie looked straight into Emma's eyes. 'I was terrified about the masterclass and Sophie offered to help. She'd do the class for me. Help me out. She knew that piece like the back of her hand and she doesn't care about an audience. She likes it. And so I said yes, that this was a good idea.'

Emma wished that she could close her ears. If this was a game on Sophie's part then it was a very twisted one. She wasn't capable of that. Emma had to believe that she wasn't.

'So she did the masterclass for me and you saw what happened. Bitch.' The final word was said with so much venom, and then Sophie flew back on the bed so hard that Emma was worried she would bang her head against the wall. She was laughing but it wasn't a joyful sound at all. It was manic and mad. Her eyes rolled and her body bucked and kicked. Emma thought she might be having a fit and was about to call for help, but then Sophie settled. Her eyes opened. She looked horrified.

'What am I doing here?' she said. 'Did I do the same thing again?'

Emma was shaking all over as she walked towards her friend. 'Sophie?' she said. Her voice was barely more than a whisper.

'Well who else did you think it might be?' She sounded annoyed. She'd always been the twin who got irritated when people mixed them up.

'You were ...' Emma didn't know how to phrase it to explain. 'You didn't seem yourself.'

The twin on the bed gazed over at her friend, and Emma wasn't sure if she knew everything she'd done and was waiting to laugh loudly at her for being so foolish. She remembered that day in the recital hall, and how she had lost her sense of who was who, and wondered if what she'd just heard explained everything.

None of the scenarios that raced around her head made sense. Her friend couldn't be possessed. It was ridiculous to think that the dead twin was coming out through her sister, trying to get a message across. Emma refused to believe it. Either Sophie was playing some kind of elaborate game at her expense, or this wasn't Sophie at all, and Matilde was playing a sick joke on the whole world and pretending to be her dead sister. Neither of these pictures fitted with the image she had of the twins. But they were the only alternatives to the supernatural explanations and she wasn't having any of that hocus-pocus. The only thing she needed to work out now was which of the twins was the nasty piece of work. Was it Matilde or Sophie who was capable of these games and deception?

That was when the strangest thing happened. Emma had no idea where it came from but she had a sudden urge to do what Sophie had done: to sing the *Ave Maria*. The desire grew in her fast; she wasn't sure where it came from but it was overwhelming. There was a part of her that thought better of it but that part was easily stilled. She opened her mouth and the music came from it. She wanted to hit the notes more than she could have explained. She felt a love for the vocal arrangement she had never felt before. It bubbled in her stomach and out through her throat.

Sophie stared at her. 'What are you doing?' Her face screwed up with anger. 'What are you playing at, Emma?'

Emma carried on singing. She didn't have an answer; she had no idea at all what she was playing at, or what Sophie had been trying to achieve either. Right now, her friend looked livid. Her eyes narrowed and she stood up from the bed, heading towards Emma.

'Stop that!' she said. She got closer and closer and at the same time her voice got louder. 'Stop it, Emma. Stop!'

Emma didn't stop, though. She hit the notes like she didn't know she was able. She had always been a decent singer but this was beyond her usual skills. She had no clue where the beauty and purity in her voice came from. She felt like she was soaring above the Conservatoire, above the university, above the world. And then she came to the end of the music and she was lost. She didn't know what she would say to Sophie, who was staring at her open-mouthed and looked like she might hit her.

'That's what you've been singing,' Emma said, as if it was an excuse for what she'd done herself.

'When?' Sophie sounded incredulous. 'There's no way I'd have sung that after what happened to my sister. It was Matilde's song, you know that.'

'Isn't there?' Emma was feeling cruel, an emotion that was new to her. It made everything warp around her; even her voice sounded different. The cruelty lit her from within and filled her with a vitality she hadn't had in weeks. 'You don't like my singing?' she said.

There was no reply; Sophie just stared at Emma.

Then Emma came to her senses. Sanity rushed in

and she was confused; what had come over her? She let herself fall on to the bed. All the energy had left her like air from a balloon. 'I'm sorry,' she said. 'You've been singing it, though, at night. It freaked me out. Henry too. He said you were playing a game.'

'He said that?' Sophie's eyes narrowed. 'I sang that?'

Emma nodded. She should tell her everything, all the things she'd heard her say before she woke up, or came to her senses. Sophie would want to know that she'd revealed the big secret about the masterclass. Emma believed it completely. There were so many things that it explained. She looked at Sophie and remembered she had been told not to trust her, and out of her own mouth as well. 'You sang it,' she told her. 'Tonight and last night as well.'

'I don't remember,' Sophie said. She seemed genuine and looked confused. She turned towards the mirror as if she might see the answer there. Maybe she thought she could ask her sister. 'I don't remember a thing.' She sat back down on the bed. 'I still don't get why you sang it to me.'

Emma looked into the mirror too. It disturbed her, seeing the girl in the mirror and the girl on the bed. The twins again. It answered one question, though. It was definitely Sophie on the bed. If anyone was scheming and deceiving people, it was Sophie. Emma found she was not surprised. 'I don't know. It was like I had to sing it. I felt compelled to, as if I could change the world, or like something really bad would happen if I didn't.'

Sophie stared at the twin in the mirror. 'She's really got to us both, hasn't she?'

'Yes,' Emma said, nodding her head slowly. 'I still can't believe what she did.'

Sophie said nothing in reply to this, but stared at the image of her sister in the looking glass. 'We have to stick together,' she said eventually. 'We're the only two people who can understand.'

'Yes,' Emma said, but her voice sounded odd and she was sure, had she been Sophie, she would have thought she didn't mean it.

'I sometimes feel like she's still here.' Sophie was staring at her reflection, her mirror twin.

'Yes, me too,' Emma said. The words slipped out before she could stop them. 'But she's not. We have to remember that.' That word came to her again. *Possessed*. It was the stuff and nonsense of fairy tales and spooky stories and Emma refused to believe in it.

Sophie was still staring into the mirror. She didn't look convinced at all. 'Ave freaking Maria,' she said. 'That's just typical of her.' She smiled, a gesture that was full of regret and nostalgia and a million more things.

Emma wanted to ask what was typical of Sophie. Lies and deception? Games mean enough to drive someone to their death? 'Yes, typical,' she said, as if she was agreeing. She looked at her friend and wondered what Henry had meant. There was something that had passed between him and the twins that Emma didn't know about.

All the common sense in the world wasn't helping Emma sort out her head on this subject. She knew that someone who had died was gone, definitively and for ever. Yet at the same time, she felt exactly the way Sophie did about it. It didn't feel like Matilde had gone at all.

Fourteen

Emma had a lesson first thing with Professor Wood. It was no more fun than the previous one, although he at least focused on a different piece of music this time. She was getting desperate to play the sonata. She just wanted to be allowed to go for it with a piece of music she could get lost in. She knew this must be part of the professor's plan, to get her riled up and desperate to play it, but it was still hard to take.

After the lesson, Emma went to her room. She wanted to be alone. She lay there staring at the ceiling, wondering what to make of what she'd seen and heard the previous evening. Matilde gone, Sophie still alive but all over the place; her world had crumbled beyond recognition in a matter of weeks. Suddenly she felt very homesick. She wanted to drink hot chocolate sitting on the sofa talking to her mum. She wanted to go shoe shopping in the Trafford Centre, all those silly, super-normal things that she had taken for granted. She would have given all her dreams in exchange for those things, right then and there, had it been possible.

As she lay there, Emma became more and more sure that she wanted to confront Sophie about what had happened the previous night. She didn't buy Sophie's act any more. She couldn't have wandered around the corridor singing that piece of music without knowing she was doing it. Henry had sussed her right away. Emma felt naïve for not seeing right through her. She was so very young and silly. The secret that Sophie had told her last night, when she was pretending to be Matilde, was playing with her head.

Finally, Emma could stand it no longer. She was either going to play the Rach or confront Sophie, she wasn't sure which. Even as she left the room, she wasn't certain. She walked on autopilot and eventually found herself outside Sophie's room. She took a deep breath and rapped on the door. It opened straight away, as if her friend had been waiting right behind it for her to arrive there.

'Hey,' Sophie said.

Emma walked past her. Sophie's room was much bigger than hers; she had no idea what form of favouritism had gone on to make this happen but suspected it was related to the fact that the twins' parents were big benefactors to the university. Officially these things made no difference, but even Emma was not that naïve. Of course, none of that money had saved Matilde. None of it had made Sophie the star of the department, for all of her sense of entitlement. Sophie was talented, there was no doubt about that, but she lacked application. She didn't practise especially hard and she wasn't excelling. Her playing had remained pretty well where it had been before she arrived here, which was a very high standard, but she should have been getting better. Emma suspected that if Sophie was playing games with her, jealousy was probably involved in that somewhere.

Emma didn't hold back this time. 'The singing wasn't the only thing you did last night, you know,' she told her.

'Oh?' Sophie had put the kettle on, adding a tea bag

to a cup without asking if Emma wanted a drink. She turned from her small table and threw a glowing smile at her. 'What else did I do, sweetie?'

As if you don't know, Emma thought. She wondered why Sophie was pretending. Did nothing ever touch her? She looked at the way her eyes shone; so blue they appeared to glow with ultraviolet. Was Sophie real? She appeared too perfect and vivid to be made of the same stuff as Emma was. 'You told me,' she said, not letting up. 'You explained what happened with the master-class.'

'The masterclass?' Sophie was strolling over, smiling as if she didn't have a care in the world, passing a cup of tea to Emma.

Emma took a sip. It was Earl Grey, which she couldn't stand, but Sophie seemed to forget this every time. That had seemed a sweet enough affectation when she'd first known the twins but now it just irritated her. She drank the perfumed brew and it tasted of money, and snobbery, and all the things she'd thought she would never buy into when she'd told her friends and her mum that university would never change her. But it had. It had changed her in pretty much every possible way, and not all of it good.

Sophie sat down on one of the several armchairs in her larger room. 'Which masterclass?' she said, cupping her drink but not taking a sip, as if the contents of the mug were a comforter.

'Oh, come on,' Emma said. 'The one where you stood in for your sister, just before she died.'

Sophie noticeably paled.

'You told me, last night,' Emma said. 'I know it's true, so don't deny it.'

'It's not true!' Sophie sounded incensed. 'Don't be so ridiculous. If I said something like that when I was sleepwalking and singing *Ave Maria*, you shouldn't take it so bloody seriously.'

A few months ago, Emma would have been cowed by an angry Sophie. But she wasn't now. She wasn't prepared to be fobbed off about this. 'You were pretending to be Matilde.'

Sophie was staring right at Emma. If it was true about liars not being able to look you in the eye, then Sophie wasn't lying. 'I was sleepwalking. Dreaming.'

Emma felt her lips curling, her expression turning into a half-snarl. 'Henry said it was all an act. In the hallway. Remember?'

'Of course I don't remember.'

There was a silence between them then. Neither said a word, or even sipped their tea. Emma imagined the walls might move in and crush them both. The warmth of the tea was flowing into her through her hands and yet she still shivered. She wasn't prepared to back down, though. 'You don't remember?' she said. She snorted. She put the mug down on the desk in front of her. 'Come on, Sophie. At least level with *me*.' She wasn't sure what right she had to honesty above anyone else but she felt that she did. Sophie owed her somehow.

'I can't believe you think I'm lying to you.' Now Sophie wasn't looking her in the eyes but was staring at herself in the mirror. At the reflection of herself. It was such a strange way to go about talking to her that Emma turned to look. 'What?' Sophie said. 'Why are you doing that?' She giggled, as if this was a light conversation over tea, or they were drinking together and having a good time. She touched her hair. Wasn't that a sign that someone was lying? Emma wished she could remember. These were the kinds of things they didn't teach you at A level, or any time during school.

'Why does Henry think it's an act, then?' Emma said. She was weakening and she could hear it in her voice. She knew that Sophie would too. Maybe the twins' private school had a bigger syllabus; something more all-encompassing.

Sophie made a strange whistling sound, blowing air across her teeth. 'Bah, Henry,' she said, playing up her French side and giving a bit of a Gallic shrug to boot. 'Him and me, we aren't on great terms at the moment. He's not exactly rational when it comes to me.'

'Yes, I got that.' Emma breathed. 'But why? I thought you two were pally as.' She heard her own accent. It was one of the strange things since she'd been at university, the sudden knowledge that she had an accent. She'd no idea before and had thought only the rest of the country did. It was yet another example of how naïve she'd been and how quickly she was learning about the world.

Sophie shrugged again. Emma couldn't help thinking that this was fake, just like everything else about Sophie, or Matilde, or whoever the posh girl sitting in this room with her was. She didn't trust her one bit. When someone told you from her own mouth that you shouldn't, then how could you? Emma felt vicious and angry. She hardly recognised herself. Then she remembered that she too had sung *Ave Maria*. She remembered feeling taken over. She thought about Sophie looking into the mirror and talking to her own reflection.

'What's happening to us?' Emma said. She didn't feel tearful but she wanted to cry her eyes out just for the sheer relief it would bring.

Sophie was bent double as if she had a stomach ache. 'I don't know,' she said. 'But it's heavy shit. I feel like I'm out of control. I'm sure it's just grief. And with you as well.' She was rubbing at her neck now.

'Yes, I think you're probably right.' Emma watched her friend, feeling sorry for the way she'd behaved. Why had she come here to confront her? Sophie didn't need that. The guilt started in the pit of her stomach and spread through her body like a cold flush.

'You should get some counselling or something,' Emma said.

'You're talking to me?'

Emma felt like looking round the room for whoever else she might be talking to. Then she realised that Sophie was just reflecting the comment back at her. She wasn't exactly sorted and settled herself. Being away from home had sent her off the rails and a little crazy to begin with, but now here she was with a dead friend and a recital to deal with. Everywhere she turned, there was more to get worried about. All she wanted was to practise the Rach until her fingers bled, until she was playing the fucking thing in her sleep, but what she got was instructions to play all those soulless études.

'Maybe we both need some help,' she admitted. She was looking in the mirror at Sophie's reflection now, at what they had both lost. How could either of them get over it with the constant reminder they had? It was dreadful; the way that Sophie was such an accurate copy of exactly the person they missed so badly.

There was that feeling then, the one Sophie had described the previous night, the feeling that Matilde hadn't gone. It seemed ridiculous and yet obvious all at the same time. Emma tried to shake herself, remember the things that made sense and the ones that didn't, but this was sticking to her psyche no matter what she tried to do about it. It wasn't just about a reflection in the mirror.

'You really don't remember anything about last night?' Emma said. She didn't know what she was hoping to get from Sophie that would be different from before, that would persuade her of anything.

'I remember suddenly being in your room. Coming to there as if I'd been waking from a dream.'

There was something about this description that was familiar to Emma; she'd had similar experiences herself recently. Sophie sounded sincere and nothing about the way she was behaving made Emma think she might be lying. The time when Sophie had touched her hand and she had felt something odd, like memories stirring, came back to her strongly. She had a sense that Sophie was thinking about the same time, back in Emma's room a few days ago. She opened her mouth to say so.

'The other day. It felt like we'd grown up together, just for a moment,' Sophie said.

Emma's mouth was still open with the thought on her tongue and she was stopped short.

'You were going to talk about that too. I can feel it,' Sophie said.

It was all Emma could do to nod in reply.

'It used to be like this with Matilde all the time, when we were on our own, though, only. We didn't need to finish sentences. People say it's just because you know each other well but it was more than that. The thoughts and feelings carry.'

This was more of the same kind of mumbo-jumbo

that Emma had never believed in and no matter what had just happened, she still couldn't. It must be a coincidence that they had thought about this at the same time. But what about how they'd felt when it happened? No, that couldn't be real either. It was just like Sophie said: they knew each other well, could guess what the other person was thinking. Married couples did it too; she'd read about it in a psychology book.

There was a loud rapping at the door and in her nervous state, it made Emma jump to her feet. She looked at Sophie as if they'd been doing something wrong, then got up and headed to the door to answer it. It didn't seem strange to be answering someone else's door. She turned and glanced back at Sophie. Her friend's mood was a sharp contrast. She looked calm and serene, sitting straight-backed on the bed, and Emma got the sense that it had been a relief for her to talk about these things.

Henry was standing outside. He looked awkward. 'Come in,' Emma said.

He cleared his throat. 'No, I'd rather not.' He looked nervous. 'I've just come with a message from Wood. He said he wants to do a masterclass for tomorrow. He's sorry for the short notice but it'll be good for you for the recital, he said.' Henry's face was screwed up in

187

concentration, as if he thought the world might end if he didn't relay the message exactly as he'd been told it. 'He wants you to play the études you've been learning.'

'You're kidding me, right?' she said, her voice rising.

Henry put a hand up in front of him as if to defend himself. 'Hey,' he said, 'don't shoot the messenger.' With that, he turned away, job done and no intention of talking to Sophie, it would appear. Emma shut the door, wondering just how badly the two of them had fallen out.

'Trust Wood to do something like that,' Sophie said. 'The old git.'

'He's all right really. Just wants to do his best,' Emma said, finding she felt defensive towards her tutor, even though she could have killed him. The last masterclass she'd attended had been Matilde's. Emma felt like she was crossing the road just after a funeral procession had gone by. Of course, that was just silly old superstition but it didn't mean that she liked doing it. In fact, she had more than once changed her route after seeing a funeral procession pass in front of her. 'I'd better go and practise,' she said.

Several hours later, Emma came to on her bed. She was confused and disorientated. She tried to piece together how she'd come to be there. She didn't remember lying down. Around the electric piano were strewn the various photocopied pieces that Wood had given her; the études and preludes and all the studies he'd wanted her to perfect. It looked like she'd been fighting with them and had lost.

Sitting up, Emma tried to rouse herself. Her eye sockets felt heavy and she was weak. The piano was still switched on, so she guessed she must have been practising, but she didn't remember at all. The last thing she could recall was leaving Sophie's room. She must have gone over and over Wood's studies, and yet she couldn't remember a thing about it. There was a dull ache in her head. She was dehydrated too; she felt the way she sometimes did when waking from an afternoon nap, her jaw stiff and sore, her heart beating so fast it felt like it was fluttering.

It came back to her with a sudden clarity about the masterclass Wood had arranged. She looked at the clock. It was ten in the evening. She didn't have much time left before the class tomorrow and as she couldn't remember practising at all, she wondered if she was ready. She doubted it. How could she be anywhere near ready to play those boring technical pieces in a public class? She wished she had never auditioned for the recital. Someone in the third year who had been charged with mentoring a group of the younger pianists had said the concert spots could be a poisoned chalice. Emma had scoffed at that idea at the time, thinking that the girl had not been picked and was bitter, but she'd found out later that she'd done several recitals. She understood, now, what she'd meant.

Climbing back into bed, Emma felt cold all over, like she'd come round from fainting. The way she'd felt in Margie's office the day she found out about Matilde. Could it really be grief causing such strong physical reactions or was there something wrong with her? These black spaces in time were disturbing; it felt like anything could have happened to her while she wasn't there.

Fifteen

Emma had locked herself in a practice room to try to prepare for the masterclass. It was the sort of situation where her mum would say 'what you don't know now, you'll never know', but it made her feel better to be there, with the piano. She touched the keys softly and it was like being teased. She so badly wanted to play her beloved sonata that she thought she might go insane with the longing. But Emma came from a place where a promise meant something. She knew it would have been different for Sophie, who would have done whatever she wanted. That was one of her traits. Emma wondered, though, if some of Sophie's lack of progress as a musician came down to this.

The studies that Wood had asked her to learn were sitting on the music stand, but she hadn't played them. She was terrified that if she tried, she'd realise how far she was from being ready for the class so instead she did warm-up exercises and scales to make sure her fingers were agile. She was building towards having a go at the actual pieces, but time was moving on and she had no idea when she'd feel ready to start. Every time she looked at the music she was supposed to be practising, she felt depressed. Each time, she wanted more and more to play the Rach. But it was no use. It was as if Wood had hypnotised her. He was powerful, in his way, Wood, the kind of way that could have been abused had he been the type. Emma was pretty certain he wasn't but she had to admit that there were times when he made her heart beat faster. He wasn't classically good-looking but he had an intensity about him that was very compelling.

Emma played some of her old favourites, the kind of pieces that might relax her. Those old ragtime blues, and then movie themes that she'd enjoyed learning as light relief from studying for her grades. This was a pleasant break from thinking, but it wasn't getting the pieces practised. She looked at them again, on the music stand, ready to be played. But she wasn't ready for them. She played random discordant combinations of notes over and over, which sounded terrible but got out some of her frustration. Then she felt tired, suddenly and overwhelmingly tired. She hated all of this. The masterclass and the recital and the Conservatoire itself. And Sophie. She hated Sophie most of all. She had a flash of violent feeling towards her friend.

Breathing out, Emma played a wedding march. It was a piece she could throw herself into, bashing out the chords like a fanfare, and she enjoyed doing that until it struck her that there was something dark about the music. It was the kind of piece that went against the theory that music helped you forget you were going to die because there was something about it that reminded you. She stopped playing. It didn't matter. The whole point of a masterclass was to learn, not to show off how you knew it all already. That had been stressed over and over since they'd arrived in October, and it was true, she knew that now.

Packing up her things, Emma felt brave and daring. She was rising above the politics and nonsense at the Conservatoire. She was doing the class the way it was meant to be done. She headed to the refectory and bought coffee and a cheese scone. Sitting there alone, with a book about Tchaikovsky, she felt empowered. She imagined she could hear the people around her whispering; chattering and gossiping about how she was being very casual. Yet when she looked up and glanced around, no one was taking any notice of her at all. It was as if they knew nothing about the masterclass.

Masterclass. The word hissed around her head like a snake inside her. And all at once, the fear came shooting back as if it had never been gone.

Emma arrived early at the recital hall. She figured it was a bit like going to the dentist; something better got over with than delayed. Wood was waiting there. He was playing as Emma came into the room, but not one of the studies he'd given her to practise; the sonata itself. She stood and watched. He was brilliant; technically amazing but he also put expression into his playing and brought the piece to life. She wondered if she would ever be that good. She watched and appreciated his playing, but she also felt cheated. He'd said she wasn't to play this piece and here he was, going for it like it was the concert of his career. She felt like she'd imagine you'd feel if you walked in to see your lover with another woman except, of course, she'd never been in love, so she was only guessing.

The professor noticed she'd come in and stopped playing abruptly. 'Sorry,' he said. 'I didn't think you'd be here yet.' He flushed slightly, and looked embarrassed. 'I love the piece myself,' he mumbled.

Emma smiled. It was endearing to see him bothered like this, and she wanted to run over and ruffle up his hair as if he was a little boy. She knew better than to act on an impulse like that, though. 'I was nervous and I'm not good at waiting,' she said.

Wood seemed to consider this and he gave her a rare half-smile. 'You should come and warm up on this piano. It's very different from the one in that practice room.'

Emma did not need much encouragement to play the recital room's beautiful Steinway. She rushed down the steps, almost tripping herself up in her enthusiasm. The excitement about playing the grand overtook her for a moment and she forgot all about being nervous for the class. She sat down on the stool and placed her hands gently in the right position. She closed her eyes. She found she was ready to play the Rach and her fingers were reaching for the right notes. She remembered herself just in time. She opened her eyes and played some difficult scales and warm-up exercises. Then she rattled through some cheerful Vivaldi, followed by the Maple Leaf Rag. When she'd finished, she glanced up at Professor Wood. He looked amused.

'That's your warm-up?' he said.

Something made her laugh, even though she felt embarrassed. 'Sometimes,' she said. 'Just a bit of light relief.'

'Good for you,' he said. 'It doesn't do to take oneself too seriously.'

Emma was suddenly struck by how good a dad Professor Wood must be. She wished she had had someone like him growing up. He was like her fantasy father would have been had she thought about it before; someone who cared and would be there for her recitals but, more, someone who knew about the music scene. A father like Wood and she could have talked to him about scales and arpeggios, about recitals and masterclasses and concert pieces. She realised she was staring at her tutor like an idiot. She turned back towards the piano.

People were beginning to arrive for the class. Emma wasn't sure how quickly word might have got round. She was hoping that it would be only a few people rather than the entire department but with people trickling in already, it was not looking good. She stopped playing and stretched her fingers. She told herself that this wasn't so bad. There was no external musician coming in with an attitude and a reputation. It was just Wood, and although he'd been up there with the best of them in his concert days, now he was focused on teaching, and they all knew him. She tried to convince herself that this would make all the difference but it wasn't really working.

The noise grew and bubbled in the room. Emma closed her eyes. When she opened them again and looked around, she realised she didn't recognise everyone. She tried to place the people she could see. There were plenty of strange faces in the crowd and a number of people who looked older, professional, not like students at all. The invitation must have been circulated widely by email. There were also plenty of students she recognised who she knew were not pianists. They had come to see this working-class girl who was playing the recital, she guessed, like they thought it was some kind of freak show. Usually she would get away from these anxieties by losing herself in the piece, but as she'd be playing Wood's special exercises, that wouldn't be possible this time.

The general bubble of gossip and chatter grew but Emma stopped looking into the crowd. She couldn't bear to see how full the room was getting. Nerves did a dance inside her stomach and made her feel queasy. She stretched her fingers until the joints popped; being active made her feel better. She wondered if Sophie was there. On one hand, she hoped so, but she didn't want to see her, so she didn't look around for her.

The hall was beginning to hush by itself, but then Wood brought proceedings to a head by standing up in that commandeering way he had and waiting for everyone to quieten. The room went completely silent in moments. At this point, Emma made the mistake of looking up into the audience. The room was packed; far more people than she had ever played to before. She wondered how that had happened and what they were all hoping to see. There were stragglers arriving at the last minute, closing the doors behind them as softly as they could and tiptoeing to their seats. Worry really set in as Emma saw all the earnest faces, staring, waiting for something from her.

Wood began to address the audience. Emma turned

her attention to her professor. Seeing Wood standing and talking made her feel better. While she could focus on him instead of the people watching her, she would be okay. She watched him introducing the masterclass, explaining in turn each of the pieces he'd given her to practise, and how they prepared her for the sonata she'd be playing in the recital. That was when Emma remembered she would have to play all those pieces and have her performance torn to bits, and that she hadn't practised them enough. And yet she stared at Wood and she wasn't afraid. She was really glad he hadn't brought a musician in from outside. She felt safe with him.

Emma was gazing at the professor like a fool and then realised he'd said twice that he'd like her to play the first of the four pieces. She shuffled the music around in front of her and steadied herself. She was dizzy. She poised her hands over the keys and hit the first chords. She felt her fingers slip against the ivory and she could feel herself playing all the right notes. It was surprising; she didn't remember practising that much, or it feeling this smooth and fluent, not even once. But now she was here, it came out like she'd worked and worked at it. She had no idea how she'd managed to master it.

Wood looked over and raised his eyebrows. He

looked thrilled, and encouraging. She finished the piece and the room breathed out, then he was off. Full of praise, although with points for improvement; it was a class after all. One or two of her transitions had been slightly off beat, and she had rushed the adagio, but that was okay. Even though she knew she'd done a decent job, she could see his point with almost all of the comments, and for the first time ever, she found she could have gushed about how useful it was, how much she was learning, the way she'd seen other students do. She didn't get involved in a conversation, though, and listened carefully. All she had to worry about now was the three other pieces.

The next went well too. Again there were points for Wood to make but he had lots to praise too. He was beaming and that made Emma smile. She was basking in his approval and yet she felt unworthy of it. She was sure now she thought about it: she hadn't practised these pieces to this standard. How was she pulling this off? She knew before starting the third piece that it would be okay and by the time she got on to the final one, Wood was struggling to find the teaching points. After she'd finished the final étude a second time, he stood back and held out his hands to her, and beamed at the audience, who clapped like crazy. Emma wasn't sure what to do then. It didn't feel right to stand up and bow at the end of a masterclass.

Now she'd finished playing, Emma allowed herself the luxury of looking around the recital hall. That was when she spotted Sophie, sitting at the back. She was looking at Emma but then so was everyone in the room. There was something different about the way Sophie was staring, though; as if she knew that Emma would look back and hold her gaze. And she was doing exactly that. Sophie was smiling but it wasn't the broad smile that Emma had seen on the professor's face at the end of her last piece. It was much more half-hearted than that, and she wasn't clapping. The way she was smiling at Emma made her feel like Sophie was sending her a message. *I know your game*, her eyes seemed to say, all the way from across the room. Emma went cold all over. She looked away, at a different part of the audience.

When she looked back, Sophie had gone. She must have snuck out of the back. With the noise of all the clapping, Emma hadn't heard the door go.

Sophie came to call on Emma soon after the class was finished, and persuaded her that they should go out and celebrate. Champagne, she insisted, for the new star of the department. Everything she said was so positive on the face of it and yet Emma didn't buy it. There seemed to be an undertone. Like Sophie's lack of clapping and her half-hearted smile, there was something about her reaction that seemed to be saying she wasn't so impressed with Emma after all.

They went to Arctic, right in the city centre. It was one of Sophie's favourite places. As she sipped the champagne her friend had ordered, Emma remembered that Matilde hadn't particularly liked it here. The twins had argued a few times about going to the trendy bar. It was expensive. Being in places like this had thrilled and intimidated Emma in equal measure when she'd first come away. She couldn't really afford to drink at Arctic. She could only come because the twins insisted on paying. Half of the first year were there tonight. Emma couldn't care less about the fancy bar and the expensive champagne. She was full of the joys of how well she'd done; happy to have come out of the masterclass not just alive, but with her reputation enhanced.

Music was pumping out from the speakers. It was too loud to speak to each other. There was no dance floor so the only thing to do was to stand or sit around looking cool. Emma was getting fed up with the place and wished she could be back in her room, listening to her own music and basking in her memories of the class. She was concerned that the loud noise would damage her hearing, which was the last thing a serious musician needed. You had to be able to listen hard to your instrument, hear the nuances. It was one of the reasons they were discouraged from playing in bands and getting involved with gigs. Some people ignored that anyway, but Emma didn't want to take any chances. She put down her champagne and walked out, keen for some fresh air.

Outside, Henry was having a cigarette. He offered one to Emma but she declined. She wasn't a smoker, although she had tried the odd cigarette on nights out. That was Sophie's influence; who considered smoking part of her French heritage. Sophie shouldn't have been a smoker, not really; the flute being her first instrument, she couldn't afford to play games with her lung capacity. Emma wouldn't have been surprised if this was exactly why Sophie chose to smoke, because she wouldn't be dictated to. Emma found she wanted to have a cigarette after all, and she turned back to Henry and smiled.

'I've changed my mind,' she said. 'Give me that.'

He looked taken aback for a moment, then passed her the cigarette. Emma took a big drag and it didn't make her cough. She felt like she'd been doing this all her life. She was thrilled and shocked with herself.

'So you're a smoker now?' Henry said. His voice sounded teasing and full of fun.

'I'm whatever you want me to be.' Emma heard her own voice as if it was someone else's. It sounded deep, and sexier than she was expecting. She smiled at Henry and thought she must be glowing. She felt more glamorous than she was used to. Perhaps it was the champagne, or the cigarette, or both. She wouldn't have had the guts to chat this way to a posh boy like Henry, not usually.

She blew smoke out through her teeth and smiled, passing the cigarette back.

Henry's face clouded over slightly. In fact, he looked like he'd seen a ghost. Emma wondered what was wrong with him.

'Come on, Harry,' she said. Her voice sounded much posher than usual. Was she changing the way she spoke? She'd hate to think she was. She had definitely sounded more like one of the twins than herself, though.

Henry had gone pale. He looked like he wanted to throw up. 'Who told you to call me that?'

'What?' Emma couldn't even remember what she'd said. 'What are you talking about?' She could hear the harder tones of her own accent now, the eau de ship canal.

Henry was shaking his head. His face had reddened. 'Did *she* tell you to say that, her highness?' Emma didn't need to ask who he meant; she knew right away he was talking about Sophie. 'She bet with you or something? It's not a funny game. She thinks it's all a fucking game.'

Emma stared at Henry. His face had tightened into an angry scowl. She had never seen him angry, or even particularly irritated. 'What's wrong?' she said. But Henry had turned away and was off back into the building. She followed him inside, calling after him, but he didn't turn around. He dumped his drink on the table and said something to Sophie, then stormed out and off into the night.

Sophie sidled over to Emma. 'What on earth did you do to Henry? He's accusing me of all sorts!' She looked more amused than concerned.

'I don't know,' Emma said. She struggled to

remember what had happened and grasp at anything that could have upset him, but she couldn't. 'I think I called him Harry,' she said, trying to work out if there was anything offensive about that.

Sixteen

The masterclass had been a triumph for Emma, but she still had to play the Rachmaninoff sonata in the recital hall in a few days' time. That wasn't something she took lightly. She hadn't played the piece for over a week and it was a bigger deal going back to it than it had been learning it for her audition. She sat in the practice room feeling hungover but ready to play it again, and found that she felt afraid. There was something about the sonata that dragged her in. It was almost sinister, the hold it had on her. She tried to dismiss this feeling. She was being silly and thought it might have something to do with Sophie saying that the Rach was Matilde's audition piece.

She tried to put all of the nonsense out of her mind. She needed to focus on playing. She studied the first phrase of the music and had a sudden appreciation of what Wood had given her with the studies. Looking at the notes on the stave now, it was as if they'd been translated; colour-coded and highlighted and labelled. The techniques she had tried to get just by reading the music and listening to other people play the piece were now clearer to her. She had her own muscle memories that mirrored the techniques she needed to perfect. She sat straight on her stool and began to play. She found the right notes far more easily than before, so that, without having been near this piece of music for an entire week, she was playing it better right away. The professor was a genius. She was filled with gratitude, not just for the help she'd had from Wood with this piece but for being here at all. It was the opportunity of a lifetime and there was nothing to stop her making the most of it.

It struck her then that there was something, an obstacle in her way: Sophie. They were supposed to be great mates but was that really true? Everything Sophie had done since Emma got the recital had been destructive, even the drinking last night. Emma wasn't a drinker and she didn't like the way her head throbbed. She needed to keep her mind clear for practice but Sophie was talking about more drinks later. She was campaigning for them to have more fun, like other students. What a time to be suggesting that. Almost like she was trying to sabotage her friend. Emma remembered Henry's comments, and how competitive Sophie could be. She remembered what she'd learned from Sophie about her part in her sister's undoing.

One thing she was becoming certain of was that Sophie was a destructive force. As she sat and readied herself to play the Rach the entire way through for the first time in eight days, she decided she would avoid Sophie. Emma wanted to be all about the music and Sophie was getting in the way. She wanted to be proud of what she'd done; make her mum proud, and Professor Wood. This was far more important than a friendship with a girl who she was beginning to realise she didn't know at all.

Emma took a deep breath, and then she played the Rachmaninoff Sonata in D minor. At first she was in control, and then that changed and she let it play her, let it take her elsewhere. Far away into the past and future at the same time; to a place where no one died.

When she finished, it was like waking from a dream. She remembered being there, and the music happening, but not very precisely. She felt muggy, as after sleep, and her head throbbed even more. It was like a drug, though, and all she could think was that she wanted it again, again. And so she played once more, throwing herself back into the sonata and losing herself completely.

It was much later that Emma returned to her room, exhausted from playing. Her fingers were used to the constant exercise but even so, they felt sore and worn. She stretched and cracked them in the quiet hallway. She enjoyed the sound they were making and the relief as her joints loosened.

She arrived at her room and pulled her key from her pocket. As she went to open the door, though, something felt odd. It was just a feeling, a sense, that her room wasn't empty. She tried the door without turning the key and found it was unlocked. *How strange*. She wouldn't usually leave it like that while she went off to practise. It wasn't that she worried about thieves so much as her privacy. She didn't imagine that the rich kids in the dorms here would want her precious things but she hated the idea they might mess about with them and laugh at her. She pushed the door open and there was Sophie, drinking a beer and chewing gum, sitting on her bed. She was rifling through Emma's CD collection like she owned the place. Emma was so taken aback by this that she could hardly think what to say.

Sophie looked up from the bed and smiled. 'Is it you, my love?' she said.

'Of course it's me.' Emma threw down her bag in irritation. 'What are you doing, Sophie?'

Sophie's face fell then, and her eyes went down. She looked very disappointed with the answer, as if she had been expecting someone else. She recovered herself. 'I'm chilling, like you said. We're going out. Remember?'

Emma didn't remember. She had no idea at all what Sophie was talking about.

'I know you wanted to.' Emma's voice was quiet as she spoke. 'You mentioned it last night. But I told you then that I need to focus on my practice.'

Sophie moved to the edge of the bed and sat up straight. 'But earlier today,' she said, 'you agreed we should have more fun.'

Emma thought back to before practice. Her head

felt heavy from how deeply she'd thrown herself into the music and nothing from early morning was clear. She didn't think she'd seen Sophie but her friend appeared to be sincere.

'You said yourself that we don't have as much fun as the other students here. That we need to get out and about.' Sophie was pressing buttons on the CD player, messing with a disc in her hand. Emma felt tense as she watched her. Just who did she think she was?

'No,' Emma said. 'You said all that.'

With a flick of her hair, Sophie pressed the play button and turned towards Emma, looking confused. She focused for a moment on putting the CD she'd taken out back into its case and on to the shelf. 'You agreed, though,' she said.

As if I had any choice, Emma thought. Sophie was prone to stating her own opinions as faits accomplis, and Emma was used to nodding. She felt particularly manipulated by her friend right now, and violated by the way she was using her room, her things, without asking.

'Who let you in here?' she asked, her voice carrying some of the irritation she felt.

'What?' Sophie turned to her looking incredulous.

'You said I could stay here while you went back to practise!'

'Back to practise?' Emma's head was spinning. 'I've been practising all morning.'

Sophie giggled. 'No you haven't, silly. What are you talking about?' Her eyes darted to the desk and Emma followed their gaze. There were two mugs sitting there, staring at her. She was pretty sure she hadn't left dirty cups when she went off after breakfast. She walked over and picked up her own mug; it had her lipstick marked on it, fresh. She placed her lips against it and they fitted; she had no doubt she'd used the cup. But she remembered washing it, along with her bowl, after eating cereal and before she'd put on her make-up.

There was a shuffling sound from over by the bed and Emma turned to see Sophie putting her shoes back on. There was a lightness to her. *A lightness that hides something dark*, Emma thought. Her friend picked up her cardigan and waltzed to the door. 'I don't know what's going on with you, but it's strange,' Sophie said. 'Like you're losing the plot.' She turned, her left foot slipping from her shoe as she tried to right it. 'It's that piece. It sent Matilde round the bend and now it's doing the same to you.' Her voice was quiet and carried little weight but the comment felt very pointed. Sophie caught Emma's eyes with her own and held her gaze for a moment. Then she shook her head and left the room.

Emma wondered if you could practise a piece so much that it sent you insane. Sophie seemed to think so. Or did she think there was something inherent in the music, a demon put there to trap young women and hold them in its thrall?

Somehow, she had agreed to go for a drink with Sophie that evening. She didn't want to but her friend had hunted her out and pinned her down about it. She had insisted and insinuated in ways that Emma found made her agree to meet. She could only imagine what it was like to be a man around Sophie's fluttering eye-lashes and she felt for Henry, beginning to get a sense of why he might be so angry. So now she was going out to drink, which was the last thing she wanted. In the meantime, she was doing her best to keep out of Sophie's way. The drinking was bad enough but Emma had a feeling that Sophie would try to sabotage her further, deeper, more, given half a chance.

Locked away in the practice room was the safest place to be. Not that Emma was practising. She was too distracted. If Sophie was plotting against her, then what she was doing was working. Emma tried to tell herself that she was being paranoid, that Sophie was her friend and it was ridiculous to think she would do anything to harm her. For some reason, though, it didn't reassure her. She felt strongly that Sophie was working against her. She worried about the missing time from her day and where it might have gone. Like the few times she'd got mindlessly drunk since she'd been at university, it was terrifying. If you didn't remember what happened, then it could have been anything.

Emma pressed down middle C with a thumb. She remembered when she'd first been teaching herself to play the piano. She'd borrowed a book from the library with cartoon characters that had made it fun. The crotchets and quavers had personalities, and danced across the page. She remembered the first music she'd read; lines and lines of middle Cs hopping along the treble clef at different rhythms. It had moved slowly on. Middle C on the bass clef too. Swapping between one thumb and the other. It had been dull, that part, but the cartoon pictures and lively text had brought it alive enough to get her through it. She found it amazing to think she had ever been at that level, and that she had progressed to where she was now. Time was like magic and transformed everything.

Emma pressed down chords. C major, B minor, A seventh. She listened to the contrasts and she remembered learning those for the first time too. It was sad to think that she'd made all those discoveries now. She understood music and how it worked and there was nothing more to know. She smiled; she knew that was wrong. Every time she'd ever thought there was nothing more to learn, she'd discovered there was another level, a whole quantum jump to make next. There had to be fewer of those leaps to master but she wasn't done yet, of this she was sure.

Emma was startled as the door flew open. She had been sure she'd put on the light outside to show that the room was busy. She was ready to tell the intruder off and point out that she had booked this room all day. Then she saw that it was Sophie and not some random accident.

'Is it you, my love?' Sophie said. She had taken to calling Emma 'love' recently.

Emma didn't reply. She stared at her friend.

'Of course it's you,' Sophie said, looking at the floor and finding a place to sit, the chair where Wood usually sat or leaned on his knee during Emma's lessons. She seemed rushed, flustered even, and Emma wondered what was stressing her. 'Of course it's you.' Sophie's voice came like an echo, and Emma was sure she should remember something from what her friend was saying, but it wouldn't come. It felt like she had missed a cue.

'I'm practising,' she said. She was determined to resist whatever it was Sophie had in mind for her.

'Of course,' Sophie said. She had got up again and was shutting the door. 'That's fine but I have this.' She pulled out a package from her pocket and showed it to Emma. A pungent, green smell came from its wrapper and Emma looked at it closely. She might have been naïve, but she still recognised the fronds and curls of weed being held out to her.

'I don't do drugs,' she told Sophie.

'Yes, I know, DARE to say no and all that.' Sophie was sitting again, rolling her eyes and a joint at the same time, her voice mocking and sing-song. 'But it's nice,' she said, lifting her gaze and looking straight at Emma. She stared, all intent, for what felt like several minutes, then dissolved into giggles. 'Don't take everything so seriously. This is just what you need. Chill you out some.'

Emma watched what Sophie was doing. She had to admit she was fascinated. But no, she mustn't. Life was mad enough right now. This was the last thing she needed. What kind of friend was Sophie anyway, bringing drugs to her, when she had a recital to prepare for? Not a very good one, that was for sure. 'I'm not interested,' Emma said. But she knew her voice lacked conviction and that Sophie would see straight through it.

'Of course you are,' Sophie said, with another little giggle. She narrowed her eyes. 'You don't fool me.'

'I'm not doing it,' Emma said. This rang more true. In fact, she sounded deadly serious.

An amused light still danced in Sophie's eyes. She thought she knew better and that she could change Emma's mind. Emma was irritated from the inside out. It was a little like having an allergic reaction; every part of her itched. She wanted to get at her friend, say something that would hurt her.

'Why does Henry hate you?' Emma was shocked at the words that came running from her mouth.

'I don't know what you're talking about.' Sophie sounded confident and poised but she had slumped, and Emma knew she was hitting her target.

'What's the Harry thing about?'

Sophie shrugged. She'd recovered herself and her eyes were shining with mischief as she lit the joint.

'You can't smoke in here,' Emma said.

Sophie seemed to breathe in deeper in reaction to this comment, as if she had to disobey it. She looked like a cheeky little girl, and Emma could imagine growing up with her again. She could picture running around getting up to mischief, playing tricks on neighbours. She could see it all in her head as if it had happened to her, which was disconcerting. She found herself changing her mind about trying the weed. Something kicked off in her brain when she smelled the smoke. She indicated to Sophie to pass it along to her. It felt right in her hand as she held it and she put it naturally to her mouth, taking a big drag. The drug rushed to her head and she felt it having an effect right away. It was strange and yet familiar, like she had tried it before. She dropped the joint.

Picking it up quickly, Sophie gave her a wry half-smile. She seemed to be searching for something in Emma with her eyes. After a while, she turned from her, her lids heavy and mouth curled. Emma couldn't work out if this was the effect of the drugs but she looked disappointed.

Emma felt light-headed and strangely absent from the room.

'Henry doesn't like to be called Harry,' Sophie told her. 'That's all. I used to say it to tease him.' Her voice sounded all wrong. She didn't sound like she was telling the truth. Emma wondered if she was becoming paranoid with the drug. She sat back and smiled at that. So soon? Surely, it wasn't that. There were lots of reasons to be paranoid, and the drug was the least of all of them. She thought about having another drag and found that Sophie had passed her the joint already. She looked at her hand and saw it there. It felt like a foreign object between her fingers. She still knew what to do with it, though. She took several drags, until it was smoked right down. Then she passed it back to Sophie, who considered it dubiously then stubbed it into the floor.

Emma stared at the piano, which looked fascinating and useless all at the same time. Playing the piano suddenly seemed a ridiculous thing to do. To play in a recital, where people came to watch and clap, was so silly that it made her start to laugh. The giggle grew in her stomach and took her over. It bubbled up inside her like vomit and she needed to get it out. She wanted to go outside and run through the gardens with the wind in her hair. She wanted to laugh until she collapsed in a heap on the ground. Everything was so incredibly funny, and she couldn't believe she hadn't noticed that before.

Seventeen

It was dark, and cold. Emma had no idea where she was. She reached out in front of her, into the shadows, and found a wall. Her head was filled with pictures of a huge house, with turrets and a lake, like a stately home, and of being there with Sophie. She hugged herself. She was wearing her flimsy pyjamas.

Grasping at the wall, she found a switch and pressed it. The room flashed and stuttered into light. She looked around and blinked. She was in the great ballroom, right at the other end of the Conservatoire. It was a place that was used maybe twice a year for big public events. There was a stage with the coat of arms of the university, and the floor was polished so well you could slide along it in your bare feet. Emma realised that this was what she could smell, the wood polish. It reminded her of being in church, weddings but especially funerals.

What was she doing here? She tried to remember but she couldn't. She tried to work out how she'd got from the other end of the Conservatoire all the way here. Did they even leave this room unlocked? She guessed they must, as she was in here, and she had no keys. She must have been sleepwalking. She used to sleepwalk, when she was younger. She remembered dreaming about a Victorian house and working as a chambermaid there, getting beaten for doing something wrong, then bumping into a dressing table and waking up. That dream still haunted her. She'd been tiny at the time.

That was years ago, though, and Emma hadn't been a sleepwalker since she was a little girl, so why now? Grief for Matilde; stress, perhaps? Random people she met in the hallway said, 'Oh, you look stressed' when they'd never even spoken to her before and knew nothing about her. She would be glad when tomorrow night came and the recital was over so people wouldn't have an excuse to talk to her as if they knew her. Even Professor Margie had suggested that the pressure could get too much and that Emma needed to be careful, that pulling out would be understandable. Emma wondered what it was with Margie. Maybe because she hadn't become a successful musician and had to teach, she was trying to find ways to help Emma fail. She seemed kind and sweet but she was a bit pathetic. Emma stopped, surprised at herself; why was she having such bitter thoughts?

The ballroom looked ghostly and deserted. It was a room built for lots of people, for events, so it was especially eerie to see it empty. Emma walked across the floor and the boards lifted and flexed as she went. She could feel them under her feet. She crept across the room, although the building felt so dark and quiet that she couldn't imagine for a minute that there was anyone around. It was the middle of the night; the dead of night, as they called it, but she didn't want to think about why. She found a door and pushed it. It swung readily open. The hallway ahead of her was pitch black. She turned back towards the ballroom, thinking she should switch off the light. Dust motes danced in the beams from the chandeliers and as Emma looked, she felt that time had stopped right in front of her. She shivered. She couldn't plunge the place into darkness; she was too afraid.

Keeping one hand on the wall to help her, Emma crept down the corridor. She felt for light switches but found nothing. Then there was a soft shape. A warm shape. The lights came on so suddenly that Emma's body went rigid. Standing right in front of her was Sophie. Emma screamed. Sophie grabbed her arm. 'For God's sake,' she whispered. 'You'll wake everyone up. Calm down!' She didn't seem surprised to see Emma at all. She didn't ask what she was doing there or explain why she was roaming the hallways either. She just shushed her and led the way out. They left the building and headed to their halls of residence, not talking.

Back in the halls, Sophie kissed Emma on the cheek and headed to her room. Emma stood, watching her leave. What had Sophie been doing in that area of the building with her in the middle of the night? It was too much of a coincidence to be down to random chance; they must have gone there together. She wanted to ask Sophie, demand to know, and yet she found she couldn't call after her. She was paralysed as she watched her walk away.

A small thought danced in her head, one she didn't much like. It wouldn't go away, though, and grew and danced like it belonged to her. It was to do with why she hadn't asked Sophie. *You don't wan-na kno-ow*, it told her in a sing-song playground voice. *You don't wanna find out why-y!*

Emma tried to ignore the voice. She was so tired. She opened her door and went inside. She pulled the bolt across hard. She had never bolted herself in before, but something was bothering her. She didn't feel safe at all. She lay back on her bed and relaxed, drifting off towards sleep surprisingly fast. Then it felt like the bottom dropped out of the world, as if she was dying, and she jerked awake. She thought about the ballroom. Had she been dreaming? She remembered the dust motes dancing in the light. She couldn't be sure. She could find out in the morning. The light would still be on. She could find out now; she would see it from the window, just the far right end of the Conservatoire lit like a beacon. But she was so, so tired. She just couldn't pull herself from her bed to look.

Emma was woken by a rapping sound. It was coming from the door. She sat up straight in bed, remembering

right away that it was the day of the recital. This woke
her up faster than she was used to and she felt light-
headed. She looked at her alarm clock: eight thirty in
the morning. She had plenty of time to practise and to
get dressed and made up, to consult Sophie over her
look and accessories. She breathed. She needed to hold
it together. It was only the morning of a very long day.
She remembered that someone had been knocking on
the door. 'Coming,' she mumbled, and she pulled on
her dressing gown from beside the bed. She reached for
the curtains and opened them to let in some natural
light. Rain sobbed down on to the window. Emma
hoped this wasn't an omen.

Of course, it was Sophie at the door. She stood there
looking impatient, as if Emma should have been
expecting her. She kind of was. Emma didn't exactly
have a legion of fans and friends knocking her door
down. More surprising was that Henry was with her. He
looked like a schoolboy who'd been made to go somewhere with his mother. Sophie swept past Emma and
into the room, settling herself on the bed as if she
owned the place. Henry followed looking sheepish.
Emma caught Sophie's gaze, and it threw her back, to a
hallway, to the huge cold ballroom the night before. She

turned to put on the kettle. She wanted to ask Sophie if they had really been there but she didn't want to talk about it in front of Henry.

'You're not to practise today,' Sophie told her.

'What?' Emma was still bleary-eyed, and what her friend said was not going in at all. 'Of course I'm going to practise.'

'No, darling,' Sophie said. The crackling bumps of the water beginning to warm filled the room. 'It's a rule. No practice on the actual day. It'll just make you nervous.'

Emma tried to focus on getting cups and tea bags. What was Sophie doing here so early in the morning anyway and why was Henry with her? Not that Emma had a problem with being woken up, not at all, not today. But now Sophie was telling her what she could and couldn't do. She was dictating to her over practice, which was definitely overstepping the mark. Emma was not having that, not even for a moment. 'Of course I'm going to practise,' she repeated. The kettle was boiling, so she poured hot water into the cups and got milk from the fridge.

When Emma turned to pass tea to her friends, Sophie looked like she was sulking. Her bottom lip even pressed out a bit, like a parody of the kind of face a child pulled when she didn't get her own way. She nudged Henry and giggled, giving the impression that the two of them were sharing a joke. Henry didn't appear especially amused, though, when Emma looked again. He took the tea from her and looked as though he wanted to walk straight out of there and leave them to it.

'Can you believe it's the recital already?' Sophie said. She glanced at Henry and Emma got that sense of her trying to force a private joke on him. Henry hadn't said a word since he'd been there, and Emma wondered why he'd come. He didn't seem to be friends with Sophie any more, never mind anything romantic, and she couldn't imagine how Sophie had got him here.

'I really can't,' Emma said. It was true. The days had passed by in a blur. There had been practice, and the masterclass, and drinking. Big chunks of time had seemed to go missing. She was playing piano so much that when she tried to sleep, she spent several hours with the notes running around in her head. People said that they ate, slept and drank their professions, but Emma was dreaming hers too. There was no escape. Not that she wanted to escape from the music, not really. As she sat drinking tea, all at once the only place she wanted to be was the recital hall, with the Steinway. It was the kind of piano she had dreamed of playing her entire life, and tonight she would be playing it in a concert. It was hard to take in that all her dreams had come true. Almost too much to believe. Her stomach jerked with nerves and excitement as she thought about it.

'I had this crazy dream last night,' Emma said, no longer worried about what Henry would think of her. 'I dreamed we were over in the ballroom, walking around in the dark.'

Sophie's eyes twinkled with mischief. 'What a strange dream,' she said.

Emma had been hoping that something about Sophie's reaction would help, give her a sense of whether it had happened or not, but she studied her friend's face and there was nothing there.

'Anyway, you can't practise because I'm not letting you out,' Sophie said.

Emma grinned, thinking that Sophie was joking, but her smile wasn't returned. Sophie looked deadly serious. Emma was suddenly afraid of her friend, unsure what she was capable of. Then Sophie beamed, that way she could sometimes, a smile that lit up a room. Emma wondered if she'd imagined it all, the things Henry had said and the weird dreams and her sheer exhaustion adding up to a package of paranoia. She rubbed her eyes and sipped tea and tried to throw off the bad feelings.

'Have you been eating properly?' Henry asked her.

Surprised, Emma wasn't sure what to say. Of course, she hadn't. No one she knew ate properly. There was one rather overweight girl in the third year who had a terrible diet of cookies and doughnuts and was gossiped about mercilessly, but Emma rarely saw any of the other young women do more than pick at food. She wanted to fit in so she copied this, meaning her eating habits were random at best. 'I'm eating fine,' she lied. She had skipped meals a lot recently. She needed to fit into her ball dress for this evening and she wasn't taking any chances with that. She couldn't afford to buy a new dress, so she needed to be the same size as she was when she was fourteen.

The lie made Emma look at the floor and chew on a nail. She winced as she caught raw flesh; her nails were bitten right down. When she looked up, Henry was staring at her. There was something in his eyes that held her attention. She realised why he was here. He was concerned about her. Henry was a good bloke and she only wondered how he ever got so wrapped up with Sophie and did what he did to poor sweet Matilde.

Putting down her tea, Emma shuffled around the room getting clothes ready, hoping that the other two would take the hint.

'We should go,' Henry said.

'We're not going anywhere.' Sophie narrowed her eyes at Henry. Her words seemed to stop him in his tracks. How did she have such a hold over him? It was bizarre and kind of impressive to watch, in a very dark way. Emma was so desperate to get down to the practice room that she was grinding her teeth. The tension in the room was palpable.

The clock flashed from the other side of the room and Emma saw that it said 08:37. It was hard to believe that only seven minutes had passed since her friends had arrived at the door. She wondered how long before she would feel desperate enough to be rude and throw them out of the room. Another three minutes? Ten? All that wasted time when she could have been warming up and getting ready. She wondered whether Sophie was genuinely concerned or if she was trying to ruin everything. She couldn't be that much of a bitch, surely? Emma had that sense again of not knowing her friend, not at all.

Emma's pile of clothes sat on her knee and she patted them, pointedly. But no one moved. Then Sophie got up and Emma was heartened, thinking that she was going to take the hint and leave. Instead, she walked over and picked up the kettle, filling it with water. A violent thought swept into Emma's head. She could imagine herself, throwing the boiling water over her friend. Then she could see herself hitting Sophie hard on the head with the metal bottom of the kettle enough times that she didn't get up again. She tried to shake away these feelings. Why was she imagining such violence? But they were only pictures in her head. The fact was that she wasn't even capable of being rude to her friend, never mind hurting her physically.

A feeling built inside Emma, from her stomach, like nausea, and she couldn't ignore it. She needed to get to a piano and she needed to do it as soon as possible. She stood up with her clothes in her arms. She wasn't going to sit there and watch Sophie ignore her hints, deliberately trapping her in her room. She didn't care if she ended up outside in the hallway wearing her night-clothes. She wouldn't be bullied like this. She walked past the bed. Sophie watched her go and raised her eyebrows, giving her that look she did that stopped most people in their tracks. But Emma was not most people. She liked Sophie; well, most of the time she did; they were friends. But music was Emma's life and no friend was going to get in the way of that, not in a million years.

Emma opened the door and turned towards the couple. 'I'll see you later,' she said. Sophie looked incredulous but Henry seemed amused, for the first time since he'd walked into the room. Emma realised there hadn't been any secret joke. Whatever Henry's reason for being there, it didn't change a thing about what he thought of Sophie.

The bathroom on the corridor was free and Emma walked in, locking the door. She realised she didn't have a towel with her. She took off her pyjamas, then splashed water on her face and dried it on her pyjama bottoms. She would have a shower later, before the big event. Thinking about this sent a shock of fear and excitement right through her. It was tonight; she would be playing in front of a paying audience and she would be the star of the show.

Pulling on her jeans and T-shirt, Emma looked at

herself in the bathroom mirror. She felt that disconnection again, that sense that it wasn't herself she could see reflected but another girl, a different person who had a life of her own the other side of the divide. She reached for her reflection, which did exactly what it was supposed to and reached back. They touched hands and Emma smiled; it was only more of that paranoia. She slipped her fingers through her hair to untangle it; it needed a wash but would do for now. She pulled at her T-shirt so it was neat on top of her jeans, then slipped her feet into shoes and unlocked the door.

Emma walked out and right into Sophie, who was standing blocking the doorway. Sophie looked down at Emma, and the look in her eyes made the smaller girl take a step back. 'What?' Emma said.

Sophie stood there. She blocked the way but didn't speak.

'I've had enough of this,' Emma said. She pushed past Sophie, who hardly moved, but Emma ducked and bent to get by her friend. She locked her room door, then headed down the hallway without looking back. She didn't turn to see whether Sophie followed her, or watched her go, or walked away. But she could feel Sophie's gaze boring into her from behind, furious at her defiance. She could imagine the way Sophie's eyes narrowed at her, the frown that grew on her forehead. She could see it as clearly as if she was looking straight at her. It was the strangest feeling.

Even once she was down in the practice room, Emma couldn't shake the sense she'd felt of Sophie's fury towards her. It hung in the air and left a trace the way electricity left a sense of something charred in the air after lightning. She expected her friend to turn up at the practice room and drag her out by the hair. She had locked herself in, and kept getting up and checking the door wouldn't open. She wasn't sure why, but she had a sense of Sophie being capable of anything when it came to getting her own way, even breaking down locked doors. As she played, she tried to forget the way her friend had stared at her as she left the room with her clothes in her arms, but she couldn't. The narrowed eyes and frowning face that she hadn't even seen hung over her like a dark family secret and she found it hard to play anything at all.

Eighteen

The silence that filled the room sounded loud and Emma was sure it would suffocate her. She didn't know why she couldn't start playing but something was holding her back. She kept adjusting the music on the stand, as if that might make some difference. She was biting her nails and getting annoyed with herself for that.

There was a tentative knocking on the door. It didn't sound at all like Sophie's sharp, confident rap, but Emma hesitated before answering. The knocking came again, a little louder, and then a voice. 'Emma, is that you in there?' It was Professor Margie. Emma was relieved it wasn't Sophie but wondered what her supervisor wanted. She grabbed the practice room keys and got up from her seat.

Unlocking the door, Emma opened it a crack. Whilst she wasn't as wary of Margie as she would have been of Sophie, she still didn't want her practice interrupted. Not that it had been going so well but that wasn't the point. 'What do you want?' Emma realised she sounded rude. 'Sorry, but I have the recital this evening.'

Margie smiled around the gap in the door. 'Yes, I know you do. That's what I wanted to talk to you about. Can I come in?'

Emma hesitated. Then she opened the door and let Margie through. She wanted to lock it behind her to keep them both safe from Sophie but she was aware that would look strange so she refrained. Margie came right in and sat down on the chair at the side of the room. Emma hoped she didn't plan to settle. She could do without a lecture about last-minute practice. She had heard it all before and it made no difference to the fact that she wanted to play. She sat on the stool and tried to pay attention to what Margie was saying but it was a struggle; she could only think about the piano now, and the feel of its keys when she was playing well.

'I'm worried about you,' Margie told her. 'You haven't looked yourself recently. You're very pale and thin, and now I find you here, locked in a room. Why did you lock yourself in?'

'I didn't want to be interrupted.' Emma tried to say this without the annoyance she felt carrying on her voice. She didn't want to confirm anyone's theories about how stressed she was, or that she wasn't coping. This was the third conversation of this kind she'd had with Margie. 'I'm trying to practise.'

Margie didn't answer right away but sat looking at the piano, apparently deep in thought. 'You surely know the piece by now,' she said finally. She reached a hand towards Emma, who shrank away from her touch. 'I can't help thinking about your friend and how she crumbled under the public scrutiny,' Margie said. 'I keep wondering if I could have done more, and now you … well, you just don't seem well. I have serious concerns.'

Emma shuffled the music on the stand. 'Of course I know the piece.' She cleared her throat. 'But, you know, a piece is never really finished. There's always something you can do better.'

Margie was nodding at this. 'You locked yourself in, though. Was there something you were afraid of?'

The professor's head was at an encouraging angle as she waited for Emma to reply. As she sat there, thinking about that question, Emma wanted to answer honestly. She had a sudden urge to tell Margie everything about Sophie and Matilde, about her hopes and fears and confusion over the twins. She didn't, though. She shook her head. 'No,' she said. 'What would I have to be scared of here?' The note to her voice sounded false and pretend.

'Well ...' Margie hesitated and Emma got the impression she was choosing her words carefully. 'Listen, I know that Paul can be ...' She trailed off. She shrugged and her features sagged. Emma had no idea what Margie was trying to tell her.

'Professor Wood is a great teacher. I'm very happy to have his help.'

Margie was looking right at her, but she didn't seem convinced by what Emma was saying. 'Well, if you ever need to talk about anything, anything at all ...' She was getting up to leave the room. She turned back as she stood in the doorway. 'I do mean anything. I will believe you if there's something you need to tell me.'

The professor walked away. Emma stared at her retreating back and watched the door close behind her, shutting her off from view. What had she been getting at? Emma suspected it was to do with what had gone on between Wood and the twins, whatever that was. At least one good thing had come from Margie's visit. Emma was hungry to play again now. She got up and locked the door. This time she would ignore anyone knocking.

Music flowed over Emma as she practised the sonata and she honestly couldn't have said how long she'd been playing or what time it was. She remembered starting with some warm-up exercises and the usual stuff, but that seemed a lifetime ago. At some point she had got into playing the Rach and she had become completely absorbed. At last she paused for breath. That was when she heard the banging on the door. It sounded desperate; as if there was a fire or some other emergency. It sounded like whoever was knocking would batter down the door if she didn't answer it. Emma felt like she was coming round from a dead faint.

Picking up the keys, she unlocked the door and opened it. She found Sophie the other side. Her friend looked concerned. 'You need to get ready,' she said, sounding breathless.

'What's the time?' Emma could hear that her own voice sounded dreamy; half asleep.

'It's half six and you need to get ready.'

This snapped Emma out of her trance. She went cold all over. She grabbed her music and shoved it inside the portfolio case, then scrabbled around for her other things. Sophie came properly into the room and helped, gathering up the papers that had been strewn all over the place. 'You really need to get ready,' Sophie muttered, quietly this time, as if she was speaking to herself. It was all Emma could do not to snap at her friend. She knew Sophie was right but the nagging reminders were making her more anxious. She had exactly an hour to get showered and changed and to make herself look like a concert pianist. She didn't think she'd be able to do that given all the time in the world. She thought that she might cry; she could feel the tears coming. Sophie noticed and she reached for her.

The girls hugged and then Sophie pulled back, holding Emma firmly by the shoulders. 'Hey,' she said, 'it's all right. I'll help you.'

Emma felt reassured. She felt cared for and looked after and it was good. It reminded her of how much easier things had been when she lived with her mother.

'Come on,' Sophie said. 'I have everything we need in my room.'

Emma smiled and let her friend take her by the hand, as if she was a child. She followed Sophie, not questioning how she'd got hold of her ballgown and all the things she needed for tonight. It must have meant breaking into her room but that was okay. It was easier to let someone else do everything for her.

Up in Sophie's room, Emma admired the view as Sophie flapped around her. No matter how hard she focused on it, it was impossible to believe she would be playing the Rachmaninoff in front of a large audience that evening. It was a bit like the idea of Matilde being dead; nothing about it rang true. She felt sure she'd bump into her friend walking down the corridor any day now. She wondered what she needed to see to get it straight in her head. An open coffin? A body mouldering in a grave? Even then, she didn't think she'd be able to believe Matilde had gone.

'Shower,' Sophie said, pushing Emma into the en suite. Sophie's shower room was a fair bit bigger than Emma's. Her room was in an old wing of the building, and everything about it was larger. Emma looked

at the picture window beside her. It was still raining and the fat, pregnant drops ran down the window
and formed streams as they joined and sped faster.
Instead of showering, Emma watched this for a while.
Then she remembered that she had very little time.
She quickly took off her clothes and got into the
shower. She stood there, under the water. It was
warm and pleasant. She could have stayed there for
hours.

'Get a move on!' Sophie's voice came from the
other side of the door, and Emma found she was hurried by her friend's urgency. She turned off the water
and stepped on to the mat, drying herself on a towel
left out for her. It struck her as odd then that she was
getting ready in Sophie's room. Now she thought about
it properly, she was very bothered that Sophie had been
through her things without her permission.

Coming into the main bedroom, Emma had steeled
herself to say something about this but that was when she
saw the dress. It was hanging on the side of the wardrobe,
red with tiny sparks of colour from sequins that spread
through its full skirt. It was beautiful, far more stunning
than anything Emma could have afforded. It was amazing, but it was Matilde's. Emma took in air too sharply

and her breath caught. There was no way she was wearing Matilde's dress for the recital.

'It's perfect for you.' Sophie's voice was quiet and it was like she had anticipated the protest that would rise from Emma's stomach and stick in her throat.

'It's not mine.' It was all Emma could say. She knew that if she said her dead friend's name her mouth would seal right up and she'd have no chance of making her point and getting out of this horrible situation.

'You don't have time to mess around, and this one's ready,' Sophie told her. She was undoing buttons and pulling the dress from the hanger. Emma watched her, everything inside her appalled at the idea of wearing the dress. But Sophie's actions were hypnotic, and the dress was so beautiful, much more so than her own, hanging in her wardrobe downstairs. Besides anything else, Sophie was right. She didn't have time to get back to her room and find her own dress. She definitely didn't have time to argue. She needed to let Sophie dress her.

Moments later, Emma was wearing the dress. It no longer felt like Matilde's dress but her own. She looked down at her slim waist and the pretty red décolletage and saw the skirt flow from underneath. She stopped fighting it. It *was* perfect for her. It was exactly what she should be wearing for the recital. Sophie ushered her over to a chair in front of the mirror and plugged in the hair dryer. Then she set to work on Emma's hair with the dryer and a hard-bristled brush, pulling it rather harshly out from her scalp. Emma sat and let her, all the fight gone.

When Sophie had finished, Emma's hair was piled on the top of her head like a bride's. Sophie started on the make-up then, being far bolder than Emma ever would have; a darker lipstick, more shadow and a dramatic sweep of eyeliner that extended out beyond the usual boundaries of the lids. When she had finished, she stood back as if to admire her work. 'Well?' she said.

Emma stared at herself in the mirror, trying to recognise anything there. 'I look like a different person,' she said.

Sophie took this as approval and smiled, standing back and looking right around Emma again, clearly pleased with her work. The reality hit Emma that she'd be on stage playing within half an hour. The nausea came again, harder and stronger than before. She tried to stand up but became light-headed and had to sit straight back down again.

'Are you okay?' Sophie said, drawing closer. Her face was right up in Emma's, as close as she'd been to put on the make-up.

Emma waved a hand across her face as if she was fanning it. Sophie moved backwards. 'Just got up too quickly,' Emma said. Then she thought about the question, really thought about it. 'No,' she said. She could feel the tears welling, and struggled hard against them because she knew she'd ruin the make-up. 'I'm not all right,' she said. 'Weird things keep happening to me, Soph. I'm losing bits of time and finding myself places but don't remember getting there. It's like I'm sleepwalking half my life away. Sleep-playing it, too.' She looked up at Sophie and tried a weak smile.

'You're working too hard, honey. I've told you this before.'

Emma shook her head. She tightened her mouth to keep from crying. 'I don't think it's just that. It's like I'm not in control any more and something else is taking over. God, I think I'm going mad.'

Sophie sat next to her and placed an arm around her shoulder. It was unusual for her friend to be so physically close to her and for some reason it made Emma feel uncomfortable. Closed in on. 'It'll all be fine,'

Sophie told her. 'Once you've played the recital you can relax. It'll be good for you.'

Emma tried to believe Sophie that things would be better after the recital but it wasn't how she felt. When she looked ahead like that she was filled with nothing except dread. So she stopped thinking about what would happen after the recital and focused on the fact that she needed to get there. She didn't feel like she was controlling her body as she made to stand up again.

'Take your time,' Sophie said. She helped Emma to her feet, then took a step back and stared. She sighed, long and deep and full of meaning. 'You look stunning,' she said, her voice soft and tender. 'Come on, we're taking you to the ball.'

Despite everything that had happened recently with Sophie and all of Emma's reservations, she felt close to her friend again now. She smiled. She wouldn't want anyone else in the world to be helping her through her first big recital.

It was only as Emma walked through into the green room next to the recital hall that she remembered she was wearing Matilde's dress. Fear hit her in the throat and flowed through her. What had she been thinking?

She felt cold all over. She sat on a chair and shivered. She realised she should be inside the hall warming up but she couldn't move to do it. Soon they would be letting people in and the chance to get the feel of the Steinway again and flex her fingers a little would be gone. She still couldn't bring herself to get up and go inside. She felt if she went through the door, something bad would happen. It was because of the dress.

A few moments later, Wood walked into the green room. He looked at her then did a double-take. 'I hardly recognised you,' he said. He seemed to be examining her closely and bent forward to take a look at her face. 'So that's what they've done to you.' He looked cross; like he wanted to tell her to go and wash her make-up off, as if she was still at school. He hesitated. 'Well,' he said. 'I suppose it's okay. You look very beautiful and sophisticated. It's a shame it's sucked all the innocence out of you.'

Catching a glance of herself in the mirror on the other side of the room, Emma realised this was exactly what Sophie had done. All of the home-scrubbed, common-or-garden, clean look she knew people saw in her was gone. Now she looked like Sophie or Matilde or any one of the private-school girls who studied here with her.

'It's a shame,' Wood said, once he'd reflected on it. 'It was charming, the way you were. Never mind.' He paused, still staring at her. 'It's about playing the piece, in the end,' he said. 'No more, no less.'

Emma thought she might crumble then and be unable to move ever again. She breathed deeply and hoped above hope that she would be able to do justice to what she'd promised in choosing the Rachmaninoff sonata. And that she would do justice to having been chosen at all, above all these well-trained, well-groomed young musicians with the right connections. She knew in her heart that tonight was make or break. If something went wrong, if she didn't perform or made a mistake, then it would be the end of her. She wouldn't be able to face the people here again. Even the building seemed to echo around her and insist that she do well.

Looking down and seeing that she was shaking, Wood came over and put a hand on her shoulder. 'Nerves are good,' he said. 'The day you stop feeling nervous, you might as well give up.'

Emma nodded and gritted her teeth. Now she could feel the dress buzzing against her skin with its own expectations. It wanted her to do this for Matilde, for her dead friend. She wanted to tear the dress right off. It felt like it was burning against her skin. She scratched at its edges and saw red patches there.

'Come on,' Wood said. His voice was soft and gentle. It felt like a lullaby and she followed him to the door into the hall.

Professor Wood was in the hall, introducing her. Emma could hear his voice echoing around the room, although she couldn't focus on what he was saying. He was a compelling speaker, and the audience were responding to him the way they always did. She could feel the expectation that filled the room like smoke. She felt choked by it. She considered turning heel and running out the other way.

There was a roar of applause and Emma knew that this was her cue. The piano was a lonely instrument. It was too self-sufficient. Because it didn't need others to make the harmonies like single-tonal instruments did, it was very often played without accompaniment. She was used to being on stage alone and she would be tonight. She walked out and took a small bow, the way she'd been taught. She told herself she didn't need to look into the audience, and yet she couldn't help herself. Her eyes scanned the room for faces that she knew. There were plenty of them, scattered in small groups around the seats. She wondered which of these were on her side and who was waiting for her to fall.

It was as if time had slowed down. Emma heard every sound and felt every breath as she made her way to the grand piano. She sat with her hands on the keys. They felt cold against her fingers. She still felt the nerves from her gut upwards but she wasn't shaking now. She knew she would be okay once she started playing. And yet she couldn't quite begin.

There were a few coughs around the room. Emma could feel people stirring. She heard a whisper from near the back, stifled giggles. She didn't look. She refused to care. She checked that the music was where it should be. She felt the professor's breath as he joined her, ready to turn the page when she needed. She shut him out. The sense she got of his expectation was almost too much for her. She pushed out the thought that she was wearing Matilde's dress. She got rid of all of that, everything she had been thinking and feeling, and she thought just about the sonata. She closed her eyes and smiled and was somewhere else entirely.

And then she began to play.

Nineteen

Emma was in a room full of people. It was loud and there was a strong smell of alcohol, and she had no idea how she'd got there. The last thing she remembered was the first few chords of the sonata washing over her and resounding around the room. She must have done a good job in losing herself in the piece of music because she didn't remember leaving the recital hall, going back via the green room, or walking from there to wherever she was now. She looked around. The room had been spruced up for the evening but it was basically the Conservatoire bar. She realised that what she'd perceived as a smell was actually the taste of alcohol in her mouth and on her breath. She had been drinking again.

There was a glass of champagne in her hand and it found its way naturally to her lips, as if Emma wasn't in control. She tried to track back through the things that had happened earlier that day but between sitting down to play in the recital hall and finding herself here at the reception, there was a big, black space. She was standing opposite Henry, who looked trashed too. He also looked like he was waiting for her to respond to something.

'I feel a bit sick,' Emma said. It wasn't a lie but it was all she could think to say to distract Henry from the fact that she had no idea how she'd got here, never mind what he'd just said to her.

Henry leaned in, full of concern. 'Do you want to sit down? Go back to your room?'

Emma was shaking her head. She tried to assess her options. She needed to know how she'd done in the recital. She could deal with anything else she found out, just as long as that had gone well. She guessed it couldn't have been a total disaster; this was the reception, and she was here, and people were enjoying themselves. She thought about how to frame her question. She knew that

Henry must have said something about her performance, and that he was kind, so she second-guessed.

'Did you really think I did okay?' she asked him.

Henry looked back at her as if he'd been asked the most obvious question in the world. 'You don't know?' he said, sounding incredulous. His face changed. 'Or are you just after that positive affirma-wotsit or something?' He was smiling broadly.

Emma laughed. 'No,' she said. 'I really don't know.'

'Man.' Henry rolled his eyes, like he was indulging her. 'You were just amazing, babe.' With that, he placed a territorial hand on her waist. This gesture startled Emma but she tried to take it in her stride. How arrogant was this man? First Matilde, then Sophie, and now their best friend. It didn't gel at all with the impression she had of him as a rather sweet boy.

Everything about how Henry was acting was as if the two of them were a couple. He leaned in to talk to her, and sent her special smiles, ones that felt like they were just for her. He moved his hand to rest on a shoulder, an arm, her waist, but all the time making contact. He was behaving as if he was her boyfriend. She remembered how he'd turned up that morning full of concern, trying to control Sophie, always a thankless task. Were there other things she had forgotten, other black patches of time that she didn't even know she'd lost yet?

'I have to go to the bathroom,' she said, waving Henry away and staggering off.

There was another young woman in the toilets, washing her hands, and Emma tried to smile as she came past her. She stared into the mirror and saw Sophie's handiwork, the confident sweep of eyeliner and shadows making her face look like someone else. It startled her. She turned from her reflection, flinging herself into a cubicle and locking it tight shut behind her.

This idea of missing time resonated inside her. Something about the thought felt true and like it explained things she had noticed but ignored. Waking up in different clothes to the ones she'd been wearing when she fell asleep. Sophie saying things to her that didn't make sense, referring to conversations Emma could not remember having. There were no explanations that fitted entirely. She couldn't be sleepwalking, not to that extent and anyway, sleepwalkers didn't, as a rule, make sense and have coherent conversations; they certainly couldn't play recitals. She didn't think it was something wrong with her memory either. She was as sharp as ever, could remember hundreds of pieces of music, could have sat down there and then and reeled them right off. She remembered the periodic table of the elements and the names of all the novels she'd studied at A level.

A thought came to her then. A possible explanation. But it was even sillier than the others. Still, it danced in her head for a few moments before she was able to completely dismiss it. What if she was being taken over in some way? Her body used by some other force, some other spirit. Then, almost as soon as it had come, the idea seemed so utterly stupid that she could have laughed out loud for even thinking it. She was more logical than that. She didn't believe in ghosts and voodoo.

Emma felt properly ill, like she might throw up any moment. She heaved. The nausea abated a little. She came out of the toilet cubicle and was glad to find the room empty. She splashed water on her face. She felt cold and clammy. She stared at herself in the mirror and it really did look like a stranger staring back. She grabbed a paper towel and soaked it, then began rubbing at her face. She wanted to remove every trace of what Sophie had done to her. Whatever was happening, Sophie was involved in that too, Emma was certain. She scrubbed at her eyes with the paper towel. The colours smudged and spread, making her look like a clown. She scrubbed some more. The paper was breaking up and coming off in little balls and her skin felt sore, but she kept rubbing.

Emma cleaned her face until the eyeliner and lipstick were gone, and there was just a trace of the eyeshadow and foundation. Her cheeks and eyelids had gone pink from the rubbing and her skin stung. But she looked in the mirror and she saw herself again. She splashed cooler water on to her face and took a step back from the basin. She blinked. Her eyes felt gritty, as if she wasn't sleeping at night. And yet she was. She had no problems falling into long, sweet, dreamless unconsciousness.

After another splash of water on her cheeks, Emma was ready to face the crowds again. What Henry had said came back to her. He had said she was amazing. She felt a thrill rise in her throat that was almost choking. She had done it. She had proved that she deserved to be here. The only problem was that the person who needed to see this the most had missed it all. Herself.

Taking some deep breaths, Emma straightened up and brushed imaginary fluff off Matilde's dress. She tried to remember how Sophie had managed to persuade her to wear it, but she couldn't. It was a beautiful piece of clothing but it was wrong to be walking around in a dead girl's ball gown. Emma shivered, although she wasn't cold. It was time to go back to the reception. Her reception. The reception in her honour because she had played the Rachmaninoff and had been 'amazing', even if she couldn't remember a thing about it.

The room was sparkling and glittery with the clothes people were wearing and the smell of champagne. Emma could appreciate it now. The bubbles almost rose in the air in front of her and she could taste them; the taste of success. She grabbed hold of the feeling and promised herself to remember this at least. She knew that she couldn't count on these moments for the rest of her life. She could hope for more but it could end any time.

Professor Wood was walking towards her. She didn't know what she'd say to him. What if he wanted to do a post-mortem, or asked her about something she couldn't remember? She held her breath as he approached. He beamed as he came towards her, holding out both arms as if to lift her up with them. Emma tried to smile back at him but it felt faked.

'How is the star of the show?' Wood's voice boomed out into the room.

Emma actually looked behind her, which made Wood smile.

'So modest.' He leaned in and examined her face. 'You've taken off the slap,' he said. 'Good.' He was whispering, as if it was a secret. 'You look better without it.'

Emma realised how close his face was to hers, and then there was a sudden image that flung itself into her mind. It came from nowhere and slapped her around the head. It was a picture of herself with Wood. They were kissing; he was removing her clothes. That wasn't a memory, surely? Emma felt sick to the stomach.

'What is it, my darling?' he said. It was as if it carried on his voice that they had really done those things. His smile no longer appeared fatherly but sinister, and seedy. She had to get away from him. She needed to be out of the bar and back in her room, or further away; back home. This was not right at all. She had liked Wood; seen him as a father figure. But those things hadn't happened. It was just some warped part of her imagination. She felt like she'd been infected by some weird disease. *Taken over.*

Emma rushed from the room and into the quiet hallway. It was dark there, and she felt seriously unsettled. She walked as fast as she could, away from her own celebration. She didn't care what anyone thought. She couldn't stay there any longer. She needed to go to the doctor or see a psychiatrist. She dashed along the corridor as if she was being chased.

She wouldn't let it pull her under. She wouldn't even believe in it. Emma rushed through the main hall, which felt ghostly with the lack of people, washed out, and burst through the main door and outside. The cool air was so sharp it was close to painful. Emma threw herself across the courtyard and towards the halls of residence. She would lock herself in her room. She would hole up there until her mother could come and get her. She would ring her and ask her to drive through the night to take her home. It was all wrong being here. She had made a big mistake ever thinking she could fit in at a place like this.

Arriving back at her room, Emma realised she had no idea where her room key was. She pushed against the door and it fell open. She hadn't locked it. The key must be inside. How careless of her.

The other side of the door, she shut herself in. At last she could breathe normally again. She closed her eyes and leaned back against the door. The drink hit her in waves and images of Wood danced around her head. She tried to stop them. Her eyes snapped open. She knew before she looked that something wasn't quite right. She stared at the bed in front of her and blinked, as if that might change what she saw.

Sophie was there, sitting on the bed. 'Had enough of all that?' she said with a smile. 'I don't blame you, my love.'

It took a few moments for the scene to sink in. Emma stood there, staring at Sophie, trying to work out how she'd got here before her. Her first reaction was to make a fuss but something made her stop short. There was no sign of a break-in from the doorway; Emma realised that the only way Sophie could have got into the room was with her key. She could have stolen the key but Emma realised it was just as likely that she'd given it to her, somewhere in the period of time that she couldn't remember.

'Hey,' she said, as if it was no big deal to find Sophie sitting there on the bed. She wanted more than anything to throw her friend out and lock herself away but something stopped her. An old loyalty, maybe. The idea that perhaps, if she went to sleep, she would wake up tomorrow and everything would be normal again. She sat down on the chair beside the desk and heard the dress fabric crush underneath her.

'Be careful with that dress,' Sophie said. 'Mama will be furious if we get it creased up.'

Emma nodded. It was Matilde's dress and that was fair enough.

Sophie lay back on the bed and closed her eyes, a wistful smile playing on her face. 'Do you remember when we bought that dress?' she said. 'You'd twisted your ankle and London was ridiculously hot, but then it rained.'

Emma stiffened on her chair. Sophie was talking to her like she thought it was her sister in the room. She wasn't sure what the right thing to do was in this situation. You had to be careful with insane people, didn't you? She didn't want to contradict Sophie but she couldn't play along. She said nothing.

'I miss you when you're not here.' Sophie's voice was sweet and crazy as she carried on speaking. 'You should be here more. As much as you can,' she said.

Emma's throat contracted as she listened to Sophie talk.

'I wish I could explain all this to Mama, so that she could talk to you again too. But she wouldn't believe me. She'd think I was making it all up. I didn't believe it at first. After the funeral, when Emma was acting all strange, I thought I could sense you there but I thought I was imagining it. Seeing what I wanted to see.'

The more Sophie said, the deeper Emma sank. She could see her phone. It was just a short distance away; she could have reached for it and called home, or the police. But she was scared. She wasn't sure what Sophie was capable of if she broke the spell and told her that her sister wasn't there. She tried to reach across subtly, pull it in front of her to send a text, but she saw Sophie's eyes follow her hand and she didn't dare.

'We can stay here tonight, sleep in this bed,' Sophie said. 'It'll be just like before you were gone. We can cuddle up like we used to when we were babies.'

Emma's breathing came in sharp at the idea that she wouldn't be free of this until morning. She wanted to shout out that she wasn't Matilde, tell Sophie she was losing the plot, but there was something in her friend's eyes; something manic. She was becoming more and more convinced that Sophie was capable of bad things, stuff she didn't even want to imagine. All of the weird memories she had, the stuff with Henry and Wood, she was sure that Sophie was involved in that. Everything that was happening to her was thanks to Sophie somehow.

The girls didn't undress or get under the covers. Instead, they lay on top of the bed in their formal wear. Emma faced the wall and stared at it as if she might find answers there to what was happening to her life. Sophie placed an arm around her. Emma could feel the other girl's warmth and she felt her fall asleep too, the change almost imperceptible, a slipping away. She wondered if that was what it was like to die. She wondered if that was how Matilde had gone, quietly into the night. But then she had a sudden vision of a struggle, a fight, that made her jerk in the bed. Sophie didn't stir.

Minutes later, Sophie was snoring lightly, not an unpleasant sound. Emma was nowhere near to falling asleep, though. She couldn't stop thinking about what had happened that night. She had played the sonata but she could not remember; there was just a big black stamp of time. And Sophie, she had been talking to her as if she was Matilde. She tried not to think about the pictures she had of Wood but they flashed up in her head no matter how hard she tried to repress them. Emma had always had a vivid imagination but this was beyond anything she'd twisted from reality before. When she thought through the facts, they seemed to add up to one thing. But it was impossible; the conclusions she came to were about something that could never happen.

All the same, it was the idea that danced around her head. Sophie thought she was Matilde and so maybe she was. Not now, not tonight in the room here, but maybe when she was playing the sonata and, afterwards, getting drunk at the reception. All the times recently that had gone missing or been blanked out, when she was playing, when she came to in the middle of the Conservatoire ballroom and had no idea how she'd got there. Had Matilde been there, those times? Was that why Sophie had thought she was Matilde tonight?

Emma gritted her teeth and stared at the wall. These thoughts were completely ridiculous. There was something strange going on; something out of her control that warped the world and meant it didn't make sense any more. But it wasn't about spooks or ghouls or dead girls coming back and taking her over.

Possession. The word whispered through her and hissed inside her head.

Twenty

It was early the next morning when Emma woke up feeling cold and disorientated. She was still wearing the ball gown, and it dug into her arms and neck. She tried to calculate if she could get out of the embrace with Sophie without waking her. She reached for the catches at the back of her dress to try to release them but it was no good and she was very uncomfortable. In the end, she slid from Sophie's grasp and around the end of the bed, then stood up. The other girl reached for her once, then was sound asleep again. Emma felt like she breathed for the first time in hours.

It was awkward, trying to undo the dress on her own

without waking her friend, but Emma managed to reach round and get hold of the clasp. It hurt her shoulders but she kept on at both fasteners at the top of the dress until they came undone. Once the top was released, the rest was easy. She pulled the dress from her and dropped it to the floor. Then she walked carefully over to her wardrobe. She took out jeans and a T-shirt; clean underwear. Trying to be as silent as she could, she dressed. She didn't feel as desperate as she had in the night. She was no longer ready to run away. In a way, it had been a blessing that Sophie had been waiting in her room and had stayed the night, because otherwise Emma might have gone home and not looked back. She had a sick feeling in her mouth about the night before, especially the missing chunk of time, but the pictures of Wood were no longer haunting her. She had imagined those; of that she was now pretty sure.

It was the first morning in a very long time that Emma did not feel compelled to practise. In fact, she had nothing to practise for, except for the hell of it, although that had not often stopped her in the past. Today, though, she didn't want to play. She headed towards the Conservatoire but she was planning on coffee in the refectory rather than time locked away in the dark with a piano. As she realised this, she was shocked at herself. What was happening to her motivation? *Going the same way as my sanity,* a little voice told her.

The café was just open. The lights were half dimmed but there was someone behind the counter putting coins into the till and ready to serve. Emma ordered a latte and took it over to a corner of the seating area. She cradled it and it warmed her hands. She wasn't hungry and could still taste the tang of old alcohol against her lips, on her own breath. She didn't like the flavour at all. She thought about the night before. Maybe it was the alcohol that was stealing her memories; she'd been pretty drunk. She'd heard people talk about this before and had always wondered if it was an excuse to not account for how they'd behaved. She had always found this stupid; like a child imagining they couldn't be seen if they covered their eyes. Whether they remembered or not, the embarrassing events had happened. Perhaps they simply didn't remember everything, though. She had been drinking much more than she usually did recently, so it was a possibility that this was what was causing her gaps. Emma was happy to blame this; it made sense but it was rather worrying that she might be drinking enough to have so many blackouts.

The coffee was too hot and she blew on the top of it. She was falling back into a trance again and made an effort to pull herself out of it. She'd had enough of losing time and memories. It was then that a commotion broke out in one of the main hallways. A cleaner came running out from the area around the professors' offices, shouting about something. Emma tried to ignore her and relax, enjoy her drink, but the woman got increasingly frantic and it became clear something serious had happened. The woman who worked in the café abandoned her post and rushed after the cleaning lady. Emma got up and followed.

The women ran down the hallway to the main staff room. Emma didn't feel right coming here. It was the staff room; not a place for the students. She was only just over being at school, and had been a good girl. She ignored her discomfort, though. Something big was happening here, something scary. She followed the women into the room. Nothing could have prepared her for what she saw there. She gasped, and stepped back.

Professor Wood was lying across the floor. His eyes were wide open and his right hand clutched to his left arm. Emma knew as soon as she looked at him that he was dead. She knew it in her heart and without a single doubt about it. His lips were tinged with blue and something about the colour of his skin and its shiny pallor was enough for her to be sure that he was gone. The two women were bent over him. One of them, the lady from the café, was opening his shirt and undoing his tie. Emma felt a strange compulsion to touch him. She needed to know what his dead skin felt like. Before she could stop herself, her hand shot out. She grabbed the professor by the wrist and dropped his arm just as suddenly.

'He's stone cold,' she said. She heard her own voice, but it was like she was listening to someone else, a report on the radio or TV. 'You're wasting your time,' she said. She sounded uncaring and callous but she knew she was right.

The woman from the café looked up at Emma, narrowing her eyes and frowning. 'Help me,' she said. She was trying to turn Wood on to his back. Emma shrugged, but she was still a good girl and so she did what the adult asked her to. She had to touch the professor again, and the feel of his stiff arms and legs, his waxy skin, made her heave. They managed to turn him and he dropped on to his back. There was a thud as he hit the floor. Then the woman from the café was on her knees, ready to give mouth-to-mouth.

'He's dead,' Emma said. The truth of it hit her as she said it, and she found that tears were in her eyes. She had no idea why the woman was trying to revive him. It was so obvious. He wasn't just dead but had been for some time. It was far too late to do anything for him. Emma noticed he was still wearing his dinner jacket. He had died the previous evening, after the reception and before he'd managed to find a taxi and go home. She thought of his wife and their children. Then she thought of herself, and all the other students here, and what they'd all lost. She was hit again with the finality of death, when it came for the people you cared about. She would never hear his voice again, never have a piano lesson with him again. He would never smile as she played a phrase in exactly the right way.

Emma wanted to shout at him to get up. She wanted to scream that he should stop messing around and pull himself up from the floor. But she looked at his wide-open eyes and noticed their dullness. She sat down, then, on the floor and curled up into a ball. She was rocking back and forth and making some kind of wailing sound. The woman from behind the café counter was still trying to revive him and she turned and gave Emma a look of utter disdain. The other woman, though, the cleaner, walked over and bent down, placing a hand on Emma's shoulder. Emma looked up. There were tears in the cleaner's eyes too.

Paramedics appeared, it seemed from nowhere, and rushed down the hallway towards the staff room. The woman who'd been tirelessly trying to revive Wood moved aside. The paramedics surrounded him. Emma could see them going through their routines, checking for pulses, opening airways. Moments later she heard the word 'clear' loud across the room and the loud sound of the defibrillator charging, then discharging. It filled the air with a burnt metal smell.

And then they were leaving; Wood's body and head were covered on the stretcher. Someone had put a blanket around Emma and was leading her to an ambulance too. She felt like a complete fraud. Nothing had happened to her. She tried to take off the blanket and walk away but one of the paramedics, the only woman, held on to her firmly by both shoulders. 'You're in shock, love. We need to keep an eye on you.'

The ambulance smelled like hospitals, that over-disinfected smell. Emma let herself be led in and sat down. She stayed there for a while. They gave her hot, sweet tea and she drank it all, even though the sugary taste was abhorrent to her. Then she was determined to go. 'I'm okay,' she said. She stood up and shrugged the cover off, then climbed out of the ambulance. She turned to look at the paramedic; she was no more than a girl really. Emma wondered how many people she'd seen die by now. More than she should have, probably. 'Thanks,' she said. She tried to smile but it came off like a grimace.

All of the strange things that had happened the previous evening were put into perspective by Wood's death. None of it mattered. In the end, it would all be over, like it was for Wood and for Matilde. It was depressing if you let yourself think about it for more than a minute. Emma couldn't stop thinking about it. Those pictures came back to her of herself with Wood, taking off clothes, touching, kissing. More. She didn't want to see them, so she worked hard to think about something else. Her warped imagination was disturbing her. Why would she create these scenarios with cosy old Wood, her boring, married piano teacher who had never once behaved in a seedy way towards her?

It was Sophie she turned to. Despite all the weirdness between them, Sophie remained the person she was closest to at the Conservatoire. She left the ambulance and looked for Sophie in her room. When she didn't find her, she headed up the stairs to Sophie's. She rapped on the door. Her knocking sounded like the police coming with bad news. Sophie opened the door and beamed at her. But the smile faded as she saw the state that Emma was in. 'What's wrong?' she said.

Emma pushed past her and into the room. She didn't know where to start. She sat on the bed with tears in her eyes. 'It's Wood,' she said. 'He's dead.'

'The nutty professor?' Sophie's voice snapped at the words. 'Dead?'

Emma was nodding.

'Wow. That's a shock.' Sophie sat down on one of her armchairs. She didn't sound surprised. It was like she'd been expecting it.

'Yeah, heart attack or something. That's what the paramedic told me. She said it probably happened last night. He'd been dead for a while.' At the time the woman's talk had washed over Emma and annoyed her a little, but now she found it was all coming back to her.

'Did you find him?' Sophie said.

'No, it was the cleaner. I heard her shouting and came to see.' Emma remembered the coldness in Wood's eyes, their glassy consistency. 'It was horrible,' she said. She shuddered.

'Ah, well, he was quite old. These things happen.' Sophie's voice was very matter-of-fact. She sounded like she was talking about her mark in a test or some other minor disappointment. Emma could hardly believe what she was hearing.

'He wasn't that old, Sophie. And he was my tutor. I couldn't have done the recital without him.'

Sophie huffed. 'He helped lots of people with lots of things.' There was an undertone to what she was saying, implications again, like the first time they'd talked about him.

'How can you be so callous about it? You knew him. He was a decent bloke.' Emma was crying as she spoke, her face screwing up with it and mangling the words. 'He was one of the good guys and he's gone.'

Sophie gazed across at the bed, her stare level, her

face set hard. She looked capable of anything, untouched by the news she'd just heard. 'You didn't even know him,' she said. 'He was just your teacher.'

Emma found she was racked by sobs now. She couldn't speak and her body was heaving with the force of them. Her throat felt dry and scratched. Sophie's mood broke and she came over to the bed. She reached for her friend and pulled her close. 'I'm sorry you're upset about it,' she said. She held Emma to her chest and let her cry.

The sobs subsided after a while and Emma's crying was much less hysterical. Her eyes felt sore and she was tired to the bone. 'Don't worry, my love,' Sophie was saying, over and over again. She stroked Emma's hair. Emma found she was lulled by this and became sleepy. She wanted more than anything to sleep, deep, deeper than she had in years. She felt herself dropping off the end of the world.

Emma woke with a start. She was lying on Sophie's bed. She tried to piece together where she'd been, what had happened. She was disoriented. She couldn't remember getting there at first. She remembered the recital reception, seeing Wood dead on the floor, but it was misty, like it had been a dream. Then she remembered the scratchy blanket the paramedic had placed around her shoulders, the cold of the morning air, the disinfectant smell of the inside of the ambulance, and she was sure it hadn't been. She remembered walking trance-like to Sophie, and her friend's strange reaction. She sat up slowly, rubbing her eyes, and looked across the room. Sophie was sitting at her desk. She was leant forward, over her laptop, and had headphones on. She seemed to hear the sound of Emma moving on the bed, though, and turned towards her, pulling them from her ears. 'Hey,' she said. Her voice was soft and kind. 'Is it you, my love?'

The question had been phrased so gently and yet it shot through Emma like an electric shock and she sat straight up, suddenly awake. 'Why do you keep asking me that?' she said. Her voice sounded very abrupt after Sophie's tenderness.

Sophie looked a bit taken aback by Emma's reaction. This was a novelty; to see Sophie thrown by something. Emma noticed that her friend's cheeks were flushing slightly. 'No reason,' she said. 'I just like the way it sounds.'

Sophie made it sound so reasonable but Emma didn't believe her. Something felt strange about that question. It was as if Sophie was waiting for a particular answer, some specific combination of words that would unlock the code and reveal the mystery. Emma searched in her brain to try to work out what the right answer was. She felt sure she knew deep inside the words that Sophie wanted to hear but she couldn't pull them from the mire, from the blackness of the forgotten things and lost time.

Outside, the sun was shining, at odds with the way Emma was feeling. Despite the darkness she felt, her resolve to leave and go home from the previous night had disappeared. She wasn't prepared to run away from what had happened to Wood. She needed answers to all her questions. If she left now, she'd never find out about the missing time. She'd never be certain that she hadn't had a sordid affair with the professor. Last night she'd felt in danger but looking out of Sophie's window into the sunny day, she couldn't believe there was anything to worry about.

Turning to Sophie, though, and seeing the hard look on her face, Emma wondered again. 'Don't you feel even a little bit sad about Wood?' she asked her friend.

Sophie shrugged. 'He was nothing to me.' She got

up from her seat and picked up a hairbrush, burying it in her thick locks and pulling it through with some force. 'Matilde had a soft spot for him. He taught her piano before. Years ago.'

'I remember that you said she liked him.' It had been the first evening they'd spent together. Sophie had been digging at Matilde, Emma remembered that too. She had implied more than just a 'soft spot'.

'He gave her a really hard time when she switched to flute.' Sophie tugged at her hair and then, happy with it, began to put on make-up. Emma watched her, fascinated with her expertise. Sophie was naturally very pretty, but she also knew how to use cosmetics. 'Like I said, you don't even know him.' With that, she pursed her lips to apply gloss to them, and sucked them in to smudge it down. Emma felt like she was doing more than putting on lipstick; signalling the end of the conversation in some way. Sophie smacked her lips and then closed the gloss pen with a loud snap. 'Come on,' she said. 'Let's do something with the day.' She was admiring her reflection and flicking her hair out to fluff it up. She turned from the mirror and towards Emma. 'Something decadent,' she said, narrowing her eyes. Emma knew right away that it would involve drinking.

There couldn't be any more gaps in her time. Emma was determined. Whatever happened now, she wanted to stay with it and remember it all. There was a strange feeling dancing around inside her about Wood and his death. It was an emotion really, an abstract feeling of guilt. She had no idea why she felt this way. Surely she hadn't done anything to harm her professor? Anyway, the paramedics had said it was probably a heart attack. It wasn't as if he'd been murdered. The problem was not being able to account for her time. How could she be sure she wasn't involved in some way when she kept going missing inside her own body?

Sophie was at the door and she turned back towards her. 'Come on, my love,' she said. Emma wondered why she called her that, and what the question she kept asking was about. *Is it you, my love?* Who was she expecting? A name came to her when she thought about that. *Matilde.* But Matilde was dead.

Emma wasn't sure what to believe but she did as she was told and followed Sophie from the room.

Twenty-One

They were drinking champagne again, at a bar in town. Sophie had insisted it must be champagne. She said that they needed the bubbles even more when bad things were happening and that the two of them were young and needed to get on with living. She talked about them like this a lot: *the two of us*, as if they were a natural unit like she had been with her sister. The taste of champagne felt acrid and biting against Emma's tongue. It was the taste of being with the twins together, which would never happen again, and it was the flavour of a triumph she couldn't remember, the previous evening, before the professor dropped dead.

But then Emma had never really liked the taste of champagne. It had been the idea that had appealed to her.

Sophie was in her element. Young men they knew flitted around her and she flirted for as long as it entertained her, cutting them dead and coming back to Emma whenever she felt like it. There had been times that evening when Emma had stood on her own for an hour, waiting for Sophie to get bored of whichever boy she was playing with. She always came back but that was not the point. And now she was talking to Henry, of course. It felt like more was at stake when Sophie talked to Henry. Emma wasn't close enough to hear what they were saying. All she could tell was that Henry looked drunk and engrossed with Sophie, hypnotised by her presence. Emma was jealous. Somewhere inside her, there were warm feelings towards Henry. Maybe they had ignited at the party the night before or in the dark, blank spaces in her memory, she didn't know, but she did find that she gripped her glass until her knuckles went white as she watched them together.

Then Sophie was back, and Henry was walking off into the night in a temper. Sophie was all smiles and

bubbles as if nothing had happened, chinking glasses
with Emma and grinning all over her face.

'What's wrong with Henry?' Emma asked her. She
really wanted to know.

'What?' Sophie looked genuinely surprised at the
question. 'Nothing!' She batted her hand in front of her
face as if to dismiss the very idea that something could
be wrong. 'Henry's always fine,' she said.

Emma looked at her friend and tried to work out
how she could lie so blatantly. She must have convinced herself of what she was saying. Maybe, in a way,
it was true. Sophie could make Henry fine; force him to
be. She had a talent for getting people to do whatever
she wanted them to. Emma had a sudden ache to know
the answer to the question Sophie kept asking her. *Is it
you, my love?* There had to be a right answer, something
that would unlock this puzzle.

Another young man arrived at Sophie's side, bringing more champagne. She ignited in front of him, all
full of *thanks so much* and *darling* and kissing him
brightly on his cheek. 'Isn't this kind?' she said to
Emma, who nodded in answer. Then she was flirting
with the boy. He was another music student, two years
above them, a cellist. Sophie reached for him, landing

butterfly flutters of her fingers on his back, shoulders, arms, and he responded to this and glowed. Emma had only met him tonight and yet there was something about the look on his face that jogged her memory. She stared, trying to work out when she'd seen this boy with this kind of expression on his face. It had been in the recital room, she was sure of it.

There were flashes then, in her head, like strobe lighting. Snapshots of moments came back, of her, in Matilde's dress, playing the sonata. There were pictures of the audience in her field of vision, like photos in a family album. Then she remembered her fingers on the final chord, and looking up into the big breath out of the crowd just before they erupted into applause. That was where she recognised his face from. He had been there, in the crowd; he had clapped and cheered and it had been the same look on his face, the glow of it. She reached for the memory and tried to see more but the moment she focused on it, it was gone, leaving lights behind her eyes and a slight nausea. She put down her drink and excused herself.

In the toilets, Emma leaned over the sink. She thought she might throw up but managed to hold that back with big, deep breaths. She felt like she'd been on a fairground ride and had reached with her feet for firm ground only to find that it was moving. The blank pieces of memory were coming back to her and she wasn't sure that was a good thing. She wasn't at all sure she wanted to remember everything.

A phrase came to her then, words she couldn't quite make out, as if she'd overheard them the other side of a door. *The course, it's he, farming dear.* It didn't make any sense and yet something inside her said it was important and that she just needed to listen harder. She wetted her hands and pressed them, cold against her cheeks. She stood upright. Most of the sickness had waned. It was probably caused by too much to drink; she'd had rather a lot of champagne. She felt wicked, out drinking when Wood had dropped dead and his poor family had that to deal with.

Back in the bar, Sophie was alone again. She was sitting at one of the tall tables on a high stool. Emma sat down next to her. She didn't reach for her glass but Sophie passed it to her. Drunk likes company, Emma knew that. She remembered the strange guilty feelings she'd had about Wood's death and the idea that it might not have been an accident stuck in her head. She looked at Sophie and again she felt like her friend might hold the key.

'What do you think happened to Wood?' she asked her.

'He had a heart attack?' Sophie's eyes said that she was bored of this topic and she stared, heavy-lidded, into the distance. 'A stroke? I don't know, I'm not a medic.' She turned her gaze on Emma then, full of disdain. 'Why are you asking me?'

Emma shrugged and realised she didn't know why she thought Sophie might have the answer. 'I'm just not sure it was a natural death. It was too sudden, the timing was too strange,' she said.

Sophie let out a shriek of laughter, as if this was the most ridiculous thing she'd heard all year. 'Of course it was natural. For God's sake Emma, you sound like something out of a fucking Nancy Drew story.' Her voice was brittle and unkind. Emma was stung by the tone of it.

'He really helped me,' she told Sophie. 'He seemed kind.'

Sophie snorted. 'Oh, pul-lease,' she said. It was the exact same phrase and tone as the girl who'd burst in on Emma practising the Rach, dismissive and disdainful all at the same time.

'What, so I'm not supposed to be grateful that he

helped me and chose me to play the recital?' Emma said. Her own voice sounded different from usual; hard and nasal. She sounded like some of the estate girls who lived where she grew up and she had never sounded like them before, not really.

'Listen, Wood was pretty famous for picking his "pets",' Sophie said, punctuating the last word with two fingers from each hand. 'You're not unique and you're not even the first. The man had his ulterior motives, as I'm sure you well know, and he wasn't a decent chap, not by any stretch of the imagination, so excuse me if I don't shed too many tears.' She took a breath, and then a furious gulp of her champagne. She slammed the glass back down.

'Wood never had any motives with me,' Emma said. She listened to her own voice and realised it sounded like she was trying to persuade herself.

Sophie looked at her doubtfully. 'Wood was who he was, and that's the end of it,' she said. 'You just want to believe different because he's been playing with your ego. Making you believe you're special or some shit.'

These words came out cruel, and they hit Emma hard. She felt like she'd been slapped. She stared at her friend. 'What are you trying to say?'

'I'm not trying to say anything,' Sophie said. She looked tired now, and stared into her empty champagne glass as if the answer might be there somewhere, if she just looked hard enough. 'You believe what you like about him.'

It was quiet for a moment then. Emma wanted to break the silence but she didn't know what to say. She couldn't get over the bitterness in Sophie's voice when she talked about Wood, the dreadful things she thought about him. And the worst thing about it was that it all fitted with the snapshots of memory she'd had of herself and Wood. She had another flash of it then, as real as if he was in the room, her body wrapped in his between the scratchy sheets of a college bed. Had she slept with him? Surely not. She had seen him as a father figure, as someone above all that. She did not want to adjust her world view about this. And Sophie was right. It wasn't because of some sacred memory of Wood. It was also because it would have meant he was less interested in her as a pianist than she'd thought. His ulterior motive.

'We should go home,' Sophie said. She waved at the barman and made a signature in the air; he nodded and went to the till to prepare the bill. Emma watched

Sophie take her credit card from her bag, secure in the fact that Daddy would foot the bill when it arrived in a few weeks' time. Sophie's head was down, though, her spirit gone. Emma thought that you wouldn't have recognised her as the person who had been flirting with all the young men in this very same bar earlier in the night. She thought how you never knew the people around you, not really, not when it came down to it. Sophie's bitter words had had an undertone to them; more had happened to the twins than she would ever reveal to Emma. They might have had every little material thing they'd needed growing up but there were other things, bad things, that had made them grow up far too fast. Emma couldn't believe she hadn't noticed this before.

They left the bar and got into a taxi. Just one more expense they both knew Sophie would cover. They sat in silence as they drove through the peaceful city. There were so few people on the suburban streets near the university; it felt like the whole world was asleep. It had never struck Emma before that she was a kept woman but it did now. If Sophie had been a male friend, she would never have accepted all the things she paid for. She would have assumed that there was some motive, some reason she was prepared to pay. So why was Sophie doing this for her? There was probably still a reason. Sophie didn't need to buy friends. She was the kind of girl people flocked around whatever she did.

The thing was, though, that Sophie didn't have lots of friends. When Emma thought about it, the twins had never had *any* other friends. They'd had boyfriends but never let them get too close, and admirers who they kept at arm's length, and lots of acquaintances they could drink with. But not friends, not except Emma. It would have made her feel special except that, after what Sophie had revealed about Wood, Emma was wary of allowing herself to feel special. People judged by their own standards and if Sophie always looked for the ulterior motives of others, that said it all. Emma wanted to know what was in this for Sophie. She wanted to find out why she was being bought and paid for.

The soft tones of a clarinet filled the air in Emma's room. She sat down on her bed and closed her eyes, leaning back against the headboard. If she fell asleep before getting changed tonight, it didn't matter. That theory she'd read about music and forgetting, it must be right. Certainly the lovely sounds that filled the air were helping her forget the bad things that had happened that day, soaking her clean of them. She let herself drift and not worry about anything. The music became so real to her, it was like a world, a foreign place that she'd immersed herself in. It was like a different kind of air, all soupy and fragrant. As she drifted off with the music, there was nothing else.

And then there was. Her head had cleared and more of the weird, dreamy snapshots came to her. Herself and Sophie, dancing in a garden, naked and covered in mud. Sophie laughing manically, throwing mud around, moving like she'd been taken over by the devil. And the question Sophie kept asking her came into her head so vividly, it was like her friend was in the room asking it. *Is it you, my love?* Then her own voice, lilting, talking back. *Of course it's me, my darling dear.* These were words she would never use, though.

The words and images that her brain had conjured up startled Emma from her reverie. Was that the answer Sophie had been waiting for each time? She was almost sure it was. She turned the CD player off at the wall and the music stopped abruptly. Silence filled the room but it felt oppressive rather than peaceful, like it was pushing in on her from all sides. She could hear her own breathing. She wanted to know what the question was about, unlock the mystery that had settled over her life like fog. If what had come to her just now was a real memory, then she knew the response that Sophie was looking to get from her. But what would she do if she was right? Did she really dare to go to Sophie now and test out her theory?

It seemed that not only did she dare, she was compelled to. She stood up and checked her reflection in the mirror. She fluffed up her hair and wondered why she was doing that. She never used to care about what she looked like, had never been that kind of vain, preening girl, not like the twins. She had noticed this change recently and caught herself fussing with her hair, reaching for the lip gloss.

The hallways were dark and quiet. Emma's footsteps echoed as she walked. The high ceilings floated above her, looking sugar-iced with the cornice work, and she felt part of the history that was plastered into the walls. Where Emma had grown up, they didn't have high ceilings. The light bulbs hung down so that you could reach and touch them, if you stretched on tiptoes.

When she thought of her childhood home, she thought of being boxed in; a small space with little windows. Here she had felt the sense of space at first, the sense of freedom, but it had turned to this. She realised now that the small, cosy home she grew up in had been built close to protect her against the world, not as a prison.

It was after midnight, and Emma stood outside Sophie's room about to knock. She had a moment's doubt; what if she was imagining all of this, the question, its importance? But she was sure that she wasn't. She rapped on the door, three hard taps. It came out louder than she'd intended. There was the sound of shuffling about inside the room and eventually the door swung inwards. Sophie looked dishevelled and annoyed as she poked her head around the door. It was clear that Emma had woken her from sleeping.

Then Sophie looked up and saw who it was. Her expression changed completely. She brightened, then smiled. 'Is it you, my love?' she said.

Emma's stomach lurched. It was now or never and she felt sick inside. 'Of course it's me, my darling dear,' she said. Without even thinking about it, she found her voice adapting to the words, becoming like Sophie's, a girl who was far more likely to say a phrase like this.

Sophie was beaming now, a full-on smile that took over her face and lit up the hallway. 'Come in, darling,' she said. 'It's been a while. I was with Emma all evening bored out of my skull and hoping you would come, and you didn't.'

The change in Sophie was palpable, as if someone had flicked a switch inside her. Emma flinched at the reference to her evening. She had to check her reflection in the mirror. She walked over to Sophie's full-length ornamental looking glass, one of her prized possessions and like something out of a fairy tale. She examined her face and fluffed her hair.

'She doesn't give you much to work with, does she, love?' Sophie said, glancing over. She was searching underneath her bed and pulled out a bottle of whiskey. Emma hated the stuff but the twins had always drunk it. Sophie took out highball glasses and dripped a decent-sized dram into each one. 'God, she was hard work tonight.' She wiped her brow as if it had been a physical effort to be with her in the bar. Emma was so shocked by the way she was talking that she wasn't even angry.

Sophie was insane. She had lost her sister and now she had lost the plot. Emma took the glass from her with a half-smile. The drink that Sophie would expect her to want. She took a sip of the whiskey and tried not to pull a face. She found it tasted better than she was expecting. Sophie was fiddling with her computer, which was connected to speakers. She put on some music; rock music, the kind of tracks that Emma would never usually listen to.

Sophie grabbed Emma by both hands and pulled her over to the bed. She bounced there, pulling her friend down and wrapping her arms around her, hugging her like she hadn't seen her in days. 'I'm so glad to see you, I miss you so much when you're gone,' she said. 'My darling, dear, lovely little sister.' She kissed Emma hard on the side of her face. 'Oh Matilde!'

Emma forced herself to smile, the same way she did when she was having her picture taken for the paper. She felt its falseness strongly and thought that Sophie would surely know too. She didn't seem to notice, though, as she chattered away about all the things Matilde had missed, at the same time looking for something on her bed. Nothing important now, nothing more about Emma, and she was thankful for that, but silly gossip about which girls had kissed which boys. Emma smiled and nodded and tried to look surprised.

She sipped the whiskey, drinking it down as fast as she could.

Sophie turned sharply and stared right at Emma. 'Matilde? It is really you, right?'

'Of course,' Emma said. She felt like her voice must be shaking.

Sophie paused, then waved a hand across her face. 'I'm being silly,' she said. 'Of course it's you. You knew our code.' She settled down on the bed and whatever she'd been looking for was forgotten. 'Emma's so confused. She's been telling me how she blanked out when she played the Rach, like she really thinks it was her who played it. Even when I saw her audition, I knew it wasn't. In fact, it was watching you play that made me certain it was you inside her.'

Emma smiled. She didn't know what else to say and was sure that if she opened her mouth she would give herself away.

'You know, I think Wood might have been up to his old tricks with our Emma.' Sophie was sparkling at her now, revelling in some shared secret.

'You think so?' Emma hardly dared whisper in case her voice gave her away.

'Yes.' Sophie giggled. 'He had out all those old

études he made you slave over.' Her eyes flashed. 'He likes them young and naïve,' she said. 'Bloody pervert. He must have thought himself so much the stud having one of us and then the other. And now our friend.'

There was a silence between them as Emma heard her fears about her professor's relationship with the twins confirmed. 'I'm so tired,' she said as soon as she dared. 'I have to go.'

Sophie's face crashed with disappointment. 'Not so soon!' she said. 'I've missed you too much. I'm sorry, I won't talk about Wood any more. I know how much he hurt you.'

'No, I'm really sorry, I have to go,' Emma said. She put down her glass and rushed from the room.

Twenty-Two

Emma leaned on an elbow, gently pressing down keys on the Steinway, hardly making a sound. She shouldn't be here, in the middle of the night. She'd be in trouble if she were found. But she needed to be somewhere Sophie wouldn't come looking. She'd been itching to get back to the recital room, to touch the Steinway again and reassure herself that it was real. Her thoughts raced. She had always been so sure of how she saw the world. There was what you could see and hold and touch and nothing else. She had always thought that stories of ghosts and ghouls and witchcraft were ridiculous. She hadn't even been able to stomach the Harry

Potter books that everyone at school had loved so much because they were too far from her world view, even if they were supposed to be fantasy. But she couldn't deny the evidence in front of her face any longer. Strange things had been happening for a while and it all fitted together, even if the explanation was so hard to believe.

Sophie had acted as if Emma was Matilde. She had spoken about things only the two of them would know, whispered secrets. What had happened with Wood was so similar to the Henry incident that Emma couldn't help seeing a pattern and wondered if Sophie went after anyone who got close to Matilde. Even Emma. The short half-hour she'd spent in Matilde's shoes had been enough for her to understand far more readily the complex reasons why the quieter twin might have killed herself.

The ceiling here was freshly painted, its cornice work perfect and ornate. Not like in her room, where the paper was peeling. This kind of neglect was typical of quite a lot of the non-public space at the university, she knew, although not Sophie's room, or the room Matilde had lived in for such a short time. Emma knew now why they got special privileges. She knew why Sophie didn't care to practise as much as she could and wasn't so bothered about wasting the opportunity. She even knew why Matilde had switched to the flute. She wasn't sure what disturbed her more: the twins' history with Wood or the fact that she'd been Matilde for a night. And Sophie had asked her that question so many times before she'd answered it correctly; that she remembered, at least. How often had Sophie seen Matilde inside her? Well, it would certainly explain all the missing blocks of time.

Emma tried to dismiss it. There had to be a logical explanation. Sophie was seeing what she wanted to see. Emma herself, disturbed by recent events, was having some kind of psychological breakdown and acting out. But all the logical explanations in the world didn't explain to her why she saw some of Matilde's memories. She had touched Sophie and seen a childhood together so vividly she could smell the summer grass they'd run through. No matter how she tried to rationalise it, she couldn't get past what she'd seen and felt. A word that had whispered through her head before was now set in concrete there. As crazy as it sounded, she had become possessed. Matilde continued to live, through her, and she came alive when she wanted, outside of Emma's control.

Emma's breathing had become faster, and she tried to slow it down. She could still feel the bitter tang of whiskey on her breath; the taste of the dead twin inside her. She tried to calm herself. If she thought hard enough, she would be able to find a way to stop this happening. What had changed to allow Matilde in? Sophie hadn't been so surprised to see her in the middle of the night, which probably meant she was used to it. How long had it been happening? She remembered now that more than once she'd lost herself when playing and that was when things had gone black. Like the recital. The Rach; it had been Matilde's audition piece. On the recital day, she'd worn Matilde's dress and her make-up, done by her sister. Sophie had acted afterwards like she was Matilde, as if she'd been there all night.

Emma could hear music. It was simple, haunted single notes held and let die, as if someone was pressing down on a piano and leaving their finger there until the sound faded each time. She looked down at her hands. She realised it was her; she was making those sounds without even realising it. She recoiled from the piano in horror. That was it; the key to it all was the piano. She mustn't play any longer. She pulled herself up from the Steinway with some regret and crept out of the room into the hallway.

It was chilly in her room and Emma pulled her night-clothes on quickly, wrapping her dressing gown tightly around and tying its belt firmly. She had been spooking herself but now, back in her own space, it all seemed ridiculous. She put on the kettle. The bumping sounds it made as it warmed were reassuring; as if everything was normal. She wondered when life would really be normal again. She would have killed to be at home, sitting in the kitchen drinking coffee with her mum. She wasn't sure what was stopping her from calling her mum right then and there and leaving this nightmare behind. But something did stop her. Something stalled her every time she went to pick up her mobile phone, like her actions were being controlled by someone else's will.

The keys on her electric piano glinted at her from across the room. She longed to play. In fact, more than anything else, she wanted to play the Rachmaninoff sonata. She checked herself. It was that very piece that had caused her so many problems in the first place. Or maybe not. Maybe it had already been happening to her and choosing the Rach was a symptom, not a cause. She poured water into her mug and mixed in hot chocolate. Then she sat curled in her desk chair, staring out of the window.

She drank the chocolate and let it warm her. She had a plan now. She wouldn't play for as long as it took to make Matilde go away, and she would never touch the Rach again. Life would be hard but at least these bad things would stop happening. But even as she sat there with the mug in her hand, she was desperate to play the sonata. She felt that if she didn't play soon, she might die with the effort of stopping herself. There was something about piano keys, for Emma, that was as much of an addiction as any drug could have been.

Emma came to on the chair and it was like no time had passed. She was still holding her mug but when she looked inside, it was emptied of drink. She hadn't spilled any so she must have drunk it and she had lost some time again. Maybe she had just fallen asleep? She tried to persuade herself that this was all that had happened.

As she came back to full awareness, Emma realised she must have been sleeping because she could remember a dream. It was about Henry. At least, she thought it was a dream. She sat up and opened the curtains and saw that it was light outside. She rubbed her eyes, which were sore. She went cold. She tried to remember the dream. She had been with Henry, by the lake. They had been kissing and he'd wrapped her in his arms. She had felt happy and so close to him. And he had given her something. She remembered now; it had been a stone, reddish, round. She had placed it in her pocket. She rushed to where her coat was hanging and checked. She gasped as she felt its cold, smooth shape in the pocket.

Emma stared at the red stone in her hand. So it hadn't been a dream at all. It had happened. She had been right in her suspicions that there was something romantic going on with Henry. How could she sleep through something like that? Did Henry think Matilde was coming through her too, the way Sophie had seemed to? She tried to remember what he'd said, by the lake. Whether he'd called her Emma or not. But none of his words would come back to her.

She was supposed to have a piano lesson today but she needed to get out of that somehow. Then she remembered that Wood was dead, so the lesson would be cancelled anyway. The fact of her teacher's death hit again, that cold, hard, permanent reality.

With a heavy heart, Emma took clothes from her drawers. It didn't matter what she wore. None of it mattered at all. She pulled on a pair of jeans and a black T-shirt and found some socks. She thought about having a shower, but that didn't matter either. It was all she could do to put on her clothes and drag a brush through her hair. She wondered if Sophie would come to her lectures today. She often didn't, if she'd been drinking. Emma realised that part of the haze that was enveloping her was a simple hangover. She wondered if there would be more news about Wood. She wanted to know why he'd died; she needed an explanation.

The hallways were busy as she left; students flitting from their rooms to the toilets and bathrooms, getting ready for the day. She walked through them in a daze. She had this romantic picture of herself wearing a long flowing nightie, walking towards her fate like a victim in a vampire movie. She smiled at her silliness in imagining this. Then she realised, she wasn't imagining it at all. She had done that: floating down the corridor in her night clothes. She hoped that no one had seen her.

It was chilly outside, like the weather reflected

her life. Her coat wasn't thick enough, but she only had to walk a few hundred yards. She looked at the Conservatoire building across the landscaped gardens. Its dome shone in the morning light and it reminded her of a fairy-tale castle. It was a beautiful building and yet there was something cold about it. She shivered. She wished she had never come here.

Inside the main building there was an air of anticipation that was more pronounced than the usual morning buzz. She looked at the noticeboard. She thought there might be something there to say what would happen about her piano lesson, but there wasn't. There was a notice, though, calling all students to an important meeting at ten a.m. in the recital hall. She knew this would be about Wood's death. Emma didn't want to go and hear about what had happened all over again, but she knew she had to. She didn't want to hear about what a great teacher Wood had been after what she'd learned from Sophie the night before.

Emma had nothing to do until the meeting. Usually she would have found a practice room and played in the intervening time. She couldn't, though. She couldn't risk losing herself again. She had no idea how she'd live without playing. What time period would be enough to stop this? She walked along the hallway and into the refectory.

As soon as she entered the refectory, Emma remembered the previous day, and how she'd found out about Wood's death. She stopped abruptly in the doorway. Then she told herself she was being silly. She would have to get used to being here again. She had another two and a half years at the Conservatoire to go and she couldn't avoid the refectory and the recital hall and the staff room and everywhere that would remind her of Wood. Holding her head up high, she walked over to the counter to order something. She was relieved to see that it was a different woman from the one who'd tried to revive her professor. That woman was probably off sick; she might be off for weeks trying to recover from the shock.

Emma wasn't particularly hungry but she ordered a muffin and coffee, as well as a banana. She thought that all the ready sugar, together with the caffeine, would perk her up and keep her going. She moved over to a table and sat down. The room was dotted with groups, sitting together and chatting. Everything seemed ridiculously normal, considering what had happened. She found it surprising that the place wasn't sombre and subdued, the way she felt.

That was when Sophie came in. She sashayed into the room like she owned the place, looking up and around for the people she should say hello to. She was fully made-up and wore a pair of jeans with a sparkly, low-cut top. She looked stunning. Emma stared then, glancing around the room and realising she wasn't the only person who had noticed. Sophie came over to her table and sat down. She didn't get food or a drink from the counter, as if she was above all that.

'Hey,' she said. She smiled at Emma, but she also looked like she was staring, trying to work something out. Emma hoped she didn't ask the question. Now she knew the right response, it was too tempting, but it was not a good idea. She didn't want to know any more of the twins' secrets. Then Sophie seemed to have decided and she turned away. 'It feels weird here today,' she said. Clearly she had seen no sign of her sister in Emma.

'It is weird here today,' Emma said. She felt angry. The negative things Sophie had said the night before came back clearly to her. She knew now how false her friend was. Their closeness was entirely based on the idea that Matilde could reach Sophie through Emma.

She felt such a surge of temper that she could have slapped her. She controlled herself, though. She didn't want Sophie to know that she'd deceived her.

'Are you coming to this meeting thing, then?' Sophie was looking at her nails, as if she was talking about nothing more serious than a date or a disco.

'Of course I am.' Emma tried not to let her feelings carry on her voice. 'Are you?'

Sophie sighed. She twisted a finger through her hair. 'I suppose I ought,' she said.

'Well, don't go just because you think you have to.' Emma heard an edge to her own voice. 'I've been thinking about what you said.'

'Oh?' Sophie looked up from her hands.

'Yes, I was thinking that you were right. I didn't really know him at all.'

A half-smile played on Sophie's lips, as if she was pleased with herself about something. 'Well, if we're going, we should get on,' she said.

Emma looked at her watch. It was ten to. She couldn't believe how quickly the time had gone. She felt like she'd been here ten minutes at most. She saw that people around her were collecting together their things to go off to the meeting too. She kept looking at her watch, and then around the room. Then she shrugged and stopped. 'Let's go,' she said.

The recital hall was filling with people. The noise of so much chatting blurred into a hum, and it rose and fell, buzzing in Emma's ears and making her feel sick. She sat down, about halfway up the hall, and Sophie sat next to her. It seemed she wasn't so keen to be right at the front for once. The room continued to fill. It was hot inside the hall, and Emma had her head in her hands. She couldn't look at Sophie, didn't want to. She didn't want to watch the front of the hall.

Professor Margie came through the door behind the stage. It was the same door that Emma had walked through for the recital, with Professor Wood. She watched Margie make her way across the stage with her head down. She remembered those meetings with her supervisor and wondered how different things might have been if she'd taken her advice and gone home. She might not have come back but that wouldn't have been such a bad thing at all. She suddenly felt very tired indeed.

Margie cleared her throat and began to speak. 'For those who haven't heard, I'm afraid that I have some rather bad news,' she said. Emma could have laughed out loud at the way she phrased it; it was just so typical of all of these middle-class and private-school types she was surrounded by. Margie was still talking but Emma wasn't really listening. It wasn't like she didn't know everything about what had happened. She caught the odd phrase. *We're deeply saddened and our thoughts go out to his family.* The usual platitudes. Then there was a whole sentence that seemed to rise from Margie and over the students. 'The police thought at first that it was natural causes but have found reason to doubt that.' The professor was still talking, saying that certain individuals would need to be questioned, and Emma knew right away she would be one of them.

They thought Wood might have been murdered. Emma remembered something she had felt; a sad ache of guilt about her teacher. She remembered the pictures, of them together, far closer than a student and tutor should be. And she added that up with the missing shafts of time. She turned towards Sophie, as if she might find clues from the set of her eyes. Her friend was staring right at her with an expression that was impossible to read. Sophie looked away, quickly, as if embarrassed to be caught looking. Emma wondered if she had been searching for her sister again. This thought took her over and made her shiver.

She stared at Professor Margie, still talking from the front. She was droning on and on and the words weren't going in at all any more. Emma made a real effort to keep her eyes open, and they felt sore with it. They were watering and making the room swim around her. She felt them closing and pulled herself up, jerking in her seat and making several people around them turn to look at her. She turned towards Sophie, making eye contact with her friend again. Sophie nodded at her, as if she was trying to encourage her before a performance. Emma's eyes were going again. She was so tired she couldn't help closing them. All she wanted was to let herself slip far, far away.

There was nothing she could do as her eyes closed again and she let whatever it was take her, not caring any more, just wanting to let herself go.

Twenty-Three

Emma was dreaming of music, of singing, the beautiful voice of a soprano filling her head. She was enjoying the sounds, letting them soak into her, helping her to forget that she would die. Then she was waking. Her eyes fluttered open and she realised that it was her singing the piece, and it was Schubert's *Ave Maria*, of course. She was sitting up in bed but there was something unfamiliar about the dark space around her. She reached for her lamp, where it usually was, but grabbed at fresh air. She was breathing fast and her heart was pumping. This wasn't right; what was going on?

Then the room flooded with light and she saw that

it was Sophie's room. She let out a small yelp, and all at once Sophie's hand was over her mouth from behind, which made her struggle and panic. She could feel her friend wrapped around her. 'Shhh,' Sophie said. Emma calmed herself and Sophie let go, falling back on the bed. Emma was sitting dead upright. She was fully dressed. She got up and walked over to the window, pulling the curtains wide. Sun streamed in; it was the middle of the day.

'Did you have a bad dream, love?' Sophie said. She paused. 'Sorry to grab you like that but you made me panic. God knows what other people must be thinking.'

Emma turned towards her friend, who was lying on the bed. If she hadn't known better, she'd have said it was quite a provocative way of lying there; the kind of pose she'd expect Sophie to pull for a man. She was staring up at Emma through her eyelashes and she seemed to sparkle at her. She looked drunk. Emma made her way back to the bed and sat down. Sophie let her head fall back and stared at the ceiling. There was a faint smell of alcohol around the bed and, on the floor, used whiskey glasses.

'I was singing,' Emma said.

'In your dream?' Sophie was rocking her head back and forth as if she could still hear the music.

'No, here, in the room. I heard my own voice.'

Sophie laughed. 'Darling, I think I would have noticed if you'd been singing. You were asleep, bless your heart, and snoring lightly. You look so lovely when you're sleeping.'

Emma tried to level what Sophie was telling her with what she had experienced. She was sure she'd been singing as she woke up. She was losing her trust, though, in her own memory and senses. They were letting her down so often.

'What were you singing?' Sophie asked her.

'Just a little aria I learned when I was young.' Emma wasn't exactly lying, but it wasn't truthful, how she put it. She couldn't tell Sophie that she'd been singing the *Ave Maria*, though. Not *that* song, not Matilde's. Even dreaming about singing it felt wrong. 'Can I get some water?' Emma said. Her throat felt scratched and sore.

Sophie gestured towards a glass of water that was beside the bed and Emma grabbed it, drinking hungrily. She had no idea how she had got to Sophie's room and she wasn't even shocked. The last thing she could recall was being in the recital hall. That was it; Professor Margie had been talking about Wood. Emma had felt ridiculously tired. She must have fallen asleep.

'I dreamed Matilde was back again, here in this room. We were talking for hours.' Sophie's voice was strange. She sounded completely taken over and in a way that frightened Emma. She wondered if Sophie was testing her.

'It must have been nice, to see her again,' Emma said.

'It really was.' Sophie was curling hair around a finger and staring at the ceiling. She looked like she was somewhere else entirely in her head. Then she came back and stared right into Emma's eyes. 'It's horrible to wake up and find it's all a dream.'

The words felt pointed. They seemed to fly across between them and straight into Emma's face. She wanted to go then, get out as fast as she could. She stood up from the bed so quickly that she came over dizzy. Sophie grabbed her by the elbow.

'Are you okay, love? You're not going, are you?' Sophie's voice was thick and heavy.

'I have to,' Emma said. She tried to think of a good excuse, a reason, but nothing came and so she didn't explain. 'I have to go,' she said. She grabbed for her coat.

'Don't go,' Sophie said. Her voice was musical and hypnotic. She really did sound quite drunk. She held firm to Emma's elbow and pulled her towards the bed again. Emma found she was falling and put out a hand. Then she was back on the bed and the soporific feeling she'd had earlier, in the hall, was coming back, taking over. She forced her eyes open, determined to stay awake, to stay conscious inside herself and not let go. Sophie was pulling hard against her, though, and the look on her face was frightening. Were they both going mad?

Then something seemed to break in the room, like the first roll of thunder. Emma felt wide awake. Sophie snapped out of her mood and sat up. She picked up Emma's coat and bag and passed them to her. 'I miss her so much,' she said. She seemed sad but in control. Emma breathed again. She put on her coat.

'I miss her too,' she said.

'What do you think happens when you die?' Sophie had lost her veneer, her whole sense of sophistication. She sounded like a child.

'I don't know. I used to think it was the end but I'm

not so sure any more.' Emma paused and thought about it. 'Maybe I just want to believe that since I lost someone close.'

'I know what you mean,' Sophie said. She sighed. 'But I do think she's here with us, somehow. I just feel it.'

'Maybe,' Emma said. She had started to consider all sorts of things possible that she would have laughed at before. 'I have to go. They'll need to talk to me about Wood. I was there when they found him.' It was true, she realised as she said it, but it wasn't why she wanted to go. She wanted to be out of this room and away from Sophie.

'Oh, stay,' Sophie said, grabbing her arm again. 'Just for a bit. You don't know anything and they can wait to hear what you saw.' Her eyes were pleading.

Emma couldn't stay, though, and she pulled herself away. 'I need to talk to them or it might look like I'm hiding something,' she said. She surprised herself with how easy she found it to lie to Sophie, and how much she wanted to be away from her. A few weeks ago, she would have said nothing could shake the friendship they shared. She rushed out of the door as fast as she could. She felt that if she didn't move fast, then Sophie would somehow suck her back in, charm and hypnotise her with those subtle ways she had. Or even use force to make her stay.

Out in the hallway, Emma leaned against the closed door. She breathed, deep. She walked away from Sophie's room as calmly as she could, somehow resisting the urge to run, to sprint down the corridor like a mad girl.

Emma headed straight to Margie's office. It was as if her excuse to Sophie had to be followed up on. She hated being dishonest. She found her lecturer already meeting with a detective inspector. It was a young woman; younger than the professor, anyway. She was sitting with a notepad, facing Margie and nodding. She turned and stared at Emma as she burst through the door.

'I'm sorry,' Emma said. 'I don't mean to interrupt but I thought I should give a statement. I was there when he was found.'

The detective smiled at her. 'You must be Emma?' she said. 'Yes, we do need to talk.'

The way she said this sent a chill through Emma. She felt that nagging doubt again, that guilt, and the weight of all the lost time she would not be able to account for.

The woman stood up and walked over. She held out a hand, which Emma took, unsure still about hand-shakes. 'I'm DI Anne Martin.' She seemed friendly now. 'I'm just finishing up here and then I'd really like to talk to you. Will you wait outside?'

Emma nodded. She turned and left the room.

Outside, she sat on one of the chairs in an alcove not far from Margie's room. It wasn't far, either, from where she'd seen Wood, dead on the floor. She shuddered as she remembered the previous morning. She wondered what the police had seen or found that had made them suspicious. It had been clear to her, completely evident right away, that he was dead. But had she known more than she realised?

The door of Margie's room opened and made her start. The DI was standing there, looking at her all expectant. 'Your professor says we can use her room. Better than taking you to the station, I'd think. Is that okay?'

Emma nodded and pulled herself to her feet. Her legs felt shaky as she walked towards the door. Margie was gathering her handbag and other things, getting ready to leave. There was a voice in Emma's head that nagged at her to beg the professor to stay. She would have, Emma was sure of it. She wouldn't ask her, though. She wasn't a child. She could deal with it.

The room was very quiet once Margie had left and Emma regretted not following her instinct. She took a seat opposite the police officer, who was fiddling with something on the coffee table before picking up her notebook and glancing through her notes. She looked up at Emma.

'These are just informal questions. We're not charging you with a crime or arresting you, so you won't need a lawyer or anything.'

It had never crossed Emma's mind that she might be arrested, but now DI Martin had said it, it was suddenly a possibility. She shifted in her seat.

'You were first on the scene?' the woman asked.

'No.' Emma shook her head. 'It was some lady from the refectory. No, actually, it was the cleaner. The cleaner came running through shouting and we both responded to that. Me and the lady from the refectory, I mean.'

'Okay.' The DI was scribbling notes. Then she looked up and right into Emma's eyes. She had the kind of penetrating gaze that made Emma want to look away. 'So you hadn't seen him at all that morning?'

'No.'

'And the last time you saw him?'

'The night before,' Emma said. 'There'd been a recital.'

'Yes, I'm aware of that.' The officer paused and chewed on her pen. 'Can I ask, Paul Wood was your piano teacher, right? There have been some rumours around here about his conduct with young women. Were you aware of that?'

Emma wondered if Sophie and Matilde were the source of these rumours, or if they had just been two of many. She nodded. 'A friend of mine ...' She didn't finish the sentence.

'You know something definite about his conduct? Because it's important you tell me if you do.'

'No,' Emma said. 'God, no. It was just a rumour I heard.' Her voice in her own head did not sound very convincing.

'Was he ever inappropriate with you, Emma? Please, if he was, you must tell me the truth. It's really important that we have a full picture.'

Emma shook her head vigorously. 'Never,' she said.

As far as she was aware, she was telling the truth. Weird snapshots of something that might have happened did not count.

'And the night he died, after the party. What did you do that night? Were you with him?'

'No,' Emma said, on instinct, thinking about where she actually was. She did have an alibi. She had been with Sophie. Only Sophie had thought she was Matilde and so she couldn't say that. It would give everything away. 'I was with Henry,' she said. 'Henry Bailey-Ray.'

'Is that Ray as in r-a-y?' The DI looked up, punctuating her words, and Emma nodded. 'And if I ask him, he'll confirm that, will he?'

Emma nodded again, hoping above hope that she was right, and that he would. She was almost sure she could rely on him.

'That'll do for now.' The DI was leafing through her notebook again. 'But I may well be back later. We need to wait a few weeks on the toxicology report and another couple of things.'

Emma picked up her coat and was making to leave. She turned back. 'Did someone kill him?' she asked.

The police officer glanced up from her work, looking

amused. 'I can't comment on the details of the case,' she said.

Emma left the room. She felt like she was breathing again. She couldn't work out why she felt the heavy weight of guilt inside her chest.

The ceiling had grown misty because Emma had been staring at it for so long. She was worried that another minute or two and she'd be fast asleep and end up under some spell, not accountable for her actions. There was a soft knock on her door. She was torn about whether to answer it or not. It might be Sophie, who she wanted to see and wanted to avoid in equal measure. But something told her it wasn't. She knew her friend's sharp, certain taps. She got up, feeling dazed and tired, and opened the door.

It was Henry standing there. Emma was surprised but she invited him in. She found she felt flustered as he settled on the chair beside her bed. 'Tea?' she asked him, uncertain. 'Or coffee maybe?'

'Only if you're making it,' he said, ever the polite, well-brought-up young man.

'Well, yes, I am,' Emma said, clicking on the kettle and gathering cups. 'Which will it be?'

'Coffee, then,' Henry said. He smiled, that kind of half-smile that she'd noticed him give before, when he was nervous.

'Have you been in the practice rooms?' Emma asked. It felt a very benign question but she couldn't think what else to ask.

'No.' Henry's voice carried an air of frustration, as if he wasn't there for small talk. Emma ignored the boiling kettle and sat down. She felt compelled to.

'I've been thinking about the other evening. At Maddock's.' He was talking about the wine bar in town where he'd spoken to Sophie. Emma remembered she had felt a stab of jealousy at the time about how close they'd seemed. 'I know how it looked but it wasn't like that.' He finished his speech and looked down at the floor.

'Henry, to be honest, I really don't know what's going on between us.' It was as honest as she could be.

Henry looked like he'd been punched, though. He gazed up and she thought he might cry. She hoped he wouldn't; she didn't know how to deal with that. 'I'm sorry,' he said. Then it was as if he'd had second thoughts about that. 'Well, I'm sorry that I hurt you but the thing is, it's Sophie. She has this way of always spoiling everything. Manipulative bitch.'

Matilde had used similar words about her sister, and Emma couldn't help thinking that two people who knew her so well couldn't be wrong. 'I don't understand any of this,' she said. She had no idea how to explain to Henry the complexities of what she'd been through these last few weeks. He would think she was insane.

'What I said by the lake.' Henry paused. 'I meant it,' he said. 'Did you mean it?'

Emma stared at him. She didn't know what to say. She thought she knew the incident he was talking about; she had remembered it somehow. She reached for the stone, which she'd placed beside her snowstorm. She held it out towards him. 'When you gave me this?' she said.

Henry nodded.

Emma felt the stone in her hand and imagined it warming up as she held it. She remembered tender feelings and whispers, even though she had no idea what the words were. The way her chest contracted as she thought about it, she knew she had feelings for Henry. Whatever she had said, she was certain she would have meant it. 'Yes,' she said. 'Yes, I meant it.'

Henry smiled and reached a hand towards her. 'I'm

glad.' He straightened in the chair. 'That policewoman came to see me.'

Emma nodded. She had guessed that might be what had prompted his visit.

'She asked me if I was with you the other night, you know, after the recital. I wasn't sure what was going on but I thought you might be in trouble so I told her I was.'

'Thank you,' Emma said. She thought she should feel relieved and yet she didn't.

'But we weren't together, Emma.'

She didn't know where to look. She couldn't explain about Sophie, and what had happened that night.

'Were you with Paul Wood? Were you with ...' He trailed off. 'Were you with that bastard?'

Emma was shocked to hear Henry use this kind of language, and also that he had used Professor Wood's first name. 'Of course I wasn't.' She took a big, deep breath. 'I was with Sophie. It's complicated and hard to explain why I didn't tell them that.'

'Are you in trouble, Em?'

She shook her head. 'I don't think so.'

'You have to watch your back with Sophie, Emma. I never told you what she did to me and Matilde but I really think I ought. She knows what she wants and it's usually what someone else has got, and she'll do whatever she has to to take it from them.' Henry's voice was filled with passion and Emma could imagine him making speeches, when he was older maybe. He could never be a politician, though, she thought. He was too honest and faithful. She didn't know what was happening between them, didn't have a clue, but she welcomed that there was something.

'Tell me,' she said.

'I was completely in love with Matilde,' he began. He leaned over and placed a hand on her arm. 'I'm sorry to be so blunt about it but we've got nothing if I'm not honest.'

Emma found it did sting, but she nodded for him to continue.

'You make jokes about twins and swapping, and I did ask Tilly stories about that. We laughed about it. But I never thought it was real.' He cleared his throat. 'Stuff like that was just too much fun for Sophie.'

'She pretended to be Matilde?'

Henry nodded, his face slightly reddened. Emma was unsure if this was because he was embarrassed for falling for it, or still angry. 'Lots of times. It started after Matilde's performance, when she sang in the concert, and I think it was pure jealousy. It became such a game to her. She'd turn up at my room and act sweet and pretend she was her sister and then we'd be, well, in a compromising position and she'd let on who she really was. She found it hilarious.'

It was foul stuff but Emma believed it easily of Sophie. She could imagine the cruel smile on her face, hear her voice contort into a nasty laugh. Emma knew, at heart, that Sophie would have hated Matilde being the centre of anyone else's world instead of her. Had it been the same thing with Emma? It was around that time that she and Matilde had been growing close.

'Of course, eventually she told Matilde that we'd slept together. I tried to explain, but Tilly wouldn't believe me because Sophie told her a different story, of course. She never saw Sophie for what she really was. At least if she did, then she denied it to herself and to me.' He was crying now; his face had gone muffled and he was sniffing. Emma moved from the bed and right up to Henry, where he was sitting on the chair. She put an arm around him. It felt stiff and unnatural there. 'And now she's starting on what we have.' He had recovered himself a bit but he looked angry. 'Like that thing she did when we were drinking at Arctic, after you'd played so beautifully in the masterclass. You and I were on top of the world; the best it's been, remember? She isn't your friend. She isn't anyone's friend.'

Emma grasped to remember what Sophie had done at that bar, but there had been so many bars. Henry could have been talking about anything. She decided she was through with guessing or pretending about the moments she had lost. She would just tell the truth. 'What did she do? I don't remember.'

Henry looked incredulous. His face had gone so red that Emma was worried he would start to steam. 'You don't remember? How she got you to call me Harry? You mustn't listen to her, Emma. She knew that was Tilly's special name for me and she knew it'd cause a row between us.'

Now she understood. She remembered the incident after all, except that it had had nothing to do with Sophie. She tried to smile at Henry. 'Listen, Sophie didn't tell me that. It just came out.'

'That's not possible. I don't believe you.' He was rubbing his eyes now; it was like he was smudging the sadness all over his face. 'Are you just another part of her game? Are the both of you playing with my head?'

'No, Henry, it's not like that. I don't know how to

explain. There are so many weird things happening to me right now.'

There was a silence then between them; it stretched across the room. Finally, Henry spoke and broke it. 'I've heard that kind of thing before, so don't worry. I know a break-up when I hear it.' He stood up, clumsily, knocking his coat to the floor. Reaching for it, he tried to storm off but was held back while he got a good grip of the garment. Then he rushed towards the door without looking at Emma. It closed with a slam.

Emma stared at the space where Henry had been. It was for the best. She would have liked a boyfriend like Henry, but how could she with what was going on in her life? He hadn't understood anything she'd said, and she hadn't had the words to explain things any better. She believed everything he said about Sophie, though. Anger spiked through her body as she thought about it. Sophie had killed Matilde. Sure, she hadn't murdered her, shot or stabbed her or anything, but the result was the same. The bad behaviour with Henry and Wood and anyone who cared about Tilly had been her murder weapon. And the incidents Emma had learned about were probably just the start of what Sophie had done.

Twenty-Four

There was something Emma needed to know. She sat down on the bed cross-legged, and powered up her laptop. She opened up the browser and went to YouTube, then searched. She found the clip again, of the Rachmaninoff sonata, being played by a young girl with dark hair; a girl around her own age. She examined the clip over and over, turning the laptop as if another angle would reveal the truth. It didn't. She still couldn't work out if it was her dead friend or not. Whoever it was, she played the Rach with extreme precision and expression, better than Emma could imagine ever playing it herself. She made the clip repeat a further three times but was still unsure. She searched through the text attached to it, the descriptions and comments, but could see no name. The details must be there but she was missing them somehow.

Then she had an idea. Why not search for Matilde on YouTube? If this clip was her, it should come up. Or there would be other clues, something that would help her work it out. She needed to know if the Rach really had been Matilde's piece, like Sophie had said, or if this was just another one of Sophie's games. She typed 'Matilde Benoit' into the search box and pressed enter. *Bingo*. There were plenty of videos that related to Matilde. Someone had been busy recording and uploading; her parents maybe? Or perhaps Matilde herself, trying to build a career, a *profile*, the way the professors were always talking about in their lectures. Emma scrolled through what was there. Despite everything Sophie had said about Matilde, all the things she'd learned since her death, she was still surprised to see that all of the videos were of Matilde playing the piano rather than the flute. Many were very technical pieces. She flicked through the list and saw names of concertos she would have baulked at herself. Could Matilde really play this music?

Emma saw that there was a video of the Rach 2, the

full concerto. That would be a test. She clicked on the link and made it play. There she was, her friend Matilde. It was a better video than the one of the sonata, but there was no doubt that it was the same room and the same girl. The same piano, Emma could tell right away from its tone. She saw her friend hunched over its keyboard in a very familiar way. And then, what gave it away completely, as the girl turned and those eyes shone out from the screen, the astonishing blue of them. They were unmistakably Matilde or Sophie's eyes; she would have spotted them from the moon.

A shiver passed through her body. 'Someone walked over my grave,' she whispered, a phrase that came to mind despite her not liking its connotations. It was so spooky to see her dead friend, conjured up on the screen in front of her. *That must be how Sophie feels*, she thought. But that meant she was believing in it: *possession*. It meant she was giving credence to such a mad, stupid idea. Her logical brain was still fighting it but deep in her heart, Emma was sure that this was exactly what was happening to her.

The university library was so different to the ones that Emma had known in Manchester, and she had not grown used to it. The academic books were laid out in what seemed an undecipherable system to the untrained eye. She'd had an induction, which was supposed to help, but it had just confused her further. So it was with trepidation that she entered the building to look for a book that might help her make sense of what was happening. She just wanted a scientific explanation. She searched the lists on the wall, but she had no idea where to go to learn about something like this. There were librarians about but there was no way she was asking someone where to find the crazy people's books. She looked for a computer that was away from the others. She didn't even want someone to look over her shoulder and see what her search terms were. She would die if she thought anyone saw her as the kind of person who believed in witches and fairies.

In a booth to one side of the library, Emma used the library's electronic catalogue. A search on just the term 'possession' brought up over six hundred books, none of which looked relevant as she scrolled through. The academic titles left her cold. She wondered how people motivated themselves to write these books. She tried a different search, this one about the paranormal and psychology. A long list came up again, but these looked more relevant. She scrolled through and wrote down the code that was supposed to help her locate the books.

Emma wandered the aisles trying to find the books from the list. She watched for people she knew, trying to make sure that no one saw her trawling this part of the library. Despite the fact that most of the titles she'd seen on the list were proper, bona fide science books, she still felt like she was chasing the end of the rainbow. Luckily, this was not the busiest section of the library. There was another woman looking, someone Emma didn't recognise, but otherwise the place was empty. She sidled up to the shelves, searching for titles that seemed relevant. She pulled out books and flicked through them. She settled on two to take to a table at the side of the room. The first was one called *Psychology and the Paranormal* and the other *Possession; a delicate case*. She was rather surprised to find this kind of book in the university library. It didn't seem appropriate.

The books were heavy, and Emma dropped them on a desk near the window. Dust flew up and floated all around her like mist, and she had a strange sensation that the books were haunted. It confirmed for her that believing in anything supernatural was the beginning of the end of all logic. She began to read the first book, the psychology one. It was written in a dry, academic style but she persisted and tried to get through it. It explored the premise that all so-called paranormal phenomena could be explained by disturbances in someone's psychology, often trauma or major life change like bereavement. She wasn't entirely sure she was reading it correctly but it did seem to make a lot of sense. Many of the words there she could see applying to her own situation, although she did wonder a little if she was reading what she wanted to find. After a chapter or so, the academic language became so off-putting she could bear it no longer. She closed the book.

The second book was entirely different. It was written in plain English, for a start, but it also started from the premise that possession by a spirit or demon was a proven fact, undisputable. It took the opposite side completely from the other book, written by someone who thought the supernatural was evident, inescapable. Emma found some of the book's conceit difficult to accept. She couldn't stop reading it, though, because it described so much of what she'd been going through in eerie detail. Not just the missing chunks of time, but the flashes of memory that weren't your own and a sudden change in your likes and dislikes. Emma had noticed recently that she often went to put on red clothes. This had never been a favoured colour for her; but it was Matilde's favourite. After a while, she closed this book too but this time it was because she was seriously disturbed by what she'd read there. In fact, she slammed it shut.

Emma left the books on the table and walked away. She didn't want to be near them any longer. Now it wasn't just about what other people might see. She didn't want the ideas in the books to rub off on her, make it all true. She didn't want to believe in any of it. She was walking along lost in these thoughts when a voice roused her. She heard her name called and turned.

'Sophie,' she said. 'What are you doing here?'

Sophie laughed. 'It's not against the law to come to the library.'

Emma couldn't argue with that but she also knew that it wasn't a place Sophie frequented. In fact, she could count the times she'd been there with her friend on the fingers of one hand, most of them right at the beginning of the year, when they'd both been keen. Emma realised Sophie was waiting for her to speak. 'I still can't find anything in this place,' she said, to break the silence. She laughed, but it came across fake and contrived. She was sure she must look like someone with something to hide.

A thought came to Emma, about what Sophie was doing there. Had she followed her? How long had she been here? She could easily picture Sophie around the corner, watching her from the other side of a booth. There was something about this image that was compelling and real; she shivered at the thought of it.

It was as if Sophie noticed and wanted to put her mind at rest. 'I just came for this,' she said. She waved a music theory book at her friend. But Emma wasn't convinced. It wasn't the kind of thing she could imagine Sophie reading. Her having the book felt like a prepared alibi; proof, somehow, that she was up to no good.

'I have to practise,' Emma said, and she rushed away as fast as she could. It was a complete lie; in fact, she had been avoiding the Conservatoire building altogether since the meeting with the police officer. She didn't look behind her to see where Sophie was, if she was following. She didn't want to slow herself up at all. She had no intention of playing the piano, or any other instrument for that matter. She needed to get away from Sophie, as far as she could. She had no idea what she thought would happen if she didn't get away from her but she felt compelled to do it.

The room was dark. Emma had closed the curtains and shut off all the lights; she had locked the door tight and was not playing any music. She was just lying on her bed, staring into space, watching the dust dance in the black air. She was thinking about Sophie. The blackout and the locked door, the lack of music, was all in aid of keeping her friend out, but she was there, inside Emma's head, no matter what she tried to do about it.

Phrases from the books she'd read that afternoon came back to her. Some of the things she'd read in the science book had stayed with her but it surprised her to find that it was the other book, the crazy one, that came back to her most readily. She could picture the illustrations, vividly, as if they were etched on her brain. She tensed up as she thought about that book, the ideas inside it. These were ideas that she hated to give any credence to and yet she found she believed in them. The concept of being possessed was the kind of thing she'd have dismissed as nonsense even a few weeks before but she couldn't find any other explanation for what was happening to her.

There was a knock on the door; confident taps that Emma knew belonged to Sophie. There was no way she was letting her in. Sophie was causing all of this. When Sophie had talked about her dream of Matilde, it said it all to Emma. It was clear how much she wanted her sister back, and it was as if she was trying to conjure it out of Emma, sucking Matilde in through the void. Emma remembered how she'd felt during the funeral, and the weird dream she'd had that night. She remembered seeing Sophie downstairs, both of them looking for Matilde there. It had started then.

The knocks came again. Emma tried to stop her lungs and heart, as if their movement might give her away. The room was completely silent. She could hear Sophie breathing outside. Even from the breathing, she could tell it was her friend. She felt like she should just let her in and give in to it all. It seemed the easier path. There was a deep sigh from the doorway. The door handle moved, Sophie trying it from the outside. Then there was the sound of her footsteps as she walked away.

Emma knew she couldn't avoid her for ever. But if

Sophie was pulling Matilde through, then perhaps there was a way around it. She could give Sophie a little of what she wanted. At least, she could make Sophie think she had what she wanted. She never could have pretended to be Sophie, she couldn't have pulled that off, but Matilde had been far closer in personality to herself. In fact, when she'd answered the question correctly the previous night, Sophie hadn't thought for a moment that she wasn't talking to her sister. She could be Matilde, if that was what it took to stop Sophie drawing her sister back into the world.

It was so simple but it immediately felt like a solution. Emma was cheered by the idea things could be back to normal soon. She would spend some of her time pretending to be Matilde to satisfy Sophie's hunger for her sister. The rest of the time she could be herself. She could play again.

There was a knock at the door again; those same three sharp taps. This time Emma got up. She turned on the light so that it wouldn't look strange to Sophie when she let her in. She opened the door.

'Is it you, my love?' Sophie asked her.

'Of course it's me, my darling dear,' Emma answered without hesitation. The words weren't strange on her tongue. It was like she'd answered the question a hundred times before.

Sophie smiled at her, a big beaming smile that lit up her face. She walked past Emma and threw herself on to the bed. 'Thank God,' she said, all gravelly and cruel. 'I think I would have killed myself if it had been Emma again.' She was stretching out on the bed, luxuriating. Emma felt aggrieved on Matilde's behalf. It seemed bad taste to be joking about suicide. But Sophie turned towards her and didn't even notice. 'You have some of that whiskey left?' she said.

Emma panicked then. If the twins had stashed whiskey in her room, then she had no idea where it was. She could feel her heart thumping in her chest; she was about to be found out. 'Yes,' she said, searching her mind, the depths of her memory to try to work out where it might be. She needn't have worried; Sophie got up from the bed and walked across the room, standing on tiptoes to open the high cupboard. She retrieved a large bottle of Jameson's and placed it on the bedside table with a smile. Emma fetched two tumblers from the sink. She hadn't known she had those either but she found them easily. Sophie poured the Jameson's. Emma enjoyed the sound as it hit the sides of the glasses.

Taking a big sip, Emma realised she was acclimatising to the drink's sharp kick. She felt it warming her throat and enjoyed its heat. Sophie had thrown herself on to the bed again, and tapped the space next to her. Emma got up and sat there. Her friend put an arm around her and pulled her close. Emma felt suffocated, like she couldn't breathe, but she tried not to shrink away. It would be the worst thing ever for Sophie to realise that she was pretending. She tried to relax, leaning back and sipping her drink.

'I think Emma suspects,' Sophie said.

Emma couldn't bear the suffocation of the hug any longer and stood up, picking up their glasses as an excuse. 'What makes you think that?' She was refilling the glasses. She actually wanted more whiskey.

'She was skulking around the library today. She never goes there. She's not an academic. She spends too much time in the practice rooms maybe, but I doubt she's seen the inside of that library in an age.' Sophie was staring at her nails. She didn't look concerned; bored more than anything. 'Maybe you can take over altogether or something.' She looked up with a cheerless, intense expression on her face. A chill shot through Emma; Sophie was serious.

'I don't know if I could do that,' Emma said.

Sophie laughed. 'Always too soft. Too nice. I've told you before.'

It was a relief to Emma to hear these words coming from Sophie. At least she hadn't been wrong about Matilde. The other twin had been a good person. She had a moment of wondering if she could share her existence this way. Perhaps Matilde deserved a second chance. But she couldn't do it. She couldn't bear to not be in control of herself all the time, not knowing what she'd done, where she'd been. Like the recent events with Henry. She had no idea how far their relationship had gone and it was frightening. She could end up pregnant, or worse.

'Henry came to see me today,' Emma said. She wondered if she could fish for some of the details.

'Oh yes?' Sophie perked up, interested now.

'Seems he's fallen in love with Emma or something.' She heard her own voice talking about herself in the third person, and she wanted to laugh.

Sophie giggled. 'What a dolt. He's such a sucker for the sweet ones.' She spoke as if the very idea made her sick. Then she checked herself, tucking a lock of hair behind her ear in a nervous gesture. 'Sorry,' she said. 'I'm going to spoil things if I talk about him, so let's not.

Anyway, it's probably just that he can see you in her. I mean, why would he fall in love with Emma?' She made the question sound preposterous, ridiculous.

Emma did her best not to react. A downside of pretending to be Matilde would be hearing these things, the horrible barbed comments Sophie made about her to her sister. She found her mouth pulled hard in anger despite herself. Sophie looked up.

'Oh chill out,' she said. 'I know you don't like me slagging her off, but pul-lease. She just leaves herself so open to it.'

'Stop it!' The voice came from the centre of Emma but it didn't feel like her own. It forced its way out and she wondered how in control she really was. 'Stop it, Sophie.' She spoke more quietly this time.

Sophie threw herself back on the bed like a scolded child. 'Fine,' she said. She lay there staring at the ceiling and didn't speak. Emma watched her. She felt controlled by how Sophie was behaving, compelled to apologise for some reason. She tried to stop herself. She hadn't done a thing wrong. But the word kept pulling at her until she had to let it go. 'Sorry,' she said. She spat it out like it was poisoning her.

'You are?' Sophie said. She was batting her eyelashes

like a little girl. Her whole performance was completely affected, and Emma wanted to slap her, hard. Her hand was itching with the desire to do it. She curled her fingers up into a ball with the effort of stopping herself. 'I'm glad you are,' Sophie said.

'Of course I am.' She almost added the *darling dear*. She thought about those phrases now, how affected they seemed. She would never understand these posh girls and their ways.

'Yes you are, aren't you? You're always sorry. One of your weaknesses. Sorry for Emma, sorry for the world. Even sorry for me. Well, you should be. It's hard living without you. Of course, I know that's not your fault, but never mind.'

It was odd for Emma to hear Sophie saying this. It was hard to believe that she had the least sympathy for her sister's suicide. There was a tiny thought growing in Emma's head, like a silver thread, that there was obviously more to this story than she'd thought. It was no wonder that Matilde had felt so desperate. How did you escape from a twin sister who wouldn't let you go? Who dragged you down with her and clung on with her nails?

There was only one way. Suddenly, Emma felt like she understood everything.

Twenty-Five

It was dead dark and Emma could hear scratching at the door and an unholy whispering. She tried to rouse herself. Where was she? She sat up in bed. She remembered. She had been with Sophie. They had drunk whiskey until Sophie was drunk fit to pass out, and Emma had somehow managed to get her back to her own room. Her head was pounding now; the beginning of a hangover that she was sure would hit her hard by morning. But she had slept and nothing bad had happened. Pretending to be Matilde was weird and she didn't like it but it seemed that it might have sated Sophie's desire for her sister. Emma hoped so. She

hoped that this would be her answer, her path out of
the madness.

The scratching stopped for a moment. The silence
it left was more eerie. Then it came back with a
vengeance, along with the random, vicious-sounding
whispers that brought to mind speaking in tongues.
Emma was so scared she couldn't move. Her arms and
legs froze and she didn't know what to do. She told herself she should get up, find out what was happening
outside her door. It was probably Sophie. That thought
didn't reassure her more than any other. The room was
chilly as she got out of bed, and she pulled on her dressing gown, wrapping it tightly around her.

Opening the door, Emma saw her friend. Sophie
was on her hands and knees, as if she was worshipping,
or scrubbing the floor clean. She was dishevelled.
Under the corridor's strip lighting, her usually perfect
make-up was smudged and running; her eyes panda-
like with mascara, her lips made into one big gash by
how much red she had applied, over and over, like a
little girl playing. Her hair was knotted, as if it hadn't
been brushed for days. Emma stared down at her.
Without thinking, she let out a small shriek. Sophie
stared up, eyes wide, as if she wasn't really there.

'Is it you, my love?' It wasn't Sophie saying the words this time, but Emma. The question tripped off her tongue like she'd asked it before.

Sophie's eyes widened. 'Of course it's me, my darling dear.'

Emma stepped back with a sharp intake of breath. The Sophie-Matilde creature was crawling into her room. She had been wrong: Matilde was pushing herself through any which way she could find. Emma moved away from her friend, who pulled herself up using the desk. Her eyes were an even stranger shade of blue than usual; they looked like they could burn holes through metal. Emma thought it must be the light and the strange make-up. Sophie looked like some exotic creature; a banshee or demon, a monster with bad intentions. She stood still for a moment, then her head went back and she laughed, an evil, maniacal laugh. Emma cowered away. Then Sophie launched herself at Emma and grabbed her by the hair. 'Let me go!' But it was Sophie-Matilde who was screaming this. 'Let me go. Let me rest!' Her voice was piercing, the words like squeals.

Emma sat up sharp in her bed and tried to catch her breath. Her arms and legs hurt. The room was dark as death. She was relieved to wake up but had to convince herself that it had really been a dream. She pulled and pinched at her own flesh to make sure she was awake. She was breathing fast and could feel her heart thumping. What a horrible nightmare. She waited for her breathing to return to normal. Then questions came, things she couldn't ignore. It had seemed so real. It had happened here, in her room. She got out of bed and switched on the light.

Examining her body in the mirror, Emma could see bruises and scratches. She couldn't be sure which were fresh and which were old and had no idea where she might have got them. The missing stretches of time in her life meant it was beyond her to know. She had to find out if what she'd just seen had been real and if she'd passed out somehow, lost her way like she had done so often recently. She would go and find Sophie. It was the middle of the night, but if she pretended to be Matilde, then Sophie wouldn't care. She pulled clothes on in a hurry.

The hallways seemed emptier than Emma had ever seen them as she padded quietly along and towards the staircase. She made her way up the stairs, the odd creak making her start and feel afraid. She wished she dared switch on the light but she didn't want to wake anyone. She didn't want to be the mad girl who wandered the hallways when everyone was in bed. Finally she was outside Sophie's door. She knocked, quietly but firmly, a sound calculated to wake her friend if she was in a light sleep. There was the noise of someone moving inside the room.

The door flew open. Sophie looked dishevelled but she wasn't plastered in make-up. It was just messy hair from the bed and a bit of mascara on sleepy eyes; the same way any girl would look untidy if you woke her in the middle of the night. Emma was relieved. She found she was breathing easier. Sophie was rubbing her eyes and looking confused. Emma smiled at her, a full, happy smile with no hesitation; it wasn't something she usually did herself, but she remembered it from knowing Matilde. Sophie's expression changed.

'Is it you, my love?' she asked.

'Of course it's me, my darling dear.' Emma knew the answer so well now that she suspected it was something she chanted in her sleep.

Sophie beamed at her and opened her door wide so she could come in. Emma followed her friend into the large room. She shivered. There was a window open, and a cold breeze moved the curtains, brushing against her skin and giving her goosebumps. She settled on the bed. Sophie was headed straight for the whiskey. Emma wasn't sure she could stand much more Jameson's. She was shaking her head. 'I think I've had enough,' she said.

Sophie laughed. 'You're such a lightweight, darling. Come on, you know you want to really.' She was pouring two drinks. She bounced down on to the bed and handed one of them to Emma, who had to hold tight on to the glass to stop it from spilling. 'What shall we do tonight, then? We could mess with Henry some more. Or something else,' Sophie said. She looked deep in thought. 'Something good, because I'm bored,' she added.

Emma stared into the glass of whiskey. She found that once it was in her hands, she couldn't help but bring it to her mouth and sip. Its warmth spread through her body and took away the sting of the breeze wafting in. 'I don't know,' she said. 'I can't think of anything at all.'

Sophie sighed long and deeply, as if for effect. 'Well that's just typical, isn't it? I always have to think of the ideas,' she said. 'And then half the time you get all moral on me and don't want to have any fun.' She had turned on the bed and had her feet up, her head rested against her bent arm. Her other hand reached across and pushed at Emma's fringe, a futile attempt to flick or style her hair in some way. 'I'm sure she could do something with this mop if she made a bit of an effort,' Sophie said. She sounded exasperated. 'Poor you, having to put up with it.'

Emma shrugged. She found she was thinking of herself in Matilde's place. She was a poor substitute for her glamorous friend. 'I should get her hair cut for her,' she said. 'Do her a favour.' She heard the words come out and it was odd because she sounded just like Matilde. She was finding a voice in her attempt to imitate the dead girl.

'That is so typical of you.' Sophie sounded fed up. 'Always so bloody nice, for God's sake. Haven't you worked out yet that nice gets no one anywhere?'

Emma did not believe this and was glad to hear that Matilde felt the same way. She refused to think you had to be a bitch to get on in this world the way Sophie did.

'I know.' Sophie's voice had changed now; it had an edge to it. 'I know what we can do. A bit of fun at Emma's expense. Just a bit of fun ...' Her voice trailed off. 'Oh this is hilarious,' she said. 'It's a bit like having a dress-up doll.' She smirked. 'Only we'll do the opposite of that tonight. Tonight we'll take off all her clothes to play with her.'

Emma felt as if all the heat had rushed out of her body at once. She tried not to let out a sound. She stared at Sophie. Was she serious?

'Oh come on. It'll be fun. Just for a laugh.' Sophie got up and began brushing her hair. 'Let me just make myself presentable,' she said, pulling with vigour. Emma watched her, wondering what was coming next and what she could do to avoid Sophie's will. She wasn't very good at telling Sophie no and it felt like Matilde was even less able to do this.

Fluffing her hair, Sophie turned from the mirror. 'Okay, I'm ready,' she said. 'Let's go.'

'Where are we going?'

'Oh, don't worry your pretty head about that, Matilde.'

The girls left the room quietly, Sophie locking the door and putting a finger to her lips, then giggling as if she couldn't control herself. They went carefully down the stairs and to the main door. Sophie led and Emma followed. Emma wondered if this was what life had been like for Matilde, following her sister, doing what she was told.

Outside, the air was crisp and cool. They walked across the courtyard and then over the grassy hillocks that separated their halls of residence from the main buildings of the university. Being there at night made everything look different. The shadows played tricks, and Emma remembered how odd it had all been when she first came here. Now, the university seemed like a massive organism, a self-reliant thing that ate the students then spat them out afterwards. Maybe it was just the dark making her feel that way.

They were at the main Conservatoire building now. Sophie dug inside her clothes for her entry pass. She found it and waved it against the door. 'Open Sesame,' she said, in a theatrical voice. She laughed, seemingly pleased at her own cleverness at getting the door to open.

The two girls walked through the foyer and into the main hallway. This wasn't far from the staff room, where Emma could vividly remember finding Wood's dead, still body, and how something odd had come over her, something manic. She had a strong feeling now that this was the nearest she'd come to feeling the taking over, the possession.

Sophie led her on through the hallway, past practice rooms, and the old ballroom where Emma had woken in the middle of the night, and the offices of Professors Margie, Dyer and Wood. She led her right up to the doors of the recital hall. The door had a coded entry system. Sophie typed in the numbers and spoke as she did, her words coming out in the rhythm of the taps. 'We're just going to make her look a bit silly, that's all. Good clean fun, my love.'

Emma was doubtful that she would feel the same about Sophie's plan. She followed her into the hall nonetheless. As she came through the door she stood stock still, completely halted by the thought of being there again, where she'd played but didn't remember, where she'd practised with Wood. She was taking deep breaths but Sophie didn't even notice, grabbing her by the hand and pulling her along in her wake. They had to climb on to the stage as the steps were nowhere to be seen. Sophie vaulted up and then leaned over and pulled Emma after her. Then they were there: the stage area, the scene of the crime.

'Take off her clothes,' Sophie said.

'What?' Emma stared at her friend. 'No!'

Sophie didn't look away. She gazed at Emma, all

long and languid. 'Take off *her* clothes.' She stressed the word 'her', spat it out like it was dirty. 'Do it, now.'

Emma found Sophie's voice very compelling but she wasn't ready to be naked in the recital hall. She couldn't do it. Sophie wasn't taking no for an answer, though. She grabbed Emma and pulled at her roughly. Emma thought her friend might launch her right off the stage if she wasn't careful. For the first time since all this had begun, she felt afraid of Sophie. The look on her face was consuming. It was terrifying. Emma recognised it from somewhere. Then she realised that where she knew it from was the Sophie in her dream, the girl who'd come scratching at her door.

She pushed Sophie from her. 'Stop,' she said. 'It's fine, I'll do it.'

'Good.' Sophie smiled. It was the smile of someone who was used to pushing others around and getting her way. Emma realised she had always known this about Sophie. She had noticed it when they first met and nothing had changed.

Emma pulled off her jeans and socks, then her jacket. Her T-shirt went next, and then she was standing in front of her friend wearing underwear.

'She's a scrawny thing, isn't she? Bless her.' Sophie

turned her attention away from Emma's body then. 'I guess at least she's thin. Anyway,' she waved a hand in Emma's general direction, 'the rest as well.'

Emma did not want to remove her underwear. She stood feeling cold and vulnerable, her arms crossed over her chest.

'Silly thing,' Sophie said. 'It's not even your body.'

It was then that the idiocy of what she was doing struck Emma. What had she been thinking? Pretending to be Matilde to feed Sophie's delusion was crazy. Sophie was insane and she was fast dragging Emma into her insanity along with her.

'Play the Rach.' The words were quiet; bitter even. Something about them struck fear into Emma and made her realise just how deep Sophie's jealousy went.

'I don't want to do that.'

'Oh for God's sake, play the thing.' Sophie was pushing her towards the piano and her eyes were beginning to glow with a crazy energy.

Emma was stuck here, almost naked and with Sophie. She walked over to the piano and sat down. She didn't feel in control of her own movements. She wondered if she had hit some mid state, a strange place where she was neither Matilde nor herself. She had

seen some of the dead twin's memories, heard her
words come from her own tongue.

Sitting at the piano, her hands poised and ready to
play the Rach, Emma felt more vulnerable than ever.
She turned and looked at Sophie, realisation hitting her
in waves as she saw Sophie playing with her phone, setting up ready to record the event. She shut the piano's
case and stood up, heading towards the pile of clothes.

'What are you doing?' Sophie voice was a shriek,
the cry of a spoilt child.

'I'm not doing this to Emma. She's supposed to be
our friend.'

Sophie was examining Emma closely, as if she was
trying to work something out. Emma felt self-conscious
under her gaze. She grabbed for her jeans.

'Tilly, you know you're being stupid.' Sophie ran a
hand through her hair but her voice was calmer now.

'It's just wrong,' Emma said. As she heard her own
voice, she wondered how Sophie could think she was
her sister, even for a moment. It was stupid.

'You know you'll do it. You always do what I tell
you, in the end, Tilly.' Her voice was cold. 'You're not
about to completely change personality overnight.'

Emma stood and stared at her friend. She was

completely trapped. To leave now would give away that she wasn't who she was pretending to be and then everything would be shot. She was rigid with indecision. She wondered for a moment if the whole thing had been a test from the beginning. She looked at Sophie and tried to work out what she was up to. All she could see was her friend's determination. Then Sophie was headed in her direction.

Emma flinched away as the bigger girl threw herself towards her. Sophie tore the jeans from her hands and threw them to the floor. She grabbed Emma by the wrist and held on tightly. She twisted her arm behind her back. Emma was completely immobilised and helpless. She felt Sophie undo her bra and remove it.

'Stop it,' she said.

Sophie laughed. She pushed Emma away. 'Do as you're told then.'

'Fine.' Emma rubbed at her upper arm and turned away with as much defiance as she could muster. She stormed back to the piano and sat down.

'Good girl,' Sophie said. She sounded pleased with herself.

Emma hit the first chords and looked up across the stage. She saw Sophie standing there, one hand raised.

She was holding her phone in the air, recording everything. Emma knew this could destroy her completely but she was already into the Rach, and the Rach was taking over.

Twenty-Six

Emma woke up, sitting bolt upright and trying to get her breath. Her arms and legs stung. She looked into the dark. Was she in her own room? She wasn't sure. She remembered being at the piano, playing the Rach. But something more. She had been naked.

She reached around, pawing the bed and trying to find her phone. It wasn't in its usual spot. Then she felt something else, in the bed. Someone else. The warm, soft curves of Sophie's sleeping body. She withdrew her hand fast, as if she had burned herself. It was all she could do not to call out. If she was in Sophie's room, Sophie's bed, then it hadn't all been nightmares.

Carefully, she moved the quilt and climbed from the bed. She placed the cover back as gently as she could. She was glad to find she was wearing clothes now; a pair of pyjamas, Matilde's most likely, but at least it was clothing.

Trying to find her way around the room, Emma was banging against furniture and knocking items over. She managed to catch Sophie's alarm clock before it crashed to the floor. It still sounded incredibly loud. She wondered if she could get away with switching on a light. She remembered there was a row of lamps above the mirror like those in a theatre dressing room; Sophie turned these on when she was perfecting her make-up. Emma tiptoed over. She fumbled around searching for the switch. Finally she found it and flicked it on. She stared at the bed as she did this, tensing up. But Sophie didn't even stir.

Turning towards the mirror again, Emma couldn't help but make a sharp sound. She slapped a hand to her mouth. The dressing table looked like a war zone. There was powder everywhere. The lipstick that sat there was worn right down to a stub. All the signs were there. Emma wasn't sure how she'd missed this before. It *had* been Sophie at her door earlier in the night. It was no dream, no nightmare; the evil had taken over her friend.

Emma's breathing became so rapid she worried she might wake Sophie. She took some deep breaths and tried to bring herself back to normal. She had to get out of there. But first she had to find Sophie's phone. If Sophie's crazy behaviour at her door had been real, then what had happened down in the recital hall had too. Emma had to find the phone and delete the footage. It was more important than she could even begin to say. She left the lights on above the mirror and hunted around the room, frantic, desperate to locate it. She dipped her head under the bed to look there but it was so dark. She reached under. There was a creaking sound from above. Slowly, Emma pulled her head out. She heard Sophie's voice but couldn't make out what she was saying. But Sophie was just talking in her sleep, and tossing and turning. Emma breathed again.

Even these tiny movements sounded too loud, though, and Emma knew she needed to get out of there. She groped around some more on the floor. Finally she found the phone. It was switched off. She couldn't turn it on because it would make too much noise. The only thing she could do was to take it away with her. That was theft and Sophie would have to be stupid not to know it was Emma who'd done it. Still, it was a better option than the clip from the previous night finding its way on to YouTube or Facebook. Besides, what could Sophie say about it? As far as Emma was concerned, there had been no last night. But Sophie could call the police and point them in Emma's direction. She needed to destroy the phone, delete everything then dispose of it.

Searching around for her clothes, Emma knocked her hand against the headboard of the bed. Sophie stirred again, and then settled back into a pattern of light snoring. Emma found her jeans and T-shirt and crept to the door, undoing the catch and opening it as quietly as she could. Then she was out in the hallway. She walked, clutching her bundle of clothes. The mobile phone felt hot in her hands. She was sure that if someone saw her, aside from wondering why the mad girl was carrying her own clothes around in the middle of the night, they'd know immediately that she had stolen the phone.

Back in her own room, Emma dressed. She put on a sweater and her coat. She wasn't staying here and risking Sophie coming for her, getting the phone back. She was going to take action now. She went straight back out and headed towards the lake. It struck her then that there might be much more evidence on the phone. Things Sophie had persuaded her to do with that way she had and that she had recorded, things that Emma couldn't remember. She shivered. She had known nothing about the twins at all. She had thought they were a sanctuary in the strange world of being at university but in fact they had been more dangerous than any of it.

Sitting by the lake, Emma scrolled through menus. She couldn't find the footage from the previous evening. Had Sophie downloaded it somewhere already? She didn't understand completely how the phone worked but she did manage to find a folder of photographs. She scrolled through. They were of Sophie, Matilde and herself from the beginning of the year. They all looked so happy. Most of them had been taken in bars or clubs and they had been drinking. They struck her as the kind of happy-days shots they showed in the papers when someone got murdered or went missing; the kind of photos that were so full of potential they broke your heart. Emma couldn't bear to look at them.

The lake looked cold and solid in front of her.

Emma had had enough of trawling the phone. All she wanted to do now was destroy it. She took a step back, then threw it as hard as she could into the middle of the lake. It hit the water's surface and skimmed it, then finally sank beneath the ripples. Sophie might know that it was Emma who'd disposed of it, but that was fine. She didn't care. The most important thing was that it was gone. Who was Sophie to her anyway? She certainly wasn't a friend, Emma knew that now. She thought about the things Sophie had made her do and shuddered. Henry had been right about her; she was capable of just about anything.

For all Emma knew, she might have wandered the whole of campus naked the previous night. She had another gap of time that she couldn't account for and would never know how far Sophie was taking her manipulation. She was deliberately trying to destroy Emma's reputation. The truth was, Sophie shouldn't be here at all. She had some talent but she wasn't prepared to put in the hours that might nurture whatever was there. That was the irony, her doing Matilde's master-class for her because Matilde was by far the better musician.

The ripples were settling on the water in front of

her. Emma knew what she needed to do. She had avoided it for so long but she had no choice. If she stayed here, Sophie would destroy her, one way or another. She didn't have to give up on her dreams. She could still play, and another music school would snatch her up if she applied. She was a realist, though, and starting again wasn't an option. The finances ruled it out. She would have to build a career as a performer, the hard way. She was good enough to do it.

Emma headed back towards the accommodation block with a heavy heart but her mind was made up. She would ring her mum as soon as she got back to her room and ask her to come and fetch her. This adventure was over. She had never felt at home here, always worried that she didn't fit in. She knew she had more talent than most of her contemporaries at the Conservatoire, but this place wasn't really about talent. It was about something far less tangible than that and Sophie would always win.

Emma was shaking as she sat in her room with her phone in her hand. She felt cold, even though the day was warming up for morning. Sunshine came through the gaps in the curtain but it didn't cheer her up. She felt that same air of finality she'd experienced when she heard that Matilde had died, when she saw Wood lying prone in the staff room. Like those things, the idea that she was giving up on the Conservatoire was too terrible to believe.

Finally, she dialled the number. It was ringing at the other end and she almost changed her mind and put the phone down. She realised, though, that there was no going back. If she stayed here, it would be the end of her. Sophie would make sure of it. So she let the phone ring. It went to voicemail and she left a message. 'Ring me back, Mum. It's important.'

The phone rang a few minutes later. Emma's mother sounded terrified. 'What's wrong?' she said, her voice shaking.

'I need to come home,' Emma said. 'I need you to come and fetch me today.'

'What's happened? Are you okay?' The phone line was crackling with tension and the worry from her mum.

'I'm fine. I've just had enough, that's all. I need to come home.'

There was a silence then, a taking in of the information. 'Nothing's happened to you, though?'

'My friend died. My professor died. I just feel like

I'm jinxed here.' Emma supposed this wasn't exactly lying, even if it definitely wasn't telling the truth. Her mother didn't need to know the details. She would be alarmed if she had any idea of the state of Emma's mind and it was best she had no clue.

'Your professor died?'

Emma hadn't spoken to her mother since they'd found Wood. That was how messed up everything had become. 'Yeah. The police are investigating and everything.'

'Of course I'll get you. Listen, though, you had me scared then,' her mum said. 'I thought there was something wrong with you. That you'd had an accident or something.' She paused. 'Don't ever do that to me again. A message saying you need to talk to me. Can you imagine what I thought?'

'Well you must have known I was alive, since I was talking to you.'

'I suppose. But anything could have happened. Don't do that to me again, Emma.' Her mum left a gap and Emma guessed she was waiting for an apology, but she didn't feel like giving her one. She had left a phone message. So what? It wasn't the end of the world. She felt petulance rising inside her.

'Just come and get me, Mum, please.'

'There is something wrong. Are you pregnant or something?'

'Of course not,' she said. 'Mum, I wouldn't be that stupid.' But she didn't know she hadn't been. All the missing time, and the way Henry was with her, she couldn't be sure about that. 'Honestly, it's nothing like that. I've had enough, that's all.'

'But honey, you lost your friend and you've coped with all that. Why come home now? It's not that I don't want you back, but I'd hate you to regret it later.'

'Things are still hard about that. And I've fallen out with Sophie.'

'Well you don't want to come back just because of some silly squabble. Girls row all the time. You can't take it seriously.' Emma's mother seemed to run out of words for a moment. Emma let the silence hang down the phone line. It felt oppressive and heavy. When her mum spoke again, her voice was gentle and quiet. 'Are you sure this is what you want? This was your dream.'

These words, spoken so softly and yet so clearly by her mum, made her want to cry. Since she was about ten she'd had her sights set on going to a conservatoire to study piano, on being a pianist to the full extent of the word. When her friends had been buying and downloading pop records and listening to Radio One, she'd only had time for classical music, and for playing her beloved piano. She had forsaken everything else for her true love, for music. She had to hold it together. If she cried down the phone, her mum would lose it. She couldn't let her drive here, all alone and full of worry.

'I just want to come home,' she repeated again. She hoped her mother heard her this time. She hoped she'd just say she'd come. She couldn't bear this conversation any longer.

'Okay,' her mum said at last. 'I'll be there by the afternoon. I just have to get a few things sorted this morning.'

'As soon as you can, Mum, please.' Emma's voice was strained; she hoped she didn't sound pleading and desperate.

There was hesitation at the other end of the line. 'Of course,' her mother said. Emma could tell she had worried her. Maybe that wasn't such a bad thing; perhaps someone ought to be concerned about what was happening to her. Emma bit her bottom lip. 'Thanks,' she said, and she hung up the phone.

She looked around her room, feeling restless.

Sophie could turn up here any time, searching for her iPhone. She could come full of fury and take out her anger on Emma. She had to get out, go somewhere that Sophie wouldn't look for her. She grabbed her bag and swung it over her shoulder, heading for the door.

Pulling the door open sharply, Emma saw Sophie standing right there. She was staring blankly ahead. She didn't look like she'd been about to knock. She didn't have an ear to the door or a glass in her hand, but Emma was certain she'd been eavesdropping. She could tell by the look in her eyes that she knew Emma would be leaving soon; she had heard the phone call. She looked furious, her eyes shining with an intensity that frightened Emma.

Sophie leaned across the door and rested her arm on the door frame. 'Is it you, my love?' she asked. It felt strongly like she was forcing the question. There was no tenderness in the words like there had been before.

Emma hesitated. 'What?' she said. She wasn't ready to pretend to be Matilde right then and there, no matter how much her friend wanted it.

'Is it you, my love?' Sophie said the words louder this time, as if she couldn't believe she wasn't getting the response she'd ordered. 'Is it you?' She grabbed for

Emma, putting a hand very firmly on her shoulder as if to pin her there.

Emma shook out from under her grip. 'I don't know what you're talking about,' she said. She tried to push past Sophie but the other girl was bigger and wasn't having any of it.

'Let's go into your room,' she said.

'I was just heading out,' Emma told her. She tried again to get past her friend but met the same resistance.

'Come on,' Sophie said, sounding irritated. 'Let's talk inside.'

Emma turned, physically and psychologically bullied into doing as she was told. With a heavy heart she went back in and sat down on her bed. If only she'd thought before about Sophie coming round. If only she'd stayed by the lake to call her mum and arranged to meet her somewhere else, somewhere far from the halls of residence, from Sophie. She needed the safety of her mother's embrace; she felt strongly that only her mum could save her from this. She sat on her bed and hoped, prayed, that her mother would take a cue from her voice and know she was needed. That she would get here sooner than she'd said, drop whatever it was she needed to sort out and just come.

Sophie sat on the chair, staring out of the window towards the lake. 'You can't go,' she said. 'You have to stay here for me. You're all I've got now.'

'You were listening in?' Emma asked, although she didn't really need the confirmation.

'I didn't mean to. I just came to your door and I heard you talking. At first, I didn't want to interrupt.' Sophie began chewing on a nail. She never used to do that; not before Matilde died. 'Why do you want to go anyway?'

Emma shrugged. She couldn't admit to her friend that she knew. That she had pretended some of the time and it hadn't been real. 'I'm just so tired of everything,' she said. Again, it wasn't exactly a lie. 'People dying, bad dreams. I don't know. I don't fit in here anyway.'

Sophie didn't dispute this. She just carried on staring out of the window as if in a trance. Then she appeared to come to. 'Do you know what happened to my phone, last night? I can't find it,' she said.

A cold feeling swept over Emma, starting at her toes and taking her over. 'No,' she said. She hoped her voice wasn't shaking. 'I wasn't with you last night,' she said.

Sophie nodded. 'No,' she said. 'Of course you weren't.' She turned and looked Emma right in the eyes. 'I don't even know why I asked you,' she said. But there was something about the expression on her face that said she didn't buy it. Emma tried not to look away but Sophie's gaze was penetrating and she found her eyes turned, diverted, down to the floor, as if she had something to hide.

Twenty-Seven

It had taken Emma over an hour to get Sophie out of her room. In the end, she had promised not to go home, not today. Sophie had made her say that she'd give the place a few more days. She didn't mean a word of it but she must have sounded sincere, as Sophie went off to her flute lesson in the end. Emma was looking at her phone, considering ringing her mum back and telling her not to come. She had no idea how Sophie did this to her. She was determined to resist. She realised there was a good chance that Sophie would insist on seeing her mobile to check she'd done as she'd promised. She searched out her mother's number and pressed send, but didn't let the call last long enough that it would have rung at the other end.

Emma began packing her things. She hadn't built up a lot of possessions in her short time at university. They were mostly the things she'd brought with her; her keepsakes and clothes. She filled her suitcase, and then a big canvas bag. She looked around her room at the little things she owned and had scattered there, her stereo and her CDs, the mementos she kept on her shelves. She didn't want to pack them away. That felt like the final move, and proof she was really going. She couldn't bear it. She sat on the bed. She wondered how much of what she felt was about packing those last things and how much of it was Sophie's influence, pulling on her the way it always did, even though she knew she shouldn't let it.

It was then that Emma realised she would have to go and say goodbye to Sophie. She knew she shouldn't. In her heart, she felt it was dangerous to go anywhere near her friend again. But despite all the logic, something was pulling her back to the twin who had lived. It was as if she'd been hypnotised, or drugged, influenced in some foul way. She was on autopilot as she got up and grabbed her jacket, opening the door and heading towards the stairs that led up to Sophie's corridor.

Walking down the hallway, Emma repeated a mantra in her head. She would go and say goodbye to Sophie, that was all. She would be firm about it. She would say goodbye and leave. Go back to her room and pack those final things. She was determined. She couldn't let herself get dragged back into Sophie's madness. She had very nearly escaped. Her mum would come later and they would pack up the car and that would be the end of it. No more Sophie, no more black spaces of missing time. She could forget about Matilde and Professor Wood and all of the bad things that had happened here; write it all off as if it was just a bad dream.

Then she was in front of Sophie's door and everything felt strange. She suddenly couldn't remember why she was leaving the university, why she was abandoning her good friend. She gritted her teeth and made herself remember. What on earth was this woman doing to her? It was like the closer she got, the stronger the spell, as if Sophie was emitting some kind of gas that sent her crazy. She chanted the mantra in her head again. *Say goodbye, go and pack, say goodbye, go and pack.*

The door flew open before Emma even knocked, as if Sophie had sensed her standing there. Sophie beamed. 'Is it you, my love?' were the words that flew out of the door towards Emma. They took her by surprise. For some reason, in all of her planning and thinking about this, it hadn't entered her head that Sophie would ask her this although, of course, she was always going to. Without even thinking about it, she found she was saying those words again, the ones that she knew Sophie wanted to hear. She was pretending to be Matilde. There was a whisper inside her, just the start of an idea, that maybe this was what had happened all along and she had deliberately blanked it from her mind.

Emma was swept into Sophie's room by her friend's happiness. They rushed through the door together and it was like dancing. Sophie's joy was so palpable that Emma felt she was getting high off it. She could see how it might be addictive, this bringing the dead back to life, the way that it lifted her friend. She was beaming and her eyes lit up like lamps. She looked manic too; so full of emotion that she might burst. Emma was sitting on the bed with Sophie beside her. Sophie grabbed both of her hands and held them in her own, staring into her eyes.

'Emma's leaving,' she said. Her voice was almost a whisper. 'She's rung her mother to collect her.'

Emma tried to look suitably shocked. She hoped she was better at acting than it felt. 'But what will happen to us?' she said. Her voice sounded right, at least in her head. She was seeing herself out of here, despite Sophie's persuasive ways. She could do it; she could get away from the manipulative twin.

'We have to stop her,' Sophie said. She sounded very determined. 'We have to stop her by any means possible.'

Listening to her friend talk, Emma could well believe she'd be prepared to do anything at all. She sounded so decided about it, so firm. She was a woman who was used to getting her own way. Emma stared at her. Sophie let go of her hands and stood up, looking away, through the window and into the distance.

'I can't lose you again,' she said.

'I know.' Emma was looking at the floor, like she had earlier when she'd felt guilty about the phone. She realised she felt bad about deceiving her friend.

'What can we do, though?' Sophie said. 'Shall we lock her in her room? In here somewhere? We could keep her in the wardrobe until you come out. I'll let you know where the keys to the handcuffs are but not Emma. That could work.'

Emma shivered all over. Just exactly what was Sophie capable of? She knew she was manipulative, but this was beyond that. It was terrifying to think what might happen to her next. She didn't want to get locked in Sophie's wardrobe.

'Did she ring her mother back? She said she would. She said she'd cancel her coming today.'

'I don't know,' Emma said.

'Well,' Sophie said, looking at Emma as if she should know what she wanted. 'Hand me the phone, for Christ's sake.'

'Oh, of course,' Emma said. She reached into her jacket pocket and got out her phone. She thanked all the powers she could think of that she had made that dropped call. Maybe this could save her from Sophie. She needed time; just long enough for her mother to get here.

Sophie examined the phone. She smiled as she saw the phone call at the right time of day. But then she continued to scroll through menus. 'Sneaky bitch.' She looked up at Emma. 'This isn't a real call. She called but hung up to make it look like she'd rung her.' She shoved Emma's phone into her own pocket. 'She had a clue I might look.' She sounded surprised, and slightly admiring. 'Who'd have thought?' She looked like she was trying to work something out. 'We need to go to her room. See if she's been packing. I have to know.'

It was the last thing Emma wanted to do. She knew that Sophie would see the packed bags and then she might go crazy. Yet she found herself following Sophie through the hallways. She considered making a run for it, dashing off down a different corridor. She didn't know what was the safest thing to do. At least if she was in her own room, her mother should come eventually. Once her mother was there, she would be safe.

Emma unlocked the door, and they walked into her room. Sophie looked around, wide-eyed, at the packed bags.

'Look what she did,' she said. She spread out the words and sounded cruel. 'Look what the silly bitch did.' She kicked one of the bags, and looked around the room as if she was searching for more damage she could cause. Then she stopped. She sat on the floor and crossed her legs like a little kid in assembly. She leaned forward over her crossed legs, looking like someone attempting a ballet class. 'You have to phone her mother,' she said.

NIKI VALENTINE

It was yet another thing Emma hadn't anticipated. She wondered when she would have the measure of her friend because no matter what she saw Sophie do, it seemed that she continued to underestimate her wickedness. She had no idea how to get out of this. But before she could think much more about it, she saw her phone in Sophie's hand. She was dialling her mother. She could hear the phone ringing into Sophie's ear. Then her mother's voice as she answered. It was only at this point that Sophie handed the phone to Emma.

'Hi.' Emma told herself that Sophie wouldn't hurt her, she wasn't capable of that. She didn't want to scare her mum. She didn't want her mother's drive down south to be made dangerous because she was fretting. 'I've changed my mind,' she said. Sophie was grinning at her. She clapped her hands together, pleased with herself.

'Are you sure?' her mum said. 'You seemed so certain before.'

'Yes, yes, I'm sure,' Emma said. 'Don't come.' She willed her mother to see between the words, to read her mind down the phone and understand that she did want her to come. But that was useless; her mother would hear just the words and she would believe them. Emma's

396

security was gone. Her mother wouldn't come at all. She wanted to shout down the phone that she needed her here as soon as possible. But her mum was saying okay, and goodbye, and then she was gone and Sophie had hold of the phone again. She examined it carefully, as if she thought that Emma might have hung up and pretended to talk to her mother. It had never crossed Emma's mind to do that. She was cold with fear. The trick was to keep pretending to be Matilde. As long as she was Matilde, she would be safe. She sat down on the floor right next to the twin, so that the two of them were touching. She put her arm around her.

This seemed to be a step too far and it set Sophie off crying, quietly, as they sat there side by side. 'I miss you so much when you're not here.' She turned and looked right into Emma's eyes. 'I think about it all the time. The day you died.'

Emma was nodding but she didn't know why. She didn't dare to open her mouth in case she gave herself away. It came to her all at once what a dangerous game she was playing. She didn't know enough about Matilde and Sophie and their life outside of her to pull this off much longer. Sophie had stood up and was heading towards the bed. There was an urgency to her movements. She sat down facing Emma, then leaned down and grabbed both her hands.

'I'm sorry,' she said. Her crying had set in even deeper. 'I'm so sorry about everything.'

Emma was confused. All of a sudden nothing seemed certain, and she wasn't sure if Sophie was apologising to her, to Emma, or to the dead twin she was pretending to be. 'You don't need to say sorry,' she said. The voice that came out of her mouth sounded unlike her own, though, posher, more southern. Just like Matilde. She wasn't sure any more if she was putting it on and acting, or if something else was coming over her.

'I do.' The words came through sobs. 'I should never have done it.' More deep, deep sounds of grief came from out of Sophie. 'I miss you so much and it's all my fault.' She collapsed into her own tears.

Emma watched her crying. It felt like she was floating above the pair of them, watching from the ceiling. There was something about the way Sophie was speaking that disturbed her; it was about more than the everyday things that had led to Matilde's death. 'Are you talking about the masterclass?' she said. 'You're right, you shouldn't have done that.'

'No, my love.' Sophie had recovered herself a little.

She was stroking Emma's hair and her face looked manic. She was staring so hard into her eyes it looked like she was trying to climb in too, a third soul in an already overcrowded place. 'No, you know what I mean. The night when I cut you open.' Her voice changed with those last five words; it hardened and became threatening; her teeth were gritted.

The air in the room felt charged. Emma was about to ask her what she was talking about but realised she didn't need to. Everything was slotting together. Matilde hadn't been suicidal. Sure, she'd had reason to be, but that didn't mean she was. Emma remembered how calm she'd been about Henry. And she remembered her reaction to the masterclass, when she'd called Sophie a bitch. She had been angry but not destroyed. She probably hadn't even been too nervous to do the class. It would have been all Sophie's idea, the kind of thing she thought would be playful and fun, more of that same old manipulation. Emma didn't say a word. The silence crackled.

Sophie was still holding Emma's hands, harder and harder. 'You do remember that, don't you? You remember the day I cut you?'

All Emma wanted to do was get up and past Sophie,

out of the door. But Sophie was sitting in front of her on the bed, holding her hands tight, and she didn't look like she was going anywhere. Emma was stuck in a room with a crazy woman, someone who had killed her own twin sister. Her mum wasn't coming now, Sophie had made sure of that. She had to keep up the act and be Matilde for as long as possible. It was her only hope. She nodded her head, slowly.

'You remember what we did to Wood?'

Fear hit Emma with a cold flush. What was Sophie talking about? What had she done to Wood? She tried to hold it together, to continue to play her part, but it was too difficult. 'What are you talking about?'

'You don't remember.' The voice was completely cold, entirely certain. 'You don't remember.' Said like she was working something out.

'I don't know what you're talking about,' Emma said. 'What are you saying?' Her voice was no longer like Matilde's; now it was clearly her own. She sounded scared.

Sophie got down on her knees and moved her face right up to Emma's, so close that their noses were touching. 'Do you remember slipping him something in his wine? I wonder what the toxicology report will find.' Her voice was like a children's song as she wrapped her fingers round Emma's face and squeezed her nails into her cheeks. 'And later, in his office, he really thought he'd have us both, the idiot. Men are so easy, they're ridiculous. And that was when he began to feel ill, wasn't it? You remember how we sat there, hand in hand, and watched until he had stopped breathing?' She stopped and grinned like a maniac. 'He deserved it, you know he did.'

Emma shrank away from her friend as if there was something wrong with her breath.

'What's wrong? Can't take it? Or don't you remember?'

'Course I remember.' All Emma could hear was her own accent, and fear, and she didn't think she'd be fooling anyone.

'Okay, tell me all about it then. When did you put the little present in his champers? When was it we first decided that was what we would do?'

Emma was shaking her head now, and tears ran down her cheeks. She didn't have any answers, and not just to those questions. There were a million things Sophie could ask her that she wouldn't be able to guess.

'You were pretending,' Sophie said. She jerked right

back and disappointment seemed to make her shrink into the wall.

'No, I wasn't.' Emma couldn't look at her. 'Not at first. I don't remember what happened at first, but I worked it out and then I started pretending.'

'No.' Sophie stood up. She turned towards Emma. 'I don't believe you. You've been fooling me all along.' She looked devastated.

A flash of something hit Emma, survival instinct taking over. She remembered about Wood. He hadn't died until after Matilde had gone. If she didn't remember that, then it proved she hadn't been pretending. 'I didn't know about Wood,' she said. Her voice sounded keen and excited. 'I had no idea what you'd done, but Matilde had already gone then.'

Sophie stopped pacing. 'You weren't always pretending,' she said, digesting what Emma had said. 'Some of the time it was true. You didn't even know. I knew, when you said Harry, I knew it, and then when you played the Rach just the way she used to. Even in our house, downstairs, after her funeral, I wondered. Just for a moment, I thought I saw her, but it was still you. I must have known she was coming.' Sophie was gabbling now, the words coming out faster and faster.

She placed herself carefully in front of the door and Emma knew right away that she was blocking the exit deliberately. 'All the more reason that you shouldn't go,' she said. 'You have to stay. If Matilde can come through you, then you have to stay and that's that.'

Sophie locked the door and posted the keys underneath, so they were outside the room. She grinned and walked over to the bed. Emma rushed to the door and pulled at it, rattling it to and fro with the handle, but it was fast shut. She turned and saw that Sophie had placed herself across the window, the only other exit. She was locked in here, in her own room, with a mad girl who had killed more than once. Her mother wasn't coming to save her. No one was. She was trapped and it felt more dangerous than she could have imagined. She launched herself at Sophie but the bigger girl was ready. She had Emma down and pinned on the bed as quick as a flash. She sat on top of her. 'You're not going anywhere. We'll wait here until Matilde comes back.'

For the first time ever, Emma found she wanted to be taken over. She wanted to lose herself to Matilde because it was the only thing that could save her. She wanted to scream, but Sophie had a hand over her mouth.

'You be quiet,' she said. 'Be really damn quiet. Or I can't make any promises about exactly what I might do.'

Emma believed her. She didn't have any idea what Sophie might do; nobody did, not even the girl herself. Emma knew that she was in the presence of insanity. She had no doubt about it at all.

Twenty-Eight

Sophie had improvised with what she could find to make sure Emma was secure and unable to get away. She kept apologising, but in a manic voice, and holding her head saying, 'Let me just think.' Emma could see Sophie's demons coming out through her eyes and running around the room. She kicked and bucked to try to get free, but there was no way; her wrists and ankles were tied so that she couldn't even pull herself up to sitting. Sophie had used the pillowcase to gag her after the God-awful fuss she'd made, screaming for help after Sophie locked the door.

Now she just lay there, looking at Sophie, wondering

what her friend might do next. Sophie was sitting in the chair by the bed, rocking backwards and forwards and muttering to herself. Some of the things she said, Emma could understand. They were about Matilde, about what Wood had done to the pair of them and how he deserved what he got, and about how much she missed her sister. Emma could see clearly that her friend needed help. The sophisticated veneer that Sophie usually kept so polished was gone completely and she looked utterly lost.

It was when Sophie got up that Emma began to panic. She paced up and down the room and her muttering got louder and louder. She turned towards Emma, then rushed at her, grabbing her by the shoulders and shaking her hard. Emma's hands and ankles were bound tight with her own leather belts and she was beginning to feel like she might pass out. Sophie shouted in her face, begging for Matilde to come. Emma began to cry, making sobbing noises that disappeared into her gag. She was finding it hard to breathe as she cried harder and harder. She couldn't make Matilde come and she didn't dare pretend again. She couldn't explain to Sophie that if she let her play the piano her sister might come, because she wouldn't remove the gag. She felt completely trapped and utterly helpless.

Sophie's pacing got more and more frantic. She began picking up Emma's belongings and staring at them, looking at them with real disdain in her eyes. She settled for a moment then, perching on the chair and crying, rocking. Emma found that despite everything, she felt sorry for her. It was a strange emotion to feel under the circumstances, and right outside of any logic she could explain. The severed twin looked so sad, and somehow the fact that she'd been the architect of her own downfall made it worse. She was truly a pathetic sight sitting on the chair, more alone than Emma could imagine. She told herself that Sophie had only tied her up because she didn't know what else to do. She told herself that Sophie would never harm her. But then she remembered the truth: that Sophie had hurt the girl she was closest to in the world, killed her twin sister. If she could do that to Matilde, she could do anything at all to Emma. Even the fact that it seemed she was some kind of conduit to Matilde wouldn't save her.

The peace didn't last long. Sophie was up again. Now she was rushing around the room, banging into the walls with her shoulders. She was making a low wailing sound and it looked like she was deliberately trying to hurt herself. Emma hoped that the noises she was making would be enough to attract someone's attention. It was almost as if Sophie had read this in her head as she walked over to the CD player. She searched through Emma's albums with a look of disgust on her face. 'Do you not have anything modern?' she said, turning towards her friend. Emma shook her head.

Throwing aside CDs as she went, Sophie searched for something acceptable. Eventually, she put on some opera. *The Magic Flute*. Emma tried to remember who had made the recording, which orchestra, which opera company. She felt that if she could remember that, then everything would be all right. But it wouldn't come to her no matter how hard she thought about it. The shimmering voice of a soprano filled the room and Sophie turned the music up uncomfortably loud. Emma closed her eyes. At least if she was going to die now, there was beautiful music. But it wasn't enough to make her forget. It didn't make her forget a thing and she was very scared.

With the loud music filling the room, Sophie went on the rampage. She was running into things and screaming, but also taking Emma's belongings and throwing them. Her CDs first. She threw them all around the room and danced on top of them. Tears rolled down Emma's face as she heard the crunch of the discs breaking underneath Sophie's feet. This was Emma's music, her entire lifetime's collection. She didn't have much in life but she had her music. Any sympathy she'd felt for Sophie was gone then. She realised that the girl was cruel, nasty; whatever her reasons, she was truly foul in the things she did. Sophie toured the room, looking for more things to break. She began to play with the keepsakes next. Emma tried not to look at the little shelf where she kept her most precious things.

Sophie crushed the piece of the Berlin Wall with her foot, its history crumbling underneath her shoe. She threw the case and it hit Emma in the face. She flinched away. Her hands were tied in front of her, so she could lift them to touch her face. She was cut and it was oozing blood, but not too badly. Sophie looked at her and laughed. 'Baby,' she said. She loomed over Emma, her face like a madwoman's. She looked older somehow like this. Much, much older. Her face came so close that Emma could smell something sweet on her breath. Perhaps it was the smell of madness. 'You should have seen the blood,' she hissed. Emma knew without hesitation that she was talking about when Matilde had died. She remembered her dream, the sense she'd got of a frantic struggle, all the blood. Even then, Matilde had reached out for her. She felt sick. She hoped she wouldn't vomit into her gag because she didn't think that Sophie would save her if she choked.

It was as if a mist had cleared from the room, as Sophie stood in front of her with the snowstorm of New York City in her hands. Emma made distressed sounds but this seemed to encourage Sophie, who laughed like something out of a bad horror movie. Emma had never realised that people could laugh like that in real life. Sophie's smile dropped off her face and she threw her shoulders right back, flinging the snowstorm at the wall with all the force she could muster. Emma watched in horror. There was the sound of smashing and then glass and glitter filled the air near the wall. Pieces of the buildings flew around the room. It was pretty to watch. Emma gritted her teeth and closed her eyes.

There was just the music now; Sophie had gone completely quiet, as if smashing the snowstorm was the climax of what she was capable of. Emma knew that wasn't true, but she tried to believe it. She tried to listen to the music and forget. She opened her eyes. Her sight was blurred from her tears and she blinked rapidly to clear them. The room came into focus again. Sophie was standing very still in front of Emma's full-length mirror, which hung from the wall. She was staring into it as if the secret to all her problems was there. Emma saw it too; what Sophie was seeing. The twins stood facing each other. Sophie reached out a hand and Matilde's instinctively rushed to join it. Of course, it was just the magic of reflection. And yet it looked like something else, like something much, much more. It looked like resurrection.

As she watched, Emma realised that Sophie wasn't completely silent. She was talking to the girl in the mirror. She was muttering away but not loud enough that Emma could hear above the music what it was she had to say to Matilde. She pulled at her restraints but there was no give. Sophie had done a good job of making sure she wasn't going anywhere. Emma closed her eyes again and tried to concentrate on the music, imagine herself away from there.

She was startled by a new noise. Sophie was thumping the mirror. It made a dull metallic sound. She was hitting it harder and harder. The first split sounded like

411

bone cracking. Emma flinched. She didn't know how much of the cracking sound was the glass and how much was Sophie's hand. Sophie was making harsh keening sounds, and bashing at the mirror with the side of her fist. Emma didn't think it was the physical pain that was making her moan and wail. She had to keep reminding herself that it was all Sophie's fault, every-thing, just as much as any pain she felt from thumping the mirror. If Sophie had told her she'd made it up about killing Matilde and Wood, then, like a cheated lover, Emma would have believed her because it was what she wanted to believe.

Through Sophie's wails, words began to emerge over the music of the opera. 'I want you dead, I want you gone.' She kept repeating it as she smashed at the mirror. Her hands were grazed and bloody. Emma wasn't sure who she was talking to; herself, the girl in the mirror, or Emma. Sophie grabbed the chair from in front of the desk. Emma knew right away what she intended to use it for. She tried to call out but her gag turned her cries into grunts and mumbles.

'What's that, Emma? What did you say?' Sophie's voice sounded matter-of-fact, as if she didn't know Emma couldn't answer. 'Oh, you don't want me to smash up your mirror.' She cocked her head. 'That's a shame.' She smiled, a fake cracked smile like a broken doll. 'I'm going to do it anyway.'

Sophie hoisted the chair right up above her head and through the air with gusto. It hit the mirror with force and the glass shattered. Emma's bound hands shot to her face, to protect her eyes. The sound of the breaking glass merged with the music; it sounded at home as part of the opera. Emma felt sharp pains as shards hit her skin.

Sophie had fallen to the floor and was sitting in the glass. She didn't seem to care that she was cutting herself. She didn't seem to notice. She looked like she was in a trance, her head completely elsewhere. She turned and saw Emma, looking startled, as if she'd forgotten where she was. She wiped blood from her hands all over her face. Emma had seen this before; pictures of Henry, blooded from his first hunt. She thought it barbaric. She knew Sophie had been hunting too, and it had surprised her when she'd first found out. Now she knew it made perfect sense; it was similar to what she did with people.

A smile spread across Sophie's face with the red stain. She looked drunk on the blood, as if she needed more. She began frantically searching through the pieces of glass. Emma pulled against her bonds. Sophie stopped, stock still. She pulled a large shard into the light and stared at it. It glinted like a dagger. There was a sparkle in Sophie's eyes too.

'Time to sleep, my love,' she said. She moved towards Emma with the glass in her hands. Pictures went through Emma's head, footage she'd seen of what they did to pigs in abattoirs, and how much blood there was, how quickly the animals died. That was what Sophie was about to do to her now; she was sure of it.

Twenty-Nine

All Emma could see was the glass right in front of her face. She was pinned to the bed, with Sophie heavy on top of her. The opera was reaching its climax. The next thing, though, Sophie jerked upwards and away from her. She had been pulled right off.

There was another person in the room and they were shouting, but Emma was so disoriented that she couldn't make out the words. She recognised the voice. Her head swam and she tried to dig deep and work out who it was. She pulled at her restraints and squealed into her gag, determined to make the most of the opportunity to get away from Sophie. Her hands had started to turn blue and she was losing feeling. They were next to useless working at the bonds on her wrists, which were very tightly secured. She tried to stand up, but wasn't able to move her feet and fell forwards. She only just managed to stop herself from falling into the glass.

'Get out of here, Emma. Get help from some-where.' It was that familiar voice again, and she realised with a mix of dread and absolute relief that it was Matilde. She had no idea what made the tone so differ-ent from Sophie's that she recognised it as such, but she was certain. Matilde had come to save her, somehow. But Sophie had that massive shard of glass in her hands. Emma pulled herself up on to all fours and turned her head to see what was happening.

There was only Sophie in the room. She was stand-ing holding the glass, her eyes flat and unseeing.

'Go, quickly. Before she comes back. I don't know how long I can hold her off for.'

'Matilde?' Emma's voice was barely a whisper.

The twin standing in front of her nodded, slowly. 'Go!' she said, insistent.

Emma moved as fast as she could towards the door, pulling herself along the floor. She got caught by several pieces of glass along the way and felt some painful scratches. She dragged herself out and into the hallway.

She scratched and banged at the next door along but there was no response. It was hard work moving down the hallway. She dragged her body with her hands and arms. She felt sore and scratched from the restraints and the cuts. One of her legs felt like it might have some glass inside. She was tired and all she wanted to do was stop and go to sleep, then and there in the hall-way. But she knew that if she didn't get help soon, Sophie would be back, and that she would come after her and finish what she'd started. Emma banged on another door, then kicked it.

Further along the hallway there was the sound of footsteps. Emma pulled her head from the floor; it hurt, but she needed to get this person's attention. Then she realised she already had it. It was Henry. He stared at first, and squinted, as if he was trying to check that he was seeing what it looked like. Then he rushed over to Emma and pulled at her restraints. Even when he removed the gag, she found she couldn't speak. She just pointed. From this and the fear in her eyes, he seemed to work it out. He headed straight for Emma's door, which was swinging open.

Emma's hands felt light as air now they were freed. She could only hear opera coming out of her door, and not screams or shouts or signs of a scuffle. She leaned on her hands to bring herself to sitting. It hurt; her hands were sore from having the circulation cut off then blood suddenly rushing back in. She shook her arms and kicked her feet. She managed to push herself up and then she was standing, although unsteadily. It felt like she had to learn to walk all over again. She staggered back along the hallway towards her room. She was terrified about what she might find there but she was desperate to see, hoping above hope that Henry was all right. She made slow, unsteady progress.

The room was quieter than she was expecting when she finally walked through the door. Henry had Sophie pinned to the bed; she wasn't going anywhere. Emma's legs felt weak but she made an effort to stay upright.

'Get help, Emma, get someone from security or something.' Henry's voice was strained and he was short of breath.

'Of course,' Emma said. 'Of course.' She turned and left the room, forcing her legs to move along the hallway, down the stairs. She headed down to the porters' lodge like she had so many times before.

There was one old guy at the lodge and he wasn't keen to leave his post. He looked at Emma doubtfully as she explained how important it was. She tried to tell him what had happened, and then she was breaking down, sobbing and screaming at him to come now, before it was too late. Her emotional state made the porter jump to action. He pulled his set of master keys down from their hook and flew out of the office, locking it behind him. Emma couldn't keep up with him as he raced across the foyer and up the stairs. She hopped and limped behind him.

When she walked in through the door of her room again, Sophie was sitting up, staring into space. She no longer looked like a danger to anyone, except perhaps herself. She was seriously dishevelled. There were cuts and bruises all over her. But the worst thing was the look on her face. Emma was sure she would never forget that face as long as she lived. It was as if the soul had been sucked right out of her. She didn't look anything like the person Emma had so admired since she'd come to the Conservatoire. Emma felt incredibly sad for Sophie; her life was finished, over. She had no idea how such empathy kept flowing towards someone who had wanted to harm her so badly.

The porter was on his radio. He was asking for an ambulance and the police. Emma wondered which one Sophie needed most and could not decide. The whole place smelled of trauma. As they sat and waited for the emergency services, other students arrived at the door, trying to find out what had happened. The porter shooed them away. After a while, security guards arrived and blocked the doorway.

Henry grabbed Emma and pulled her tight to him. She was a little shocked at first by the passion of his embrace, but then she went with it. She could feel the love flowing from him. She didn't care any longer that things had happened with him that she couldn't remember. She felt close to him, as if she had been there for their courtship. Of course, she had. She had kissed him, loved him, even if she couldn't remember much about it. She had still been there, somewhere deep, which was why the crook of his shoulder felt such a comfortable place. Henry kissed her head, making her feel safe and complete.

The police arrived before the ambulance. They asked a few questions and it didn't take long before they arrested Sophie. Paramedics got there very soon after and pulled rank on the police, insisting they needed to take both Emma and Sophie to the hospital. The police escorted them. They wanted to interview Emma and Henry too, but the paramedics only allowed a few basic questions. Emma didn't want to go any-where and kept insisting she was okay but there was no arguing with them. She looked at her hands and saw that they were shaking, and very pink, from the shock and the way Sophie had restrained her. She nodded, in the end, agreeing she would do as she was told. Henry checked that they wouldn't be travelling with Sophie and was reassured.

Emma and Henry walked out to the ambulance and got in, unaided. As she ducked under the doorway, Emma looked up. She saw all the twitching curtains in the rooms above them. She didn't care. It no longer mattered what anyone thought of her. Then all of that was gone; the Conservatoire and the other students, Sophie and her sister, Professor Wood, all of it. All gone as if she'd woken up from a bad dream. Emma sat down in the back of the ambulance and felt exhausted. The paramedic suggested she lie down and relax, and she found she wanted to. Henry sat on the stretcher opposite and held on to her hand.

The sirens were going on the ambulances as they

sped down the road towards the hospital. Emma was smiling. How silly. This wasn't an emergency. She was so very tired. For the first time in ages, it felt safe to sleep. She gripped Henry's hand hard and let herself slip away.

It was much later when Emma woke up. She was disoriented. There was no sign of Henry now, and she was in a new place altogether, on one of the hospital wards. She sat up and called out. Straight away a nurse came, followed quickly by her mother, who pushed past the nurse. 'I've been waiting for you to wake up, honey,' she said. She smiled, but her smile made a tight shape on her face.

'You came.' Emma's throat was sore and dry, and it hurt to talk. She looked to her side and saw that she was on a drip. She was shocked. She didn't feel ill. Just very, very tired.

'Of course I came.' She was staring straight at Emma, looking like she could hardly believe that she was okay. She stroked her hair. 'I know my little girl and I could tell it wasn't right, that second phone call. So I came anyway. One of your friends told me they'd brought you here.'

Emma coughed; her throat felt scraped and sore. Her mum reached for a drink beside the bed with a straw in it. 'Have some of this,' she said.

Emma did as she was told. The drink made her throat feel better. 'What's wrong with me?' she asked her mum.

Her mother laughed and ruffled her hair. 'Nothing that a few days' rest and some good food won't sort out.'

Emma tried to smile. 'Is Henry here?'

Her mother nodded. 'He waited ages for you to wake up. He's just gone to get us both some coffee.' She winked at her daughter. 'He's a catch!' she said. 'You kept that one quiet.'

'So quiet I almost didn't know about it myself.'

Emma's mother laughed. It was a lovely sound that washed over Emma and made her feel better. She smiled genuinely then. It was good to hear her mother laugh and it was funny too. Her mum would never know how close to the truth that comment had been.

The man in question appeared beside the bed, holding two coffees. Emma couldn't help thinking it was typical of him, to feel the need to cater and run around after others the way he did. It was bizarre to know someone so well without remembering getting to know them. Henry put the coffees down as quickly as he could and headed over to her. He planted a kiss on her forehead and then pulled back, just looking at her. His face looked full of gratitude to see her in one piece. He had been through losing a girlfriend once, and at the same hands. She realised he didn't know that yet, about Sophie's part in Matilde's death, although he probably had his suspicions. She would have to talk to the police about it when they interviewed her. There must have been something lasting about Sophie's manipulation, because she found she was feeling guilty about this.

Emma realised she was staring at Henry. It was almost impossible for her to believe that he cared about her but he genuinely seemed to. Here he was, by the bed with her mother. The way he had held her left no room for doubt. Except that perhaps he just loved the Matilde inside her. She couldn't help thinking this. She reached for that part of her again, tried to feel it.

Not only could she not feel any sense of her friend's spirit inside her, the very thought seemed completely crazy. She wondered if Sophie had persuaded her so deeply that she'd believed it, forgotten the things she did because Sophie wanted her to. Her ways of persuading were close to supernatural.

Tears were budding in Emma's eyes. She tried to hold them in, but she felt like she had lost Matilde all over again.

Thirty

Emma clung to Henry's hand as they arrived in front of the Crown Court building. She didn't want to go inside, although she knew she had to. She felt sick. It would be better if Henry could come with her. They had settled into an easy familiarity since the incident in Emma's room and it no longer mattered that she'd missed their first kiss; their first night together. Emma loved Henry and she knew he loved her too. But Henry couldn't come with her. He was due to tell his own version of events after Emma had finished and so he wasn't allowed in court until then.

Henry kissed Emma on the forehead in that

absent-minded way he had; not as forgetful as Emma was about their first days together, though. She severed herself then; she knew she had no choice but to go into the court and do her duty. Tell the truth, the whole truth and nothing but the truth. The problem was, Emma knew, that if she told the full truth, no one would believe her. It might even end up being her they put away, because she would have to admit she'd lied about her alibi, who was still standing next to her, holding her hand. She let go. She felt colder straight away. Henry turned and left and she watched him go. She wanted to shout out or run after him and the only thing that stopped her was knowing that he'd be back, just the way he'd been at the end of every day. Constant Henry; she could rely on him, even to lie under oath for her.

At the security post, Emma's bags were X-rayed, her passport scanned. She was ushered through to the witness room, where she had to wait until called. This had been the worst part of every day, sitting in this room, dead quiet, waiting for the day to start. Knowing that Sophie was somewhere in the same building, in a similar room, waiting for everything to begin. Emma could sense her friend from across the rooms. She was sure she noticed the moment Sophie arrived, and when Sophie was there, it was like Matilde was back too. Emma bit her nails and waited nervously, and worried about staying in control.

Finally one of the clerks came to collect her. Emma stood up and brushed herself down. She felt self-conscious about seeing her friend each time. Even now, the word 'friend' was the one she used when she thought of Sophie, and even, sometimes, when she talked about her. Henry told her off about this, said she was too kind, but it wasn't kindness. It was the word that came to mind, that tripped off her tongue. There was a sense in which she looked forward to going into the courtroom. She missed Sophie. She missed the life that they'd had before Matilde had died.

The courtroom was silent as Emma entered. She saw Sophie, sitting next to her barrister. Every day, it had come as a total shock how thin Sophie looked; her face was drawn, her arms like sticks of willow. She'd always been slim but now she looked ill, like she had a disease that was eating her away. Emma kept staring at her, hoping she might look up, smile. But Sophie gazed steadfastly at the desk in front of her. It seemed deliberate and stubborn. Emma felt her eyes well up and gritted her teeth. She would not cry; not here, not now.

It was then that Emma had to put her hand on the Bible and swear to tell the truth. She felt like she might be struck down as she stood there with her hand on the Good Book. She would never have believed in that kind of thing in the past but she had surprised herself over what she could believe in. She had been so sure a year ago that she knew how the world worked. But now she got it; she was just a beginner. She had so much more to learn about life. And so she swore to tell everything she knew and she was not struck down.

The prosecutor asked Emma what had happened on the night she nearly died. She sat back and told the story. She faltered at first. She cleared her throat. Then she spoke again, all the time imagining Henry's arm around her, his hand in hers. In this way, she reached for his support in her mind and she felt him there. She couldn't look at Sophie now. Even if it was unlikely that her friend would look back and see her, Emma wasn't taking the risk. She stared at the wooden bench in front of her as she told the court what had happened. She had done the same yesterday when she'd talked about Professor Wood's death. She had avoided his wife and children in the gallery too, especially when she'd told the court what she knew about his relationship with the twins. She wondered as she spoke if his wife had ever suspected. She didn't want to see the woman's face as she had her fears confirmed.

Hours passed. There were questions about Sophie's movements that day. Questions about her own. Why had she worn Matilde's dress at her recital? Why did they move from Sophie's room to her own? Was she sure that Sophie had been a threat when she held the shard of glass? If she was a real threat, then how did Emma get away? The questions flew at Emma and she did her best to answer them as well as she could. The barristers swapped, and now it was Sophie's defence lawyer who was talking to her.

'And you say you know that Ms Benoit killed her sister? You can be certain of it?'

Sophie's barrister stared hard at Emma, as if he knew this was the question she'd been dreading. The one she couldn't answer without breaking the law. She had practised what she would say to these questions. Her throat felt very dry and scratched. She opened her mouth to speak and no words came out.

'Ms Russell?'

Emma took a big, deep breath. She remembered Mr Nicholls and his mantra, and she followed his instructions. She would lie, and by lying she would tell the truth.

'Sophie told me,' she said. 'When I was tied up in my room, she told me what she'd done. She was standing there with a shard of glass and she said she'd do the same to me. I was tied up on the floor and so I kind of believed her.' Emma heard her own voice. She sounded convincing.

The room was so silent and everyone so motionless it felt like time was standing still. Emma's eyes slipped from the wooden bench in front of her and over to Sophie. At just the same moment, Sophie looked up. Emma started as she was hit by the full force of Sophie's blue gaze. She saw her bloodshot eyes and sunken cheeks. And there was nothing there, no love or anger. Not even recognition. Emma realised that Sophie was drugged to within an inch of consciousness. There was nothing of the girl she'd known left inside the shell. Nothing of either of the twins there.

The barrister looked from his client to Emma and back again. He looked like his brain was processing what she'd said and both the girls' reactions. He hesitated for just a moment longer. Then something in his face changed. He waved a hand at Emma, a dismissive gesture. 'No further questions.' He swung around and away from her and she watched his retreating back.

And that was it. It was over, and Emma was free. She stood up and tried to walk but her legs felt weak and hollow. Her head was swimming. She realised too late that she was going down, keeling over. She was going to faint.

The room disappeared. There was a flash, and then just blackness.

When Emma woke up, Henry was there. Just like she'd known he would be. Constant Henry.

'Hey, sleepyhead,' he said. He reached for her forehead. She realised, at his touch, that she was clammy to the bone.

'How long did I sleep for?' she asked him.

'Ages,' he said.

'Did I talk in my sleep?' Emma wondered how long it would be before she would wake up and not be afraid that something had taken her over.

'No.' Henry smiled. 'You just slept. Like Sleeping Beauty.' He was stroking her head, pushing her hair away from her face. 'It's over, you know.'

'No further questions,' she said, imitating the barrister's strong, posh tones. They both smiled.

'They've sent her to the hospital,' Henry said. 'Where she belongs.'

It was only now that Emma realised he hadn't just been talking about her part of the trial. He meant the whole thing. How long had she been sleeping? 'You gave your evidence?' she said.

Henry nodded. 'My bit didn't take so long.'

'It's really over,' Emma said. She sounded like she was trying to persuade herself.

Henry nodded and smiled and stroked her hair. She couldn't feel Sophie there, or Matilde. She was free of them both. Despite everything, she couldn't decide if she was happy about this freedom or not.

Emma watched Henry as he emptied a shopping bag on to the kitchen table. It was a mundane action, everyday, and yet she felt so lucky to be here to see it. So lucky to have him. It seemed petty, the idea of a boyfriend after all that had happened to them both, but Emma was happy in her own, quiet way. They had moved away from halls and all those very bad memories. She no longer noticed missing tranches of time and could account for her whereabouts. She didn't lose herself when she performed, not any more. She stayed very much there, playing beautifully and emotionally but fully conscious.

Henry looked up from the table and caught Emma's eyes. Smiled. 'A penny for them,' he said.

Emma realised she had been staring at him, holding the butter halfway to putting it in the fridge. She shook her head. 'Miles away,' she said. She had these moments. At least once a day it would come back to her, that image of Sophie holding the huge shard of glass, and the certainty she'd felt that Matilde was there in the room. It had been Matilde who'd helped her escape, Emma was sure of it. She'd let Henry believe that he'd saved her life, the way that it appeared. He was the most modest knight in shining armour and flushed when it was mentioned. She was glad to let him play the hero because of how he took the role. Emma thanked the God she didn't believe in for her Henry every day.

Sophie was on suicide watch and Emma expected daily to hear that she had killed herself, but she never received this news. She found it shocking to realise that she'd be relieved to hear of Sophie's death. The nightmare wasn't over, not really, not until her friend was gone. *Friend*. There was that word again. Emma still felt that Sophie was not an evil person, not intrinsically bad, even if she did bad things. Henry said she was too generous but Emma wondered if she had a choice. Somehow, Sophie's influence swayed her even now and she couldn't think in purely bad terms about her. She had even considered visiting her at the secure hospital where she was being cared for. Henry had told her she shouldn't go; she had to draw a line under the past and move forward. She had listened to him. For the moment. Although she still felt the urge. Sometimes, in the night, she would wake and want her friend back.

The kettle was boiling and Henry was putting tea bags into a pot. Soon they would be sitting in the living room as if they could take this life for granted. Tomorrow, Emma had a piano lesson with the new tutor, a woman called Betty Dray, and she was looking forward to it. The Conservatoire was a different place now, somehow lighter without the presence of the twins, and yet more ordinary. Emma missed them. She felt their absence more than she could confess to Henry, or to her mother, or to anyone she knew. More than she wanted to admit to herself. It was as if the colour had drained out of her life at university without them. But she was glad to feel safe and to feel in control of herself. And to have Henry, without any rivals around for his affections.

Henry passed Emma a mug of tea and they both sat down at the table, the way they often did after shopping together. Their lives were so different now. They didn't want to live like students, or with them. They behaved like a much older couple. Gone were the nights of champagne with the beautiful people. They were serious about their studies and about their lives. They knew there wasn't always time to mess about. The things they had seen had knocked off that sheen of immortality young people had. It had scratched right through and destroyed it.

Emma was mostly happy and she didn't feel that someone else was in control of her now. She no longer believed that she had ever been possessed. It was the suffocating nature of her friendship with Sophie, especially after Matilde's death, that had caused all of her problems. She had been stressed and who wouldn't have been under the circumstances? Stress like that could do anything to a person, and she knew she couldn't rely on her memories of the things that had happened. There was an explanation for everything, you just had to find it.

Mirrors still spooked her sometimes. There were moments when she would catch a glimpse, and just for an instant she wouldn't recognise herself. She would have a sudden flash that the reflection was someone else altogether. She went through periods of covering the mirrors in the flat, or laying them face down, as if observing shiva.

There were other times when she noticed things that made her wonder. Less petrol in the car than she was expecting. Finding her shoes muddy in the morning when they hadn't been the night before. And other things. The inexplicable pull she still felt towards Sophie, and how some days she longed to visit her so much that her feet felt heavy. She didn't probe it too deeply and tried not to notice. She couldn't help thinking that you never knew, not really, where you went when you closed your eyes.